Spies Of The Kaiser
Plotting The Downfall Of England

by

William Le Queux

Spies Of The Kaiser
Plotting The Downfall Of England
by William Le Queux

ISBN: 978-93-59954-98-1

Published by

DOUBLE 9 BOOKS
2/13-B, Ansari Road
Daryaganj, New Delhi – 110002
info@double9books.com
www.double9books.com
Tel. 011-40042856

ABOUT THE AUTHOR

Anglo-French journalist and author William Tufnell Le Queux was born on July 2, 1864, and died on October 13, 1927. He was also a diplomat (honorary consul for San Marino), a traveler (in Europe, the Balkans, and North Africa), a fan of flying (he presided over the first British air meeting at Doncaster in 1909), and a wireless pioneer who played music on his own station long before radio was widely available. However, he often exaggerated his own skills and accomplishments. The Great War in England in 1897 (1894), a fantasy about an invasion by France and Russia, and The Invasion of 1910 (1906), a fantasy about an invasion by Germany, are his best-known works. Le Queux was born in the city. The man who raised him was English, and his father was French. He went to school in Europe and learned art in Paris from Ignazio (or Ignace) Spiridon. As a young man, he walked across Europe and then made a living by writing for French newspapers. He moved back to London in the late 1880s and managed the magazines Gossip and Piccadilly. In 1891, he became a parliamentary reporter for The Globe. He stopped working as a reporter in 1893 to focus on writing and traveling.

CONTENTS

IF ENGLAND KNEW

No sane person can deny that England is in grave danger of invasion by Germany at a date not far distant.

This very serious fact I endeavoured to place vividly before the public in my recent forecast, *The Invasion of 1910*, the publication of which, in Germany and in England, aroused a storm of indignation against me.

The Government, it will be remembered, endeavoured to suppress its publication, because it contained many serious truths, which it was deemed best should be withheld from the public, and on its publication—in defiance of the statements in the House of Commons, and the pressure brought upon me by the Prime Minister—I was denounced as a panicmonger.

But have not certain of my warnings already been fulfilled?

I have no desire to create undue alarm. I am an Englishman, and, I hope, a patriot. What I have written in this present volume in the form of fiction is based upon serious facts within my own personal knowledge.

That German spies are actively at work in Great Britain is well known to the authorities. The number of agents of the German Secret Police at this moment working in our midst on behalf of the Intelligence Department in Berlin are believed to be over five thousand. To each agent—known as a "fixed-post"—is allotted the task of discovering some secret, or of noting in a certain district every detail which may be of advantage to the invader when he lands. This "fixed-agent" is, in turn, controlled by a travelling agent, who visits him regularly, allots the work, collects his reports, and makes monthly payments, the usual stipend varying from £10 to £30 per month, according to the social position of the spy and the work in which he or she may be engaged.

The spies themselves are not always German. They are often Belgians, Swiss, or Frenchmen employed in various trades and professions, and each being known in the Bureau of Secret Police by a number only, their monthly information being docketed under that particular number. Every six months an "inspection" is held, and monetary rewards made to those whose success has been most noteworthy.

The whole brigade of spies in England is controlled by a well-known member of the German Secret Police in London, from whom the travelling agents take their orders, and in turn transmit them to the "fixed-posts," who are scattered up and down the country.

As I write, I have before me a file of amazing documents, which plainly show the feverish activity with which this advance guard of our enemy is working to secure for their employers the most detailed information. These documents have already been placed before the Minister for War, who returned them without comment!

He is aware of the truth, and cannot deny it in face of these incriminating statements.

It is often said that the Germans do not require to pursue any system of espionage in England when they can purchase our Ordnance maps at a shilling each. But do these Ordnance maps show the number of horses and carts in a district, the stores of food and forage, the best way in which to destroy bridges, the lines of telegraph and telephone, and the places with which they communicate, and such-like matters of vital importance to the invader? Facts such as these, and many others, are being daily conveyed by spies in their carefully prepared reports to Berlin, as well as the secrets of every detail of our armament, our defences, and our newest inventions.

During the last twelve months, aided by a well-known detective officer, I have made personal inquiry into the presence and work of these spies, an inquiry which has entailed a great amount of travelling, much watchfulness, and often considerable discomfort, for I have felt that, in the circumstances, some system of contra-espionage should be established, as has been done in France.

I have refrained from giving actual names and dates, for obvious reasons, and have therefore been compelled, even at risk of being again denounced as a scaremonger, to present the facts in the form of fiction—fiction which, I trust, will point its own patriotic moral.

Colonel Mark Lockwood, Member for Epping, sounded a very serious warning note in the middle of 1908 when he asked questions of the Minister for War, and afterwards of the Prime Minister, respecting the presence of German spies in Norfolk, Suffolk, Essex, and elsewhere. He pointed out that for the past two years these individuals, working upon a carefully prepared plan, had been sketching, photographing, and carefully making notes throughout the whole of East Anglia.

With truth, he declared that this organised system of espionage was for one reason alone, namely in preparation for a sudden raid upon our shores, for "the Day"—as it is known in Germany—the Day of the Invasion of England.

The replies given by His Majesty's Ministers were colourless, though they both actually confessed themselves unable to deal with the situation! Under our existing law it seems that a foreign spy is free to go hither and thither, and plot the downfall of England, while we, ostrich-like, bury our head in the sand at the sign of approaching danger.

The day has passed when one Englishman was worth ten foreigners. Modern science in warfare has altered all that. All the rifle-clubs in England could not stop one German battalion, because the German battalion is trained and disciplined in the art of war, while our rifle-clubs are neither disciplined nor trained. Were every able-bodied man in the kingdom to join a rifle-club we should be no nearer the problem of beating the German invaders if once they landed, than if the spectators in all the football matches held in Britain mobilised against a foreign foe. The Territorial idea is a delusion. Seaside camps for a fortnight a year are picnics, not soldiering. The art of navigation, the science of engineering, or the trade of carpentering cannot be learned in fourteen days annually—neither can the art of war.

In response, we have held up to us the strength of our Navy. But is it really what it is represented by our rulers to an already deluded public?

Only as recently as March 29, 1909, Sir Edward Grey, replying to Mr. Balfour's vote of censure in the House of Commons, was compelled to admit that—

> "A new situation is created by the German programme. When it is completed, Germany, a great country close to our own shores, will have a fleet of thirty-three Dreadnoughts, and that fleet will be the most powerful which the world has ever yet seen. It imposes upon us the necessity of rebuilding the whole of our fleet. That is the situation."

Germany is our friend—for the moment. But Prince Buelow now admits that the Kaiser's telegram to President Kruger was no personal whim, but the outcome of national policy!

What may happen to-morrow?

WILLIAM LE QUEUX

THE PERIL OF ENGLAND

WHO IS RIGHT?

SIR EDWARD GREY

In the House of Commons, March 29, 1909.

We have been informed verbally, but quite definitely, that Germany will not accelerate her naval programme of construction, and will not have thirteen ships of the *Dreadnought* type, including cruisers, till the end of 1912.

PRINCE BUELOW

In the Reichstag, March 29, 1909.

Great Britain has never made any proposals which the German Government regarded as a suitable basis for negotiations. Germany regards the question of limitation of armaments as outside the range of practical politics.

WHAT THE KAISER SAYS:

His Imperial Majesty the German Emperor declared:—

The prevailing sentiment among large sections of the middle and lower class of my own people is not friendly to England.—*Daily Telegraph, October 28, 1908.*

CHAPTER I
HOW THE PLANS OF ROSYTH WERE STOLEN

"But if the new plans for our naval base at Rosyth have already been secured by Germany, I don't see what we can do," I remarked. "What's the use of closing the stable-door after the horse has been stolen?"

"That's just what we generally do in England, my dear old Jack," replied my friend. "We still think, as in the days of Wellington, that one Englishman is worth ten foreigners. But remember the Boer War, and what our shameful ignorance cost us in men and money. Now, as I explained last night in London, the original plans of Rosyth leaked out some time ago, and were actually published in certain Continental papers. In consequence of this, fresh plans have been prepared and adopted by the Lords of the Admiralty. It is one of these which Reitmeyer informs my father is already in German hands."

"But is not Reitmeyer a German himself?" I asked.

"He's a naturalised Englishman," replied my friend Ray Raymond, drawing hard at his pipe as he stretched himself lazily before the fire of the inn-parlour. "It was he who gave the guv'nor a good deal of the information upon which he based those questions he asked in the House."

"The Government refused to admit that German spies are at work in England," I said.

"Yes, Jack. That's just why I'm down here on the Firth of Forth—in order to accomplish the task I've set myself, namely, to prove that German secret agents are at this moment actively at work amongst us. I intend to furnish proof of the guv'nor's statements, and by exposing the methods of these inquisitive gentry, compel the Government to introduce fresh legislation in order that the authorities may be able to deal with them. At present spies may work their will in England, and the law is powerless to prevent them."

I was standing with my back to the fire facing my friend, who, a barrister like myself, shared with me a set of rather dismal chambers in New Stone Buildings, Lincoln's Inn, though he had never had occasion to practise, as I unfortunately had.

As he sat, his long, thin legs outstretched towards the fire, he presented the appearance of the typical athletic young Englishman, aged about thirty, clean-shaven, clean-limbed, with an intelligent and slightly aquiline face, a pair of merry grey eyes, and light brown hair closely cropped. He was an all-round good fellow, even though his life had been cast in pleasant places. Eldest son of Sir Archibald Raymond, Bart., the well-known Cardiff coal-owner who sat for East Carmarthen, he had been with me at Balliol, we had read together, and though he now shared those dingy London chambers, he resided in a prettily furnished flat in Bruton Street, while I lived in rooms round in Guilford Street, Bloomsbury, in my lonely bachelordom.

He had been adopted as candidate for West Rutland at the next election, and his party predicted of him great things. But the long-wished-for General Election was still afar off, therefore, with commendable patriotism, he had taken up the burning question of German spies in England, which had been so lightly pooh-poohed by both the Prime Minister and the Minister for War. His intention was, if possible, to checkmate their activity, and at the same time reveal to the public the fool's paradise in which we are living now that "the Day"—as they call it in Germany—is fast approaching—the day of the invasion of Great Britain.

> — Miles N.E. of Dockyard. Half-closed redoubt for infantry—Platforms for machine-guns at angles—Wrought-iron palisading at bottom of ditch.
> G (in plan.) "Ferry Hills" Fort—Earth and concrete—Very deep ditches, flanked by counterscarp galleries and a stone caponier—Casemated—Probable armament—Two 9.2-inch guns, six 7.5-inch guns—Wrought-iron fraise below counterscarp.
> H (in plan). Evidently intended for use against torpedo-boats and destroyers—To mount ten 4-inch quick-firing guns—Wrought-iron palisading in ditch well covered from seaward—Gorge closed by stone wall (two tiers of loopholes for musketry), flanked by caponiers with machine-guns.
> I. A large and formidable work armed with—

Portion of translation of the German spy's report upon the new naval base at Rosyth.

After Sir Archibald had put the questions in the House, the purport of which most readers will remember, he had been the recipient of many letters pointing out the presence of spies—letters which, if published, would have no doubt created a great sensation. Many of these statements Ray and I had, during the past two months, closely investigated on the spot, and what we had discovered held us both amazed and alarmed. Indeed, we had secured evidence that although spies were openly at work in certain of our eastern counties collecting all sorts of information which would be of incalculable importance to an invader, yet the chief constables of those counties had actually been instructed from head-quarters to close their eyes to the movements of inquisitive foreigners!

In the investigations upon which Ray Raymond had embarked with such enthusiasm, and which I am now permitted to chronicle in these pages, he had taken only two persons into his confidence—myself and Vera, the pretty, fair-haired daughter of Vice-Admiral Sir Charles Vallance, the Admiral-Superintendent of Portsmouth Dockyard, to whom he was engaged.

Indeed, from the first I suspected that it had been her influence that had roused him to action; she who had promised him her assistance, and who had pointed out how, by watching and unmasking the spies, he might render his King and country signal service.

At dusk that day we had, on arrival from King's Cross, left our baggage with the hall porter of the North British Hotel in Edinburgh, had travelled from the Waverley Station to Dalmeny, and descending the hundred or so steps to the comfortable Hawes Inn, at the water's edge, had dined there. Thence we had taken the old ferry-boat over to North Queensferry, on the opposite shore, where, in the rather bare parlour of the little Albert Hotel, directly beneath the giant arms of the Forth Bridge, we were resting and smoking.

Outside the November night was dark and squally with drizzling rain; within the warmth was cheerful, the fire throwing a red glow upon the old-fashioned mahogany sideboard with its profuse display of china and the two long tables covered with red cloths.

PORTIONS OF MAP OF NEW NAVAL BASE AT ROSYTH DISCOVERED IN POSSESSION OF A SPY.

The notes, here translated from German, were written on the British Ordnance Map.

From my boyhood days, I, John James Jacox, barrister-at-law, had always been fond of detective work; therefore I realised that in the present inquiry before us there was wide scope for one's reasoning powers, as well as a great probability of excitement.

I was thoroughly wiping my gold pince-nez, utterly failing to discover Ray's reason in travelling to that spot now that it was admitted that the Germans had already outwitted us and secured a copy of at least one of the plans. Suddenly, glancing up at the cheap American clock on the mantelshelf, my friend declared that we ought to be moving and at once struggled into his coat and crushed on his soft felt hat. It then wanted a quarter to ten o'clock.

In ascending the short, steep hill in the semi-darkness, we passed the North Queensferry post office, beside which he stopped short to peer down the dark alley which separated it from the Roxburgh Hotel. I noticed that in this alley stood a short, stout telegraph-pole, carrying about sixty or so lines of wire which, coming overhead from the north, converged at that point into a cable, and crossed to the south beneath the mile-broad waters of the Forth.

Ray was apparently interested in them, for glancing overhead he saw another set of wires which, carried higher, crossed the street and ran away to the left. This road he followed, I walking at his side.

The way we took proved to be a winding one, which, instead of ascending the steep hill with its many quarries, from the summit of which the wonderful bridge runs forth, skirted the estuary westward past a number of small grey cottages, the gardens of some of which appeared to run down to the broad waters whence shone the flashing light of the Beamer and those of Dalmeny, the Bridge, and of South Queensferry.

The rain had ceased, and the moon, slowly struggling from behind a big bank of cloud, now produced a most picturesque effect of light and shadow.

The actions of Ray Raymond were, however, somewhat mysterious, for on passing each telegraph-pole he, by the aid of a small electric torch he carried in his pocket, examined it carefully at a distance of about six feet from the ground.

He must have thus minutely examined at least fifteen or sixteen when, at the sharp bend of the road, he apparently discovered something of which he was in search. The pole stood close beside the narrow pathway, and as he examined it with his magnifying-glass I also became curious. But all I distinguished were three small gimlet holes set in a triangle in the black tarred wood about four inches apart.

"Count the wires, Jack," he said. "I make them twenty-six. Am I correct?"

I counted, and found the number to be right.

Then for some moments he stood in thoughtful silence, gazing away over the wide view of St. Margaret's Hope spread before him.

Afterwards we moved forward. Passing along, he examined each of the other poles, until we descended the hill to the Ferry Toll, where the high road and wires branched off to the right to Dunfermline. Then, taking the left-hand road along the shore, where ran a line of telephone, we passed some wharves, gained the Limpet Ness, and for a further couple of miles skirted the moonlit waters, until, of a sudden, there came into view a long corrugated-iron building lying back from the road facing the Forth and fenced off by a high spiked-iron railing. The entrance was in the centre, with nine long windows on either side, while at a little distance further back lay a small bungalow, evidently the residence of the caretaker.

"This," exclaimed my friend without halting, "is the much-discussed Rosyth. These are the Admiralty offices, and from here the tracing of that plan was obtained."

"A rather lonely spot," I remarked.

"Over yonder, beyond that ruined castle out on the rocks, where Oliver Cromwell's mother was born, is the site of the new naval base. You'll get a better view from the other side of the hill," he said in a low voice.

"Who lives in the bungalow?" I inquired.

"Only the caretaker. The nearest house is on top of the hill, and is occupied by the second officer in charge of the works."

Continuing our way and passing over the hill, we skirted a wood, which I afterwards found to be Orchardhead Wood, passed a pair of lonely cottages on the right, until we reached a lane running down to the water's edge. Turning into this lane, we walked as far as a gate which commanded the great stretch of broad, level meadows and the wide bay beyond. Leaning over it, he said:

"This is where the new naval base is to be. Yonder, where you see the lights, is Bruce Haven."

"Tell me the facts regarding the stolen plan as far as is known," I said, leaning on the gate also and gazing away across the wide stretch of moonlit waters.

"The facts are curious," replied my friend. "As you know, I've been away from London a fortnight, and in those fourteen days I've not been idle. It seems that when the first plan leaked out and was published abroad, the Admiralty had two others prepared, and into both these a commission which came down here has, for several months, been busily at work investigating their feasibility. At last one of the schemes has been adopted. Tracings of it are kept in strictest secrecy in a safe in the offices down yonder, together with larger-scale tracings of the various docks, the submarine station, repairing docks, patent slips, and defensive forts—some twenty-two documents in all. The details of the defensive forts are, of course, kept a profound secret. The safe has two keys, one kept by the superintendent of the works, Mr. Wilkinson, who lives over at Dunfermline, and the other by the first officer, Mr. Farrar, who resides in a house half a mile from the offices. The safe cannot be opened except by the two gentlemen being present together. The leakage could not come from within. None of the plans have ever been found to be missing and no suspicion attaches to anybody, yet there are two most curious facts. The first is that in July last a young clerk named Edwin Jephson, living with his mother in Netley Road, Shepherd's Bush, and employed by a firm of auctioneers in the City, was picked up in the Thames off Thorneycroft's at Chiswick. At the inquest, the girl to whom the young man was engaged testified to his strangeness of manner a few days previously; while his mother stated how, prior to his disappearance, he had been absent from home for four days, and on his return had seemed greatly perturbed, and had remarked: 'There'll be something in the papers about me before long.' On the body were found fourteen shillings in silver, some coppers, a few letters, and a folio of blue foolscap containing some writing in German which, on translation, proved to be certain details regarding a fortress. A verdict of suicide was returned; but the statement in German, placed by the police before the Admiralty, proved to be an exact copy of one of the documents preserved in the safe here, at Rosyth."

"Then the Admiralty cannot deny the leakage of the secret?" I remarked.

"No; but the mystery remains how it came into the young fellow's possession, and what he was about to do with it. As far as can be ascertained, he was a most exemplary young man, and had no connection whatever with any one in Admiralty employ," replied Ray; adding, "the second fact is the one alleged by Reitmeyer, who was, in confidence, shown a photograph of one of the larger plans."

"Then spies are, no doubt, at work here," I said.

"That cannot be denied," was his reply. "This neighbourhood opens up a wide field of investigation to the inquisitive gentry from the Fatherland. Knowledge of the secrets of the defences of the Firth of Forth would be of the utmost advantage to Germany in the event of an invasion. The local submarine defences and corps of submarine miners have been done away with, yet the entrance of the estuary is commanded by strong batteries upon the island of Inchkeith, opposite Leith; the Forth Bridge is defended by masked batteries at Dalmeny at the one end and at Carlingnose at the other, while upon Inchgarvie, the rock beneath the centre of the bridge, is a powerful battery of six-inch guns. The true strength of these defences, and the existence of others, are, of course, kept an absolute secret, but Germany is equally anxious to learn them, as she is to know exactly what our plans are regarding this new naval base and its fortifications."

"But if the new base were established, might not the Forth Bridge be blown into the water by the enemy, and our fleet bottled up by the wreckage?" I ventured to remark.

"That's just the point, Jack," my friend said; "whether the Rosyth works are carried out or not, the Germans would, without doubt, use their best endeavours to blow up the bridge; first in order to cut direct communication between north and south, and secondly, to prevent British ships using St. Margaret's Hope as a haven of refuge."

"And even in face of the document discovered upon the auctioneer's clerk, the Government deny the activity of spies!"

"Yes," said Ray in a hard voice. "A week ago I was up here, and examined the safe in the offices we've passed. I was only laughed at for my pains. I must admit, of course, that no document has ever been missing, and that the safe has not been tampered with in any way."

"A complete mystery."

"One which, my dear Jack, we must solve," he said, as we retraced our steps back to North Queensferry station, where we luckily caught a train back to Edinburgh.

Next morning we travelled again to Dalmeny, and in the grey mist hired a boat at the slippery landing-stage opposite the Hawes Inn. Refusing the assistance of the boatman, Ray took off his coat and commenced to row to the opposite shore. His action surprised me, as we could easily have gone over by the steam ferry. It was high tide, and by degrees as we got into mid-stream he allowed the boat to drift towards one of the sets of four circular caissons in which the foundations of the gigantic bridge, with its bewildering masses of ironwork, were set.

Against one of them the boat drifted, and he placed his hand upon the masonry to prevent a collision. As he did so, his keen eyes discerned something which caused him to pull back and examine it more closely.

As he did so, a train rumbled high above us.

With curiosity I followed the direction of his gaze, but what I saw conveyed to me nothing. About two feet above high-water mark a stout iron staple had been fixed into the concrete. To it was attached a piece of thin wire rope descending into the water, apparently used by the bridge workmen to moor their boats.

Having carefully examined the staple, Ray rowed round to the other three caissons, a few feet distant, but there discovered nothing. Afterwards, with my assistance, he pulled back to the Dalmeny side, where, at the base of one of the high square brick piers of the shore end of the bridge, the third from the land, he found a similar staple driven. Then we returned to the pier and crossed to North Queensferry.

My friend's next move was to enter the post office and there write upon a yellow form a telegram in German addressed to a person in Berlin. This he handed to the pleasant-faced Scotch postmistress, who, on seeing it in a strange language, regarded him quickly.

Ray remarked that he supposed she did not often transmit messages in German, whereupon she said:

"Oh, yes. The German waiter up at the Golf Club sends them sometimes."

"Is he the only German you have in North Queensferry?" he inquired casually.

"I've never heard of any other, sir," replied the good woman, and then we both wished her good-day and left.

Our next action was to climb the Ferry Hill at the back of the post office, passing the station and Carlingnose Fort, until we reached the club-house of the Dunfermline Golf Club, which commands a fine prospect over the wide estuary eastward.

No one appeared to be playing that morning, but on entering the club we were approached by a fair-headed, rather smart-looking German waiter. His age was about thirty, his fair moustache well trained, and his hair closely cropped.

I made inquiry for an imaginary person, and by that means was enabled to engage the man in conversation. Ray, on his part, remarked that he would be staying in the neighbourhood for some time, and requested a list of members and terms of membership. In response, the waiter fetched him a book of rules, which he placed in his pocket.

"Well?" I asked, as we descended the hill.

"To me," my friend remarked, "there is only one suspicious fact about that man—his nationality."

The afternoon we spent out at the naval offices, where I was introduced to the Superintendent and the second officer, and where I stood by while my friend again examined the big green-painted safe, closely investigating its lock with the aid of his magnifying glass. It was apparent that those in charge regarded him as a harmless crank, for so confident were they that no spy had been able to get at the plans that no night watch had ever been kept upon the place.

Through five consecutive nights, unknown to the caretaker, who slept so peacefully in his bungalow, we, however, kept a vigilant watch upon the place. But in vain. Whatever information our friends the Germans wanted they seemed to have already obtained.

Ray Raymond, however, continued to display that quiet, methodical patience born of enthusiasm.

"I'm confident that something is afoot, and that there are spies in the neighbourhood," he would say.

Nearly a fortnight we spent, sometimes in Edinburgh, and at others idling about North Queensferry in the guise of English tourists, for the Forth Bridge is still an attraction to the sightseer.

Upon the German waiter at the Golf Club Ray was keeping a watchful eye. He had discovered his name to be Heinrich Klauber, and that before his engagement there he had been a waiter in the basement café of the Hôtel de l'Europe, in Leicester Square, London.

His movements were in no way suspicious. He lived at a small cottage nearly opposite the post office at North Queensferry with a widow named Macdonald, and he had fallen in love with a rather pretty dark-eyed girl named Elsie Robinson, who lived with her father in the grey High Street of Inverkeithing. As far as my observations went—and it often fell to my lot to watch his movements while Ray was absent—the German was hardworking, thrifty, and a pattern of all the virtues.

One evening, however, a curious incident occurred.

Ray had run up to London, leaving me to watch the German's movements. Klauber had returned to Mrs. Macdonald's about eight, but not until nearly eleven did he come forth again, and then instead of taking his usual road to Inverkeithing to meet the girl Robinson, he ascended the hill and struck across the golf-course until he had gained its highest point, which overlooked the waters of the Forth towards the sea.

So suddenly did he halt that I was compelled to throw myself into a bunker some distance away to escape detection. Then, as I watched, I saw him take from his pocket and light a small acetylene lamp, apparently a bicycle-lamp, with a green glass. He then placed it in such a position on the grass that it could be seen from far across the waters, and lighting a cigarette, he waited.

The light on the Oxcars was flashing white and red, while from distant Inchkeith streamed a white brilliance at regular intervals. But the light of Heinrich Klauber was certainly a signal. To whom?

He remained there about half an hour, but whether he received any answering signal I know not.

Next night and the next I went to the same spot, but he failed to put in an appearance. Then, in order to report to Ray, I joined the morning train from Perth to London.

On arrival at New Stone Buildings I telephoned to Bruton Street, but Chapman, his valet, told me that his master had slept there only one night, had received a visit from a respectably dressed middle-aged woman, and had gone away—to an unknown destination. Therefore I waited for a whole week in anxiety and suspense, until one morning I received a wire from him, despatched from Kirkcaldy, urging me to join him at once at the Station Hotel in Perth.

Next morning at nine o'clock I was seated on the side of his bed, telling him of the incident of the lamp.

"Ah!" he exclaimed after a pause. "My surmises are slowly proving correct, Jack. You must buy a bicycle-lamp down in the town and a piece of green glass. To-night you must go there at the same hour and show a similar light. The matter seems far more serious than I first expected. The enemy is no doubt here, in our midst. Take this. It may be handy before long," and he took from his kit-bag a new .32 Colt revolver.

By this, I saw that he had resolved upon some bold stroke.

That evening, after an early dinner at the hotel, we took train to North Queensferry, and on alighting at the station he sent me up to the golf-links to show a light for half an hour; promising to meet me later at a certain point on the road to Rosyth.

I gained the lonely spot on the golf-course and duly showed the light. Then I hastened to rejoin my friend at the point he indicated, and found him awaiting me behind some bushes.

Almost at the moment we met, a female figure came along beneath the shadow of a high wall. She was a poorly dressed girl, but the instant she addressed my friend I recognised by her refined voice that it was Vera, the dainty daughter of the Admiral Superintendent.

"Elsie is waiting down by the Ferry Barns," she said quickly, in a low whisper, after greeting me. "Heinrich has not kept his appointment with her."

"You have the note?" he asked. "Recollect what I told you concerning the man Hartmann."

"Yes," she replied. Then, addressing me, she said, "Take care of these people Mr. Jacox. They are utterly unscrupulous"; and she again disappeared into the darkness.

Ray and I turned and again walked back in the direction of Rosyth. But when we had gone a little distance he told me to approach the naval offices carefully, conceal myself in the bushes, and watch until he joined me. On no account was I to make any sign, whatever I might witness.

Though intensely cold the night was not very dark, therefore I was not long in establishing my position at a spot where I had a good view of the offices. Then I leaned upon a tree-trunk and waited in breathless expectation. I touched my father's old repeater which I carried and found it to be a quarter past midnight.

For over an hour I remained there, scarce daring to move a muscle.

Suddenly, however, upon the mud at the side of the road I heard soft footsteps, and a few moments later two figures loomed up from the shadow. But when about forty yards from the offices they halted, one of the men alone proceeding.

With great caution he climbed the spiked railing, and crossing rapidly to the main door of the offices he unlocked it with a key and entered, closing the door after him. As far as I could distinguish, the man wore a short beard, and was dressed in tweeds and a golf cap. Holding my breath, I saw the flashing of an electric torch within the building.

Fully twenty minutes elapsed before he reappeared, relocked the outside door, and clambering back over the railings, rejoined his waiting companion, both being lost next second in the darkness.

I longed to follow them, but Ray's instructions had been explicit—I was to wait until he arrived.

Half an hour later, hearing his low whistle, I emerged from my hiding-place to meet him and tell him what I had seen.

"Yes," he said, "I know. We have now no time to lose."

And together we hurried back over the road towards North Queensferry.

At the same spot where Vera had met us, we found her still in hiding. My friend whispered some words, whereupon she hurried on before us to the sharp bend in the road where stood the telegraph-pole which had attracted Ray on the night of our first arrival.

We drew back in the shadow, and as we did so I saw her halt and pull the bell beside a small gate in a high wall. Behind stood a white-washed cottage, with a good-sized garden at the rear. One end of the house abutted upon the pathway, and in it was one small window commanding a view of the road.

Vera, we saw, had some conversation with the old woman who answered her ring, and then went in, the gate being closed after her.

Together we waited for a considerable time, our impatience and apprehension increasing. All was silent, except for a dog-cart, in which we recognised Mr. Wilkinson driving home from the station.

"Curious that Vera doesn't return," Ray remarked at last, when we had waited nearly three-quarters of an hour. "We must investigate for ourselves. I hope nothing has happened to her."

And motioning me to follow, he very cautiously crept along the muddy path and tried the gate. It had been relocked.

We therefore scaled the wall without further ado, and, standing in the little front garden, we listened breathlessly at the door of the house.

"Get back there in the shadow, Jack," urged my friend; and, as soon as I was concealed, he passed his hand along the lintel of the door, where he found the bell-wire from the gate. This he pulled.

A few moments later the old woman reappeared at the door, passing out towards the gate, when, in an instant, Ray and I were within, and flinging open a door on the left of the narrow passage we found ourselves confronted by the exemplary waiter Klauber and a companion, whose short beard and snub nose I recognised as those of the man who so calmly entered the naval offices a couple of hours before.

For them our sudden appearance was, no doubt, a dramatic surprise.

The elder man gave vent to a quick imprecation in German, while Klauber, of course, recognised us both.

In the room was a large camera with a flashlight apparatus, while pinned upon a screen before the camera was a big tracing of a plan of one of the chief defensive forts which the spies had that night secured from Rosyth, and which they were now in the act of photographing.

"A lady called upon you here an hour ago," exclaimed Ray. "Where is she?"

"No lady has called here," replied the bearded German in very good English, adding with marvellous coolness, "To what, pray, do we owe this unwarrantable intrusion?"

"To the fact that I recognise you as Josef Scholtz, secret agent of the German Naval Intelligence Department," answered my friend resolutely, closing the door and standing with his back to it. "We have met before. You were coming down the steps of a house in Pont Street, London, where lives a great friend of yours, Hermann Hartmann."

"Well?" asked the German, with feigned unconcern, and before we could prevent him he had torn the tracing from the screen, roughly folded it, and stuffed it into his pocket.

"Hand that to me," commanded my friend quickly.

But the spy only laughed in open defiance.

"You intended, no doubt, to replace that as you have done the others after photographing them. Only we've just spoilt your game," Raymond said. "Both Mr. Wilkinson and Mr. Farrar are, I see from the list, members of the Golf Club where you"—and he looked across to the waiter—"are employed. On one occasion, while Mr. Wilkinson was taking a bath after a game, and on another while Mr. Farrar was changing his coat and vest, you contrived to take wax impressions of both the safe keys and also that of the door of the offices. The keys were made in Glasgow, and by their means the plans of our new naval base and its proposed defences have been at your disposal."

"Well—there's no law against it!" cried Scholtz. "Let me pass."

"First give me that tracing," demanded my friend resolutely.

"Never. Do your worst!" the German replied, speaking with a more pronounced accent in his excitement, while at the same moment I saw that he held a revolver in his hand.

In an instant Ray drew his own weapon, but, instead of covering the spy, he pointed it at a small, strong wooden box upon the floor in the opposite corner of the room.

"Gott—no!" gasped the man, his face blanching as he realised Ray's intention. "For Heaven's sake don't. I—I——"

"Ah!" laughed my friend. "So it is as I thought. You two blackguards, with some of your friends, I expect, have been secretly preparing for the destruction of the Forth Bridge on 'the Day'—as you are so fond of calling it. The staples are already driven in, and the unsuspicious-looking wire ropes, attached to which the boxes of gun-cotton and other explosives are to be sunk between the four caissons, are all in readiness. The boat from a German merchant vessel off Leith, signalled at intervals by your assistant Klauber, has been bringing up box after box of that dangerous stuff and landing it at the bottom of this garden; so that within an hour of receiving the code-word from your chief, you would be able to wreck the whole bridge and blow it into the water!"

The spy endeavoured to pass, but seeing Ray's determined attitude, held back, and my friend compelled him to lay down his weapon.

"Jack," said my friend, "just see what's in that box."

I at once investigated it, and discovered within only innocent-looking tin boxes of English biscuits. The three tins at the top I lifted out and placed on the floor, but those below I found were filled with circular cakes of what looked like felt, about an inch in thickness, each with a hole through it, and with a small cavity for the reception of the detonator. I showed it to Ray, pointing out that, packed with it, were several smaller tins, like boxes of cigarettes.

"Yes. I see!" he exclaimed as I opened one. "Those are the detonators, filled with fulminate of mercury."

"Let us pass!" cried both the spies.

"Not before you are searched shall you leave this house!" was the quick reply. "If you resist, I shall fire into one of those boxes of detonators, and blow you to atoms."

"And yourselves also!" remarked Klauber, his face pale as death.

"It will at least prevent our secrets falling into your hands, and at the same time bring the truth home to the British Government!" was my friend's unwavering answer.

Next moment both men made a dash towards the door, but I had drawn my weapon and was upon my guard. There was a flash, followed by a deafening report, as Ray fired at the box, aiming wide on purpose.

Then the two spies, seeing that they had to deal with a man who was a patriot to his heart's core, realised that their game was up.

Sullenly Scholtz put down his weapon, and I searched both men.

From the pocket of the exemplary waiter I drew forth a rough plan, together with some scribbled notes in German, which afterwards proved to be a description of the forts on Inchkeith, while from the pocket of Scholtz I secured the tracing he had stolen from Rosyth.

Then we allowed both the secret agents of the Kaiser to pass out, much to the consternation and alarm of the deaf old Scotchwoman, who had, at their request, posed as the occupier of the cottage, but who, in perfect ignorance of what was in progress, had acted as their housekeeper.

A swift examination of the premises revealed no trace of Vera. But we found in the cellar below the room where we had found the spies a great store of gun-cotton and other high explosives of German manufacture, intended for the wrecking of the bridge; while in an old battered portmanteau in one of the upstairs rooms we also found, all ready for conveyance to Germany, a quantity of prints from the photographic negatives in the room below— photographs of nearly the whole of the plans of Rosyth, and more especially of its proposed forts—which the men had been in the habit of abstracting at night and replacing in the safe before dawn.

Ray Raymond was in active search of something else besides, and at length discovered what he sought—two German military telegraph instruments, together with a complete and very ingenious arrangement for the tapping of wire.

"By Jove!" exclaimed my friend, who took a keen interest in all things electrical. "This will now come in very handy!"

And on going outside to the telegraph pole against the wall, he clambered up it and attached wires to two of the insulators. Then descending, he screwed a little brass box upon it into those same three holes in the black wood which had attracted him on the night of our arrival, and a moment later began manipulating the key.

"Good!" he exclaimed at last. "I've picked up Inverkeithing, and asked them to send the police over at once. We mustn't leave the place and risk the spies returning for any of their paraphernalia. The disappearance of Vera, however, worries me. I sent her here with a note purporting to come from the chief of the German Secret Service in England, Hermann Hartmann; but she has vanished, and we must, as soon as the police arrive, go in search of her."

So completely had we unmasked the spies that I stood puzzled and amazed.

Ray, noticing my attitude, made explanation.

"Several of my surmises in this case proved entirely correct," he said. "My first suspicion was aroused that if spies were about, they would probably prepare for tapping the telegraph lines, and, as you know, I soon discovered evidence of it. Then those staples in the foundations of the bridge gave me a further clue to the work in progress, a suspicion greatly strengthened by the signal light shown by the man Klauber. The two men who held the safe keys being members of the Golf Club aroused a theory which proved the correct one, and on tracing back the career of the waiter I made a remarkable discovery which left no doubt as to his real profession. It seems that while employed at the Café de l'Europe in London, he lodged at the house of Mrs. Jephson, in Shepherd's Bush, and became extremely friendly with the widow's son. Now you'll remember that a few days before the poor fellow's death he was absent mysteriously, and on his return he told his mother in confidence that there would shortly be something in the papers about himself. Well, the truth is now quite plain. During his absence he evidently came up here. Young Jephson, who knew German, had found out that his German friend was a spy, and had no doubt secured the document afterwards found upon him as evidence. Klauber was ignorant of this, though he suspected that his secret was out. In deadly fear of exposure, he then plotted to silence the young Englishman, inducing him to walk along the towing-path between Hammersmith and Barnes, where he no doubt pushed him into the river. Indeed, I have found a witness who saw the two men together in King Street, Hammersmith, on the evening of the poor fellow's disappearance. The plan which Reitmeyer saw is, I find, fortunately one of the discarded ones."

"Extraordinary!" I declared, absorbed by what he had related. "But while you've wrested from Germany the secrets of some of our most important defences, you have, my dear Ray, temporarily lost the woman you love!"

"My first duty, Jack, is to my King and my country," he declared, sitting on the edge of the table in the spies' photographic studio. "I have tried to perform it to-night, and have, fortunately, exposed the German activity in our midst. When the police arrive to view this spies' nest, we must at once search for her who is always my confidante, and to whose woman's wits and foresight this success is in no small measure due."

CHAPTER II
THE SECRET OF THE SILENT SUBMARINE

"It's a most mysterious affair, no doubt," I remarked. "Has anything further been discovered?"

"Yes, Jack," replied my friend Ray Raymond, rolling a fresh cigarette between his fingers. "On investigation, the mystery grows more complicated, more remarkable, and—for us—much more interesting."

We were seated together in our dismal chambers in New Stone Buildings, Lincoln's Inn, one wet afternoon about six weeks after the Forth Bridge affair. With us, lolling in the shabby old easy chair beside the fire, sat Vera Vallance, in a big black hat, with her muff and coat thrown aside. Her disappearance at North Queensferry had been of only brief duration, for we had discovered her hiding at the bottom of the long garden, close to the water's edge, watching the landing of two small boxes from a boat. It appeared that the two men, Scholtz and Klauber, on receipt of the note purporting to come from their director, Hermann Hartmann, in London, had asked her to wait in an adjoining room while they wrote a reply. But from there she had slipped out, and concealed herself in the garden to wait and watch.

Half an hour ago she had come to my gloomy chambers with her fiancé, in order, as he explained, to consult with us. She was at present on a visit to her married sister who lived in Argyll Road, near Kensington High Street, hence they were daily in each other's company.

"You see, Jack, very little has been allowed to leak out to the papers," Ray exclaimed as he lit his cigarette and took up a position with his back to the fire. "As soon as I read of the discovery I ran down to Scotland Yard, saw Evans, and explained my theory. He was inclined to agree with me, and at once gave orders that no facts were to be given to the Press. Upon complete secrecy, our success now depends."

"I only know what I've read in the papers," I remarked.

"Tell us the whole facts, Ray," urged the pretty fair-haired girl, who sat with her veil raised and her long white gloves laid across her knees.

"Well, dear, they are briefly as follows," he replied, with an affectionate glance at her. "Last Thursday afternoon, on the arrival at 4.51 of a train from Guildford at Vauxhall, the ticket-collector discovered lying on the floor of a third-class compartment a middle-aged, respectably dressed man in an apparently dying condition. The police were called, and he was conveyed to St. Thomas's Hospital, where it was found that he was suffering from a severe fracture of the skull, the wound having been inflicted probably with a loaded stick or a life-preserver. There was a severe cut over the right eye and a great gash down the left cheek. The man was unconscious, and still remains so. The doctors have grave doubts whether, even if he recovers, his mind will not be permanently affected. In all probability he will never regain his right mind."

"Terrible!" ejaculated Vera.

"Yes. A case of attempted murder, no doubt," he said. "But what first attracted my notice was the statement that the man had been identified as Max Steinheim, a German hairdresser employed in a shop in New Bond Street, who had been missing for nearly two months. He resided in Hargwynne Street, Stockwell, and as he owed a considerable sum to his landlady, she had given notice to the police of his disappearance. It was she who had identified him in the hospital."

"That's as far as the information conveyed by the newspapers carries the affair," I remarked.

"Exactly. But we are able to proceed a little farther, to a matter which must be closely investigated," continued Raymond. "On the arrival of the train at Waterloo the compartment, which showed signs of a desperate struggle, was searched, and under the seat was discovered a small piece of paper tightly screwed up into a small ball as though somebody wished to get rid of it unobserved. Upon it, in a distinctly foreign hand, and in violet ink—which, by the way, is seldom used by Englishmen—were traced some cryptic memoranda, a copy of which I have here," and he handed for our inspection a piece of paper which presented this appearance:

J 11864!   19505
Kingscliffe
12.15 train St. Pancras
M.R. Weldon and Corby 1 mile
Royal Pier 18
6.11
248 and 392
Harpur Street 2.30

? 8.88 M. 88

Elmar 39   X clock.

"You've endeavoured to decipher it, of course," I remarked, as both Vera and I gazed at the puzzling array of numerals and words.

"I have. For the past three days I've indeed done nothing else. Unfortunately the result is not very reassuring," he answered. "Deciphered by one of the little-known codes, the figures 19505 stand for 'January 24th,' which is four days before the murderous assault. Kingscliffe is the name of a village in Northamptonshire, on the North Western line between Peterborough and Rugby. The 12.15 from St. Pancras is a restaurant train for Derby, and takes passengers to Weldon and Corby station, by changing at Kettering, and the distance '1 mile' would bring the traveller to the village of Great Weldon."

"Royal Pier sounds like the name of a hotel," I remarked.

"No doubt. But there are a good many Royal Pier hotels in England, so there we are confronted with a difficulty. To what 6.11 refers I cannot conceive, while Harpur Street, which is off Theobalds Road, I visited yesterday, but I find there are no such numbers as 248 or 392. The next line is unintelligible, but if I read the last line aright it is an appointment made beneath the clock at Charing Cross Station at six."

I drew hard at my pipe. That strange document presented to me a very complicated puzzle.

"It seems to refer to some district in Northamptonshire, yet he was attacked coming up from Guildford, on the South Western line!" Vera remarked. "Is your only suspicion based upon the fact of the injured man's nationality, Ray?"

"That, combined with other circumstances," he replied. "As soon as I read the first announcement in the papers, I went down to Guildford and there ascertained that the injured man arrived at the Angel Hotel in a motor-car about one o'clock. The chauffeur remarked to the ostler that he had come up from the south coast, and after having a drink he started off on the return journey. Steinheim had luncheon upstairs, took his coffee and cigarette in the little room below, and idled about, telling the lady bookkeeper of the hotel that he was expecting a friend. The friend in question did not, however, arrive, therefore he walked down to the station, and left at 4.13 for London. A porter remembers seeing him alone in the compartment, and it seems quite certain that, on starting from Guildford, he was still alone. The train was an express, and timed not to stop anywhere from Guildford to Vauxhall, but, from the railway officials, I find that it was pulled up by signal about a mile from Esher, in which time he may have been joined by some one from the adjoining compartment."

"Then your theory is that the man who attacked this mysterious German got back again to his carriage, and alighted at Vauxhall," I said.

"I certainly think so, for the driver says that outside Clapham Junction the signals were against him, and he pulled up."

"It's a pity he has not sufficiently recovered to make any statement."

Ray smiled grimly.

"He would never do that, I think," he said. "It is to his advantage to conceal the facts, if my deductions prove correct."

"Are those all the known circumstances?" I inquired, much interested.

"There is one other. A week after the man's disappearance from Stockwell, his landlady received a letter bearing the postmark of Crawley in Sussex, telling her not to trouble on his account. He wrote: 'I am engaged upon an important mission, but shall return home within ten days, when I will pay all I owe you. Do not trouble after me. Burn this letter as soon as you have read it.—Max Steinheim.' The other fact I learned from the man's employer, an Englishman in New Bond Street. It appears that to the establishment there often came a stout, well-dressed, prosperous-looking German gentleman who waited for Steinheim to shave him, or cut his hair, and on such occasions it was noticed that they exchanged whispered words in their own tongue."

"Well?" asked Vera, looking up at her lover.

"The stout German's description tallies exactly with that of Hermann Hartmann."

"Ah! I see," I remarked. "You've certainly not been idle, Ray." And with my eyes fixed upon that puzzling array of figures and words, I added, "If we could only decipher the whole of these we might elucidate the truth."

"The injured man's knowledge of Hartmann, the crafty chief of the German Secret Service in London, is certainly suspicious," Vera remarked. "But cannot some information be gathered from the landlady at Hargwynne Street? He may have had visitors there."

"And if he did, they would speak in German, which the good lady could not understand," her lover replied thoughtfully, contemplating the end of his cigarette.

"There could be no harm in seeing the good lady," the girl remarked. "I'll go over to-morrow and have a chat with her."

"And in the meantime Jack and I will pursue another line of inquiry," remarked my friend.

Vera rose, a tall, fair-haired, and sweet-faced figure in black, and seating herself at the table, served us our tea. She was no stranger at our chambers, and as an Admiral's daughter, the question of German spies in England, which her lover had taken up so strongly, interested her most keenly. The Forth Bridge peril had already impressed a great and serious truth upon the Government, but Ray Raymond's success had only whetted his appetite for further exploration and discovery.

Therefore on the following morning I called at his chambers in Bruton Street—a tastefully furnished bachelor suite, the art green and blues of which were scarcely in keeping with his serious, earnest character—and together we drove in a taxi-cab to St. Thomas's Hospital, where, in the accident ward, we stood at the bedside of the mysterious Steinheim. His head was enveloped in surgical bandages, but during the night he had regained consciousness. To the questions we put to him, however, we obtained no satisfactory replies. His mind seemed to be a perfect blank as to what had occurred.

Ray read the copy of those cryptic figures upon the scrap of paper found in the railway carriage. When my friend pronounced the name of the station "Weldon and Corby," the invalid's big grey eyes started from his head as he exclaimed in German:

"Ah! Yes—yes. At Weldon. She was at Weldon!"

Who was "she"? In vain we tried to wring from him some reply to this question, but, alas! in vain.

Mention of Hermann Hartmann, the ingenious and fearless secret agent who controlled so cleverly the vast army of German spies spread over our smiling land of England, brought no responsive expression to the man's white, drawn face. It was indeed apparent that his intention was to hold back at all hazards the truth regarding the murderous attack upon him. Perhaps he himself was guilty of some offence, or perhaps he intended to hold his peace then and to retaliate at a moment when his assailant thought himself most secure.

He was a big, burly, strong-featured man, just the type of heavy-limbed German who might be expected to bear a murderous malice against any who did him injury.

"I feel more than ever convinced that Hartmann is at the bottom of the curious affair," Ray declared, as we walked together across Westminster Bridge and I crossed with him to the St. Stephen's Club, at the corner of the

Embankment. "As far as I can discover, the man was always in possession of ample funds. Yet to his landlady he was careful never to reveal that he had money. There was, no doubt, some hidden reason for this, as well as for the letter he wrote to the woman after his departure."

"The mystery surrounding the affair grows more fascinating as we proceed," I declared.

"And if the deduction I have made this morning proves to be the correct one, Jack, the mystery will still increase. There's some very crooked business in progress, depend upon it."

That afternoon I had to make an application in the Chancery Court, therefore it was not until after dinner that I again sat in one of the green velvet chairs in his art-green sitting-room.

Contrary to his usual habit, he had not dressed, but still wore the brown tweed suit which he had had on in the morning.

"You've brought what I asked you over the 'phone?" he inquired, as soon as I entered.

"Yes," I replied, opening the well-worn leather brief bag which I carried, and displaying a dark lantern, a coil of strong silk rope, and a small but serviceable jemmy. All that burglarious outfit belonged to my friend.

"Right," he exclaimed, stroking his smooth-shaven chin. "Have a pipe. We'll leave here about ten. We are going to spend the night in Pont Street." And he pointed to a silver flask and a paper of sandwiches upon the sideboard. "Vera has seen the landlady in Stockwell, but can make nothing of her. She's as deaf as a post. She returned home to Portsmouth to-night."

We smoked together until ten, he consuming cigarette after cigarette in that quick, nervous manner which showed the volcano of excitement raging within him.

"I can't think why the mention of Weldon and Corby should have so excited our friend this morning. To me it seemed as though he retained rather bitter memories of the place."

"And there was a woman in the case, without a doubt."

"I think, Jack, I shall go down there and have a look round as soon as I have a chance. From the ordnance map this place seems quite a small one. The station is at Corby, while Little Weldon and Great Weldon are about a mile distant."

"There's just a chance, of course, that you might pick up something there," I remarked.

"And yet what I surmise leads me in entirely an opposite direction. There are no defences or secrets in Northamptonshire, remember."

Once more he took from his writing-table the piece of paper whereon was a copy of the strange array of figures found in the railway carriage at Waterloo. But at last he shook his head and laid it aside with a sigh. The mystery remained as complete as ever.

"There's a good deal that's suspicious about Hartmann. I suppose that's why we are going to Pont Street?" I remarked.

"Yes. As I've explained, he's believed to be a money-lender with an office in Cork Street, and is registered as such, in order that no one should be surprised at the constant callers at his house. He receives visits from all sorts and conditions of men—and women, but observation which I have placed upon the house has convinced me that the majority of these people are German agents of whom he is the guiding spirit and paymaster, and among whom he is all-powerful. Payment is made through him for all confidential services rendered to the Fatherland."

"And the police do not suspect it?"

"My dear fellow, have not the police received orders from our Government to close their eyes to the doings of these gentry? England is the paradise of the spy, and will remain so until we can bring pressure to bear to compel the introduction of fresh legislation against them."

Soon after half-past ten a taxi-cab deposited us in Sloane Street, and together we turned into Pont Street, walking leisurely past a medium-sized red-fronted house approached by a flight of steps leading to a deep portico. There was a light in the first-floor window of what was evidently the drawing-room but the rest of the house of the arch-spy of Germany was in darkness.

As we passed the house, my friend examined its highly respectable exterior. Then we passed on to the end of the thoroughfare, in order to attract no attention. A constable passed us, and in order to avoid being noticed we walked together for some distance. Presently, however, Ray turned back, and gaining the house adjoining Hartmann's, ran swiftly up the steps into the shadow of the portico, I following at his heels.

In a few seconds he had opened the door with a latch-key he carried in his hand, and next moment we were within the wide, echoing hall, for the house was empty, and to let.

"I called upon the agent, and had a look over this place a few days ago," he explained. "On that occasion, I had the key in my hand for a moment, and obtained an impression of it," and switching on his electric torch he showed the square hall with the flight of stairs ascending from it.

Gaining the big drawing-room, Ray crossed to the long French window on the left and gazed cautiously out upon the street below.

As he did so I noticed the figure of a man in a dark overcoat and felt hat cross from the opposite pavement and ascend the stairs of the house next door. Ray glanced at his watch, which he could see by the light of the street lamp outside. Noticing the time, he became reassured.

"You see, Jack, that from here runs a balcony leading to that of Hartmann's house. We must creep along it and try and get a peep of our friend at home. I've watched that drawing-room window for a long time, and I believe that he makes it his business room."

Carefully he unfastened the French window, and bending low so as to escape the observation of any person passing by, we both crept along the narrow balcony until, by swinging from one balustrade to the other, we found ourselves standing over Hartmann's portico.

Even from where we stood we could hear voices. Forward we crept again until we were outside the windows of the drawing-room, crouching so that no inquisitive policeman could detect us.

The blind of the window at which I listened did not fit well, therefore, through the small crack, I was enabled to peer within. The room was a large, well-furnished one with a fire burning brightly; near it stood a large roll-top writing-table at which sat a fat, flabby, sardonic-faced man of about fifty-five. He had grey eyes full of craft and cunning, a prominent nose, and a short-cropped grey beard. Ray whispered that it was the great Hartmann.

Near the fire, seated nervously on the extreme edge of a chair, was a respectably dressed man, a German evidently, with his hat in his hand. The man presented the appearance of a hard-working mechanic, and was obviously ill at ease.

We watched them in conversation, but could not distinguish one single word of what was said. All we could gather was that the fat man was overbearing in his manner, and that the visitor was most humble and subservient against his will.

For a full half-hour we watched, but unable to gather anything further, we were compelled to return to the house next door and regain the street, where for still twenty minutes longer we waited for the visitor's exit. When at last he came forth we followed him to the corner of Knightsbridge, opposite the Hyde Park Hotel, where he boarded a motor-bus, from which he eventually descended at the corner of Gray's Inn Road walking thence to a house in Harpur Street, Bloomsbury, where we later on discovered he lodged, under the name of Leon Karff.

The nature of the mission entrusted to this man, if one had actually been entrusted to him, was a mystery, yet it was a curious fact that "Harpur Street" appeared upon that scrap of paper which to us was such an enigma.

Next morning at six o'clock, I was already idling, at the corner of Harpur Street and Theobalds Road, but not until three hours later did the foreigner emerge and walk toward Holborn. Thence he took a motor-bus back to Sloane Street, and calling upon Hartmann, spent another half an hour with him.

And afterwards he went straight home. It was then about noon, and having an engagement in Court, I was compelled to relinquish my vigil. But at a little after five Ray entered our chambers, exclaiming:

"As I expected! That man Karff has been to see Steinheim in the hospital. I was there awaiting him, believing that he might visit him. Apparently the injured man has given him certain instructions."

"About what?"

Ray shrugged his shoulders in blank ignorance. Then he said, "We have advanced one step toward the solution of the problem, my dear Jack. But we have not gone very far."

He took the copy of the cryptogram from my writing-table and again examined it. The figures "6.11" puzzled him. Many times he referred to them.

Four days passed, during which we kept strict observation upon Karff and followed him wherever he went. On the fifth day, Ray having spent all the morning watching him, to relieve him I walked along the Theobalds Road a few minutes before one and paused, as usual, before the oil shop at the corner. There was no sign of my friend, and though I waited through the whole of that cold afternoon and evening, continuing my wearisome vigil till midnight, yet he did not come.

Much surprised, I returned to New Stone Buildings, where I found a telegram from Ray, sent from Waterloo Station at three o'clock, telling me that all was right, and urging me to await further information.

This I did. For a whole week I possessed myself in patience, not knowing where Ray was or what had befallen him. That he was on the trail of a solution of the mystery was evident, but he sent me no word of his whereabouts.

It was apparent, however, that he was no longer in London.

Eleven days after his disappearance I one afternoon received another telegram, which had been handed in at Chichester, asking me to go at once to the Queen's Hotel at Southsea, where he would meet me at ten o'clock that night.

At the hour appointed I awaited him in my bedroom overlooking Southsea Common and the harbour, and at last he joined me. I saw by the serious expression upon his face that something unusual had happened.

"The fellow Karff has realised that I'm following him, Jack. Therefore you must take the matter up. He's in the service of a greengrocer in Queen Street, close to the Hard. I haven't yet discovered his game."

Thus there was left to me a very difficult matter, a mystery which I exerted every effort to unravel. For the next fortnight I watched the fellow incessantly, being relieved sometimes by the pretty daughter of the Admiral Superintendent, whose home was fortunately in the Dockyard. In all weathers and at all times we watched, but we failed to discover anything. Ray remained at the hotel impatient and inactive, and I must admit that more than once I was inclined to believe that he had been mistaken in his surmises. Leon Karff was, as far as we could discover, a hard-working foreigner, driven by force of circumstances into adopting the lowly calling of a greengrocer's assistant. His employer supplied with fruit and vegetables the officers' messes of several of the ships in the Dockyard, and on infrequent occasions he drove in the light cart with his master when on his rounds taking orders.

This round at last he was in the habit of making three times a week.

One Saturday morning, as I was idling along the Hard, I saw Karff and his master, a man named Mitchell, drive in past the policeman at the main gate. But though I waited for over three hours to watch their exit, they did not reappear.

Much surprised at this, I walked round to the Unicorn Gate, at Landport, where, on making judicious inquiries of the policeman on duty, I learnt that Mitchell had driven out—but alone! His assistant, he said, had been sent back on foot with a message through the main gate just when the dockyard men or "maties," as they are called, were leaving work at midday.

Now having stood at that gate when the throngs had poured forth, I was quite certain he had not emerged. But I kept my own counsel, and returned to Southsea, deep in my own reflections.

On taking counsel with Ray, he at once telephoned to Vera at Admiralty House, and an hour later we all three discussed the situation, it being arranged that the Admiral's daughter should contrive to admit us to the Dockyard that night, when all was quiet, in order that we might institute a search for the missing German.

Therefore, just before half-past eleven, we halted before the small private door in the Dockyard wall, used by the Admiral-Superintendent and his household, and as the clock struck the door opened, revealing Vera. Next instant we were within the forbidden zone.

The night was frosty and a good deal too bright to suit our purpose. Vera gave some instructions to her lover, pointing to a row of long, dark sheds with sloping roofs on the opposite side of the Dockyard, saying:

"If he's inside, he's almost certain to be hidden somewhere near No. 4 shed. But be careful of the police; they are very watchful over yonder."

And after refastening the gate she disappeared into the darkness.

In the deep shadows we both crept noiselessly forward, negotiating in safety a pair of lock-gates in the open, and pursuing our way until in the vicinity of the shed which the Admiral's daughter had pointed out we discovered an old boiler, in which we both secreted ourselves.

Hardly had we crept inside when we heard the measured tramp of a policeman, who passed actually within a few feet of us. From the round hole in which we lay we could see Gosport—a pale row of lamps across the harbour.

We waited there, scarcely daring to whisper, until at last the clock struck one. If Karff was in the vicinity of that shed beside which we were secreted, he made no sign. All was silent. Once the shrill siren of a ship out at Spithead broke the quiet. Then its echoes died away.

"I really think we might have a careful look round," Ray suggested after a long silence.

With great care, therefore, we both emerged from our hiding-place, and keeping well within the shadows, passed round shed No. 4, which we found was completely closed in from view, its door being strongly barred and padlocked.

Unable to see anything, we decided to halt in the darkness behind a heap of scrap-iron and to listen for any sound of movement.

The cutting wind chilled us both to the marrow, for a white rime had gathered on the ground. The only sound we heard was that of the measured footsteps of another constable, which advanced and then died away again. There was, however, no sign of the German spy.

"To get in by the door yonder would be impossible. Therefore, he would try the roof," my companion remarked.

"You're right," I said. "You remain down here and watch while I try and get up above."

So I left him, and after considerable difficulty succeeded in gaining the roof of the shed adjoining, crouching in the gutter between the sloping roofs of the two sheds.

On each side of me sloped upwards skylights which lighted the interiors of the building-sheds, but all were thickly coated with a composition of dockyard dust and soot, which had been poured forth from many a warship's funnel as well as from the dozens of furnaces around. All was dark below; therefore I could see nothing.

I had been in my elevated position for fully twenty minutes before I was prompted to creep along to the further end of the gulley, where, to my surprise, I saw that close to where I stood two panes of glass had been neatly removed and laid aside.

Through the hole I gazed down into the interior of the shed, when I was startled to see the small glow of an electric lamp in the hand of the man of whom we were in search.

He was standing beside the long, spindle-shaped hull of a new submarine boat which lay on a very elevated set of stocks on the far side of the shed. Another boat similar, but not so nearly complete, lay at the bottom of the dock alongside her.

As Karff with his electric lamp moved slowly and noiselessly along, carefully examining England's newest submarine, which rumour had said was the most silent and perfect craft of its kind, I was able to make out vaguely that, differing considerably from photographs of other submarines I had seen, the boat on the elevated stocks had a bow which ran out into a kind of snout, while instead of the usual small circular or oval conning-tower she had what looked like a long, narrow superstructure running along the greater part of her length. This, however, was much higher forward than aft. She seemed, too, to have a great number of propellers.

I watched the man Karff making some rapid memoranda, and so occupied was he with his work that he never looked upward. Had he done so, he would certainly have detected my head against the sky.

In a manner which showed him to be fully acquainted with the construction of submarine vessels, he moved to and fro, examining both boats. Then, after about half an hour's minute investigation, he seated himself upon a bench and with his little lamp shaded to throw no reflection he took out a piece of paper and leisurely made a rough sketch of England's newest war-craft, both side and horizontal views.

Leaving him thus occupied, I descended to Ray, and finding him secreted near the water's edge, described what I had discovered.

"Good!" he exclaimed. "So I was not mistaken in that cryptogram after all! We will allow the fellow to complete his work and then compel him to disgorge his notes. They will furnish us with very excellent evidence."

So we waited, keeping our eyes fixed upon the spot where he must descend, and hardly daring to breathe lest we should prematurely alarm him.

The Dockyard clock chimed three, but the spy had not emerged. After another half-hour of watchful silence I saw that Ray began to be anxious. At last the bell rang out four, and scarcely had the last sound died away when we were startled by a splash near us, and next moment discerned a man in white shirtsleeves swimming away.

"Why! That's him!" I gasped. "He's cut a way out of the side of the shed!"

But next moment a boat shot forth from the darkness pulled by a woman who had apparently been waiting close by. The woman was Vera!

In a moment we were both down the steps and pulling in the boat towards the swimming man, who, we saw, was being rapidly approached by a second boat which had also been in waiting until the chiming of the clock.

The spy was exerting every muscle to reach the boat, but we soon overtook him.

Ray called upon him in German to surrender, but he refused, and kept on. Quickly, however, we cut him off from the boat which he was trying to reach, while the rower, seeing the discovery of his friend, pulled away into the darkness.

For some time the spy struggled on, but at last, abandoned and exhausted, he was compelled to obey us and come aboard in order to save his life.

Half dead and helpless he submitted to our search, when in his belt, preserved in an oilskin pocket, we discovered the memoranda and the drawing which I had seen him prepare.

The man, sullen and half drowned, refused to make any statement, though he could speak English well and write it perfectly, as shown by the note on his plan of the new boat; therefore we landed him at the Stony Steps across at Gosport. Before we left him we gave him to understand that if he did not at once leave the country he would be arrested. Yet so absurd is our law that I doubt whether we could have given him in charge even though we had wished!

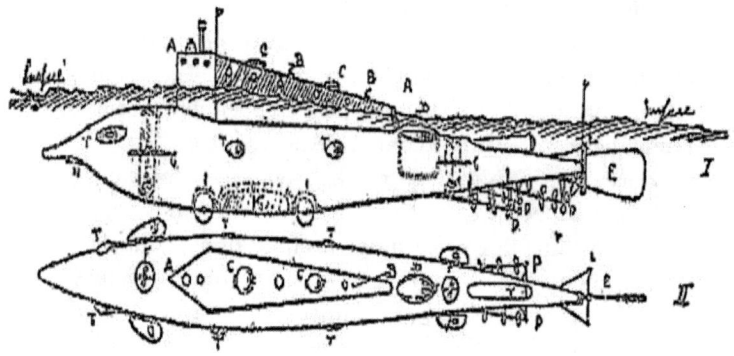

LEON KARFF'S ROUGH DRAWING OF THE NEW BRITISH SUBMARINE.
The letters refer to the notes which were also found, and which ran as follows: AA, Conning Tower; BB, Telephone Buoys; CC, Hatchways; D, Lifeboat (detachable); E, Rudder; FF, Wells with Horizontal Propellers; GG, Planes; H, Hatch from Diving Chamber; II, Wheels in Recesses; K, Detachable Safety Weight in Recess; L, Tiller; T T T T, Torpedo Tubes; P P P P, Propellers.
I. Side View (in awash position). II. Horizontal position (from above). Scale, 1/2 inch to 12 feet.

We rowed back across to the landing-stage at Portsmouth Harbour Station, and after we had seen Vera safely home we returned together to the "Queen's" at Southsea, where, in the secrecy of Ray's bedroom, we examined the spy's plan of the new submarine, and read his memoranda, which were in German, but which translated were as follows:

"Report by Leon Karff, late foreman-fitter at Kiel Dockyard, on Submarine 'F 2,' now building in Shed No. 4, Portsmouth Dockyard.

"This boat would appear to me to be of about 700 tons displacement when complete, possibly rather over. She is, as far as I am able to measure, about 180 feet long with an extreme beam a little forward of amidships of 20 feet. She is fitted with three propeller shafts with three small four-bladed propellers on each. As she is provided with what appear to me to be some kind of turbine engines, I imagine that the centre shaft is for going astern only. The propellers on this shaft seem to be attached in such a way that they could be 'feathered' by suitable gearing on board so as not to retard the vessel's way when going ahead. The engines of this boat are of a type which I have never before seen. I imagine that they are a combination of the new 'gas-producer' engine and the turbine system, the explosion of the combined gas and air being split up and passing into the turbine through a number of different channels simultaneously. This would be a very economical system if the necessary power can be obtained, and would be much safer for use below than petrol engines.

"The boat is evidently intended to operate a good deal in an 'awash' position, for there is fairly thick armour-plating over the greater part of the upper side of the bow, while the fore end of the superstructure is made of two 6-inch Krupp steel plates meeting at an acute angle, and so forming a kind of stem when the boat is moving in this way. The space enclosed between these two plates is evidently intended to be used as the conning-tower. Here there are a periscope, steering-wheel, voice-tubes, and everything necessary for the control of the vessel. There are two horizontal propellers or fans, which seem to be driven by electricity derived from an installation of accumulators, and which are certainly intended to secure horizontal immersion, so the vessel will not plunge or dive, but immerse herself horizontally by means of these propellers, which, by the way, work in vertical shafts running completely through the boat, one forward and the other aft, as was the case in the *Nordenfeldt*, *Waddington*, and other early submarines.

"Forward there is an air-lock and diving-chamber, as in the 'Lake' boats, so that divers can get in and out of the vessel whilst under water. It would also afford a means of escape for the crew in the case of accident. This is further provided for by a detachable boat or caisson at the after end of the superstructure capable of holding ten men, I should say, or possibly a dozen. There are also appliances which I suppose are telephone buoys for communicating with the surface. There are six torpedo tubes fitted, one forward, one aft, and the others two on either broadside. And there seems to be provision for six other torpedoes of the 18-inch type.

"There is a long rudder for ordinary steering, and four horizontal ones or planes which are placed abreast the horizontal screws and which, I imagine, act automatically in conjunction with them, as they seem to gear up with the shafts for these propellers. There is a big safety detachable weight which fits loosely into a recess amidships, and four broad wheels with ball bearings which do not fold up as in the 'Lake' boats, but always protrude nearly half their diameter. After all they would not obstruct her way when water-borne more than a keel—or very little more. They are quite independent and unconnected with the interior of the vessel, which while resting on them would receive forward impetus from her propellers. In the 'awash' position she would offer a very small and almost invulnerable target."

"Well," I said, marvelling at what we had translated. "What induced you to believe that the cryptogram had any reference to the new submarine."

"Those figures '6.11' puzzled me greatly," he replied; "but at last I deciphered them as 'F. 2'—F being the sixth letter of the alphabet—the number of our newest and most formidable submarine, which was being kept such a strict secret by the Admiralty. 'Royal Pier' is the name of the hotel in which Steinheim stayed at Southsea, and 18 the number of his room. From facts I elucidated, it was made plain that Max Steinheim was about to embark upon the investigation, being in secret communication with Hartmann, and was to meet Karff at Charing Cross Station. This Steinheim had already, by an ingenious device, secured from a private of engineers named James Ward—whom I have seen—certain information regarding the new boom defences of Portsmouth Harbour. Ward, whose home is at Great Weldon, suddenly discovered to his horror that the man was a German spy, followed him to Guildford, attacked him in the train, and left him for dead. For that reason Steinheim has refused to make any statement to the police. When I saw Ward a week ago, he explained how innocently he had fallen into the trap which the cunning Steinheim had laid for him."

"The evidence you have here in black and white will surely prove convincing," I remarked. "You will go and see Steinheim again, I suppose? He is still in the hospital."

"No. We shall remain silent. To show our hand will only place Hartmann on the alert. To do that is needless. We have prevented the plan of our new submarine going to Germany, and for the present that is sufficient."

And my friend drew up the blind and gazed out upon the rosy dawn across the water.

CHAPTER III
THE BACK-DOOR OF ENGLAND

"Well, that's rather curious," I remarked, closing the door of the old oak-panelled smoking-room at Metfield Park, and returning to where my friend Ray Raymond was seated.

"Was anyone outside the door?" he asked, quickly on the alert.

"Mrs. Hill-Mason's German maid. You remember, Vera pointed her out yesterday."

"H'm! and she was listening—after every one else has gone to bed!" he remarked. "Yes, Jack, it's curious."

It was past one o'clock in the morning. Two months had passed since the affair down at Portsmouth, but we had not been inactive. We were sitting before the great open fireplace where the logs were blazing, after the rest of the men had taken their candles and retired, and had been exchanging confidences in ignorance of the fact that the door remained ajar. I had, however, detected the *frou-frou* of a woman's skirt, and creeping across to the door had seen the maid of one of the guests disappearing down the stone passage which led to the great hall now in darkness.

Metfield Park, three miles from Melton Constable, in Norfolk, the seat of the Jocelyns, was a fine old Tudor place in the centre of a splendid park, where the pheasant shooting was always excellent. Harry Jocelyn, the heir, had been with us at Balliol, hence Ray and I usually received invitations to the shooting parties. On this occasion, however, Vera Vallance with her aunt, Mrs. Mortimer, had been invited, much to Ray's satisfaction.

Among the party was a well-known naval officer, captain of a first-class cruiser, two military officers, and several smart women, for both Sir Herbert and Lady Jocelyn moved in a very smart set. Several of the ladies had joined us in the smoking-room for cigarettes, and the conversation around the fire had been mainly the usual society chatter, until at one o'clock every one had left for bed except our two selves.

Over the great fireplace were the arms of the Jocelyns carved in stone, with the date 1573, and in the corner near the window was a stand of armour upon which the dancing flames glinted ever and anon. Through the long uncurtained window shone the bright moon from over the park, and just as I reseated myself the stable clock chimed the half-hour.

We had been there four days, and the sport had been excellent. On the previous day Ray had excused himself on account of the bad weather, and had spent the hours mostly with Vera.

It was of how he had employed his time that he had been telling me when I had discovered the eavesdropper.

"I wonder why our conversation should prove so interesting to that maid?" he remarked thoughtfully, gazing into the fire. "She's rather good-looking for a German, isn't she?"

"Yes," I said. "But who is this Mrs. Hill-Mason? She seems a rather loud and buxom person, fond of the display of jewellery, dark, somewhat oleaginous, and devoted to bridge."

"Harry says his mother met her in Cairo last winter. She's one of the Somerset Masons—half-sister to the Countess of Thanet."

"Oh, she is known, then?"

"Of course. But we must get Vera to make some inquiry to-morrow as to where she obtained her maid," declared Ray. "The woman is interested in us, and we must discover the cause."

"Yes, I somehow mistrust her," I said. "I met her crossing the hall just before dinner, and I detected a curious look in her eyes as she glanced at me."

"Merely your fancy, Jack, old chap—because she's German," he laughed, stretching his long legs.

"Well, what you were telling me about Vera and her discovery has alarmed me," I said, tossing away the end of my cigar.

"Yes, she only returned last week from Emden, where she's been visiting her old German governess, who, it seems, is now married to an official in the construction department of the German Admiralty. From her friend she was able to learn a lot, which will, no doubt, cause our Lords of the Admiralty a bad quarter of an hour."

"What would the British public think if they were told the truth—that Germany is rapidly building a secret fleet?" I said.

"Why, my dear fellow, the public would simply say you were a liar," he laughed. "Every Englishman fancies himself top-dog, even though British diplomacy—apart from that of our excellent King—is the laughing-stock of the Powers. No," he added, "the truth is out. All yesterday I spent with Vera, preparing the information which she forwarded to the Admiralty tonight. I registered the letter for her at the village post office. The authorities owe her a very deep debt for succeeding in obtaining the information which our secret service has always failed to get. She, an admiral's daughter, is now able to furnish actual details of the ships now building in secret and where they are being constructed."

"A matter which will, no doubt, be considered very seriously by the Government," I said.

"Oh, I suppose they treat the whole thing lightly, as they always do. We invite invasion," he sighed as he rose, adding: "Let's turn in now. Tomorrow we'll keep an eye upon that unusually inquisitive maid."

That night the eyes of the German maid haunted me. I could not rid myself of their recollection. Was it that this hunting down of German spies was getting on my nerves?

Next day we were shooting Starlings Wood, about five miles distant, but Ray having "cried off" one day, could not do so again. Therefore, at his suggestion, I made an excuse and remained at home with the ladies. The morning I spent walking through the park with Vera, a smart, sweet-faced little figure in her short tweed skirt and furs, with her bright and vivacious chatter. From her I learnt some further details concerning her visit to Emden.

"Ray is most excited about it, Mr. Jacox," she was saying. "Of course, I had to make my inquiries with great caution and discretion, but I managed to find out what I wanted, and I sent all the details to the Admiralty yesterday."

Then as we went along the wide beech avenue I told her of the curious incident in the smoking-room on the previous evening.

"Ray was telling me about it just before breakfast," she said, turning her splendid eyes to mine. "I have already made some inquiries of Mrs. Hill-Mason, and it appears that the maid Erna Stolberg was recommended to her by a friend when she was in Dresden last year. She's a most exemplary person, and has a number of friends in England. She was previously with a French *baronne*."

"Mrs. Hill-Mason often moves in a military set, doesn't she?" I remarked. "Somebody last night stated that she's the widow of a general, and is well known down at Aldershot."

"I believe so."

"If Mrs. Hill-Mason visits at the houses of military officers, as it seems she does, then this inquisitive maid would be afforded many opportunities for gathering information. I intend to watch her," I said.

"And so will I, Mr. Jacox," replied the admiral's daughter, drawing her astrachan collar tighter about her throat.

Half an hour later we drove in the wagonette out to the shooting-party in the woods, where a merry luncheon was served in a marquee. I, however, returned to the house before the rest of the party and haunted the servants' hall. With Williams the butler I was on friendly terms, and finding him in the great hall, began to make inquiries regarding the guests' servants.

"You've got a German woman among them, haven't you?" I remarked.

"Yes, sir," was his reply. "A rather funny one she is, I fancy. She goes out alone for walks after she's dressed her mistress for dinner, and is out sometimes till quite late. What she does wandering about in the dark nobody knows. But it ain't for me to say a word, sir; she's a visitor's maid."

I held my own counsel, but resolved to watch.

Tea in the great hall, over which Lady Jocelyn presided, proved the usual irresponsible function, but when I went to my room to dress for dinner I became convinced that certain papers in my suit-case had been turned over and investigated.

That night I did not go in to dinner. I heard the gong sound, and when the company had gone in, I put on thick boots, overcoat, and cap, and passed through the back way along the old wing of the house, through the smoking-room, and out upon the drive.

Behind some holly bushes where I could see any one leave by the great paved courtyard where the servants' entrance was situated, I concealed myself and waited in patience. The night was dark and overcast. The stable chimes had rung out half-past eight, but I still remained until, about twenty minutes later, footfalls sounded, and from out the arched entrance to the courtyard came a female figure in a close-fitting hat and long dark ulster.

She passed close by me, under the light of the lamp, and I saw it was the fair-haired woman for whom I was waiting.

Instead of walking straight down the avenue to the lodge-gates, she struck along a footpath which led for a mile across the park, first skirting the lake—the fishpond of the monks who lived there before the Dissolution; then, passing under the dark shadow of a spinney, led to a stile by which the high park wall could be negotiated and the main road to East Dereham reached.

As she went forward so I followed. I knew the path well. I watched her ascend the stile and cross the wall into the road. Then I crept up and peered over into the darkness. She had turned to the right, and I could discern her waiting at the roadside about thirty yards away.

From my place of concealment I could hear her slow footsteps as she idled up and down in the darkness, evidently waiting for some one.

I think about ten minutes passed when I heard the whir of a motor-car approaching, its big glaring headlamps shedding a stream of white brilliance over the muddy road. As it approached her it slowed down and stopped. Then I distinguished it to be a big Limousine, the occupant of which opened the door, and she entered with a word of greeting.

I stood peering into the darkness, in surprise and disappointment at not catching sight of the person with whom she was keeping these nightly appointments. As soon as the door had banged the driver drove across the road, backed, and turning, sped away in the direction he had come.

But while he was turning I had gained the road, advancing beneath the hedgerow in an endeavour to see the number of the car. But I was baffled. It was covered with mud.

Afterwards, much disappointed, and certainly hungry, I made my way back across the park to the Hall, where, after managing to get a snack from Williams, I joined the party at bridge.

That night the woman Stolberg returned at five minutes to eleven, and later, when Ray went upstairs with me, I described what I had seen.

Next night, instead of following her out, I waited at the spot at half-past ten, when, sure enough, the car returned ten minutes later and deposited her. The number plates, however, were obliterated by the mud both front and back—purposely it seemed to me. The man within shook her hand as she alighted, but I could not see his face. Was he some secret lover? Apparently she went no great distance each evening, going and coming from the direction of Holt.

On the following day I took several opportunities of watching the woman at close quarters. Her eyes were peculiarly set, very close together, her lips were thin, and her cheek-bones rather high. Otherwise she was not bad-looking. Mrs. Hill-Mason had, of course, no idea of her maid's nocturnal motor-rides.

Whether the woman had any suspicion that she was being watched I know not; but on the next night when Ray took a turn at keeping an eye upon her, she did not go out, but on the next she went, and Ray followed her to the park wall, but saw nothing more than I had done.

All this time, of course, Vera was greatly interested in the result of our observations. Through her own maid, Batson, she discovered the room occupied by the German, and to this I made my way, at considerable risk, one morning while the maid was busy attending upon her mistress. I had a good look through her belongings, finding in her trunk a small, flat tin box, japanned dark green, strong, and secured by a lock of well-known make. What, I wondered, did it contain?

Could I have but seen the number of the mysterious car I could have discovered the identity of her nocturnal visitor.

The same day that I discovered the tin box in her trunk, Mrs. Hill-Mason, however, returned to London, taking with her the mysterious Fräulein.

Three days more went by, and I was about to dismiss the affair as a combination of curious circumstances. Vera and her aunt had left to pay a visit in Worcestershire, and Ray I were due to go up to town that morning, when he entered my room, saying abruptly:

"I'm not going to London yet, Jack. I shall go over to Cromer instead."

"Cromer!" I echoed. "Hardly the time of year for the seaside."

That same grey chilly afternoon, in the grey falling light, we sat upon one of the seats of the pier at Cromer gazing seaward, towards where the German coast lay beyond the indistinct horizon. The place was deserted save for ourselves. On the cliff behind us stood the long red façade and many gables of the Hotel de Paris, where we had put up, while in the background rose the square old church tower, the landmark of mariners from Haisborough Gat to the Dowsing.

"There's just a chance of us falling upon something interesting about here," Ray was saying, as he pressed the tobacco into his pipe, and by the expression upon his keen clean-shaven face I saw that he had scented the presence of spies. "Has it never struck you," he went on, "that the east coast, where we now are is the most vulnerable spot in England, and the first objective of the Kaiser's army? Every soldier and sailor in Germany dreams of 'the Day'—the day when he will set foot upon this shore. For some years past our Intelligence Department has known of the German plans for our invasion. There are several, but in each one a dash, and a surprise landing along this coast of Norfolk and of Suffolk and Essex is the first step. Knowledge of this prompted Lord Roberts to resign his seat on the National Defence Committee and make those stirring speeches pointing out our country's peril."

"And what thanks did the country give him?" I interrupted. "People only laugh at him for his trouble!"

"Yes," said my friend bitterly, "the public are ignorant, therefore they do not heed. They talk glibly about the strength of our navy, forgetful that the German diplomacy is the cleverest and most cunning in the world. When 'the Day' dawns there will be no suspicion of war, and certainly no declaration of hostilities. Before we have realised that war is in the air, the enemy will have their feet firmly planted upon British soil."

"And if the enemy intend landing along this shore, it is certain that spies are active here, gathering all information likely to be of service to the invader."

"That's exactly why I've come here, my dear Jack," my friend said. "We know that our eastern counties have been divided into districts by the Germans, and in each one or more secret agents are busily at work taking notes of food supplies, forage, blacksmiths' shops, motor-cars for transport, the destruction of telegraphs and telephones, positions for artillery, and the best mode of advance south to London. One may rest assured that the ordnance map is being very much amplified just now."

That evening we spent idly in the hotel, and next day, hiring a motor-car, we drove through Runton to Sheringham and over the hills three miles further towards the back-door of England—the place neglected by those responsible for our defences, and by the public alike—Weybourne.

The road from Sheringham ran down a steep hill, called the Fox Hill, to the little village that lay cosily at some distance from the sea. Passing the church we turned sharply to the right, and in a few minutes found ourselves against a large front with a wide open beach beyond.

Having alighted, we walked along beside the surf for some distance, out of hearing of our chauffeur, when my friend exclaimed:

"Here is one of the spots which the Germans have chosen for landing. Look at it! Everything is in favour of a hostile force. That range of hills we've just come over at the back would be occupied by the landing force at once, and thus they would command the whole country from Kelling, which you see to the right, away south beyond Cromer, down to Baxton beyond Mundesley."

With my back to the long rolling breakers I gazed away landward at the long line of hills stretching in each direction. It was, indeed, an ideal spot for an enemy to effect a landing, with deep water right up to the land.

"Because of the confidence we have in our fleet and our wonderful diplomacy this place is no longer watched," Raymond remarked, standing beside me muffled in his motor-coat, for the wind was intensely cold. "Yet in days gone by, by reason of the facilities which nature has provided for the landing of hostile forces, it was carefully guarded whenever the invasion of England was believed to be imminent."

After we had strolled some distance along the beach, where the grey-green waters were breaking into foam, my friend suddenly halted and, taking a piece of paper from his pocket, stood with his back to the sea and made a sketch of the irregular contour of the blue hills facing him from the coastguard at Salthouse on the right to the rising ground behind Upper Sheringham on the left—the positions which are to be first occupied by the enemy in their attack upon us.

He made no explanation of the reason of his action, therefore I stood by watching in silence.

At last we returned to the car and drove inland to Weybourne village, a sleepy old-world little place from which the sea has receded. As we turned into the main road he ordered the man to pull up, and, descending, looked about him, first at the lines of telegraph-wire running beside the road, and then we both strolled through the village. My companion's eyes were everywhere. He appeared to be making mental notes of every feature of the obscure little place.

Just as we were returning to the car he suddenly halted, saying:

"You go on. A thought has just occurred to me." And, turning, he walked back to the small village post office situated next door to an inn, and was absent for nearly a quarter of an hour.

"As I suspected!" he remarked beneath his breath as he rejoined me. "That inn is kept by a German!"

Then we travelled along to Cley-next-the-Sea, and thence by way of Candlestick Hill and through the wooded country around Holt, back to Sheringham, where we lunched at the "Burlington."

His manner had changed. He had again become serious and thoughtful. A cycling map of the district which he had bought in Cromer that morning he brought out, and as we sat together in the smoking-room he spread it upon the table and began measuring distances with a slip of folded paper.

The car was at the door at four o'clock, and we were in the act of moving off, when by mere chance I looked up at the second floor of the hotel. What I saw caused me to hold my breath.

A face was at one of the windows watching us.

I nudged my friend, and cried, "Look!"

But when he raised his head it had gone. Indeed, the white face had only showed there for a single instant, yet it was a countenance that I too well remembered, it was unmistakable—that of Fräulein Stolberg!

I told Ray as we whirled along into the town. But he only grunted in surprise, and remarked that we were going to Beccles.

Why was that woman there instead of being with her mistress, who, we had ascertained, was now visiting at Cheltenham?

Our way lay first back to Cromer, where we joined the direct Norwich road by way of Aylsham, but about four miles after passing Cromer the road divided. The left-hand one ran to our destination, but at Ray's orders we took the right-hand one, and in the darkening twilight struck across a wide heath, which I afterwards learnt was called Roughton Heath, until we passed an old windmill, and entered the small crooked village of Roughton. We passed beyond the place for a quarter of a mile, and then descending, walked forward until we came to a good-sized, comfortable, old-fashioned house, probably of the days of Queen Anne, that lay behind a high red-brick wall.

Through the iron gates I noticed, as we paused, a wide lawn in front, with steps leading up to a portico, and behind a large orchard and meadow. The blinds were already down, but in several of the windows lights showed, and the place looked well kept up.

It differed but little from hundreds of other old-fashioned houses in the country, but it evidently held considerable attraction for Ray, because as we passed beyond the gates, and out of sight of any one in the house, he took out his electric torch and carefully examined the muddy roadway.

"See!" he exclaimed, pointing to tracks that ran in and out of the gateway. "The car's home is here!"

"What car?"

"The car which used to meet the German maid at Metfield," was his matter-of-fact reply. "For the present we know sufficient. We must look sharp if we are to be in Beccles before eight. If we're not there before, it will be of no use."

So we hurried back to our own car, and our driver, by taking a by-path, brought us out upon the main road again at Thorpe Market, and just after half-past seven we pulled up before the hotel in the old Suffolk market town of Beccles, under the shadow of the stumpy square old church tower.

The car was garaged, and after a drink we went forth for a walk along the quiet old-world streets, until suddenly upon a corner we came to the post office, a large old-fashioned two-storied house with steep tiled roof.

"Wait about here," my companion said; "a dark-haired man in a light grey overcoat and golf-cap will probably come to post a letter just before eight. He has a dark brown beard, and usually wears a white muffler. When he comes follow him, and see where he goes. He may know me, so I must keep out of sight."

Therefore I lit my pipe, and idled up and down, keeping the letter-box in view. In the window, directly above it, was a clock which showed it then to be a quarter to eight. I took a pretended interest in the small shops near, until about four minutes to the hour a closed motor-car swung round from the direction of the Public Hall, and pulled up before the post office.

From it two men alighted—one a youngish fair-haired man, and the other, dark-bearded and much older, wore a thick grey overcoat and a white muffler. He was the man of whom I was in search.

I entered the office directly after the pair, on pretence of buying stamps, but already the elder of the two had handed in a letter to be registered, the address of which I failed to discern.

Both seemed to be in a great hurry, for as soon as the receipt was written out they re-entered the car and drove back in the direction they had come, leaving me standing helpless on the opposite side of the road.

Immediately I returned to the hotel where Ray was waiting, and reported to him, whereupon he seized his hat, and walking with me back to the post office halted in the centre of the road examining the wheel-tracks, which were still quite plain upon the damp roadway.

Then, as he walked back, he said:

"Do you know, Jack, that this town Beccles has been decided upon by the Germans as the head-quarters of the Army Corps which lands at Weybourne? It's a natural position, standing upon high ground and commanding the whole of the surrounding country. Signals made from that church tower yonder could be seen very far afield."

Then, as we sat together in the coffee-room of the hotel, eating a hasty meal, he remarked:

"We'll go back to Cromer to-night, but I shall go to town to-morrow. You'll wait till my return, won't you?"

So I was left alone for nearly a week; and on his return he announced that we must at once shift our quarters to Lowestoft. So south we went that same night, arriving at midnight, and putting up at the many-balconied Empire Hotel.

The town interested my companion not at all, but from there we went forth each day on long motor excursions, scouring the whole country as far south as Aldborough and as far west as Bury St. Edmunds. All the roads round Southwold, Bungay, Saxmundham, Stow Market, and many other towns we reconnoitred, apparently always with the same object—to discover wheel-tracks of a mysterious car.

The garages of every town Ray visited alone, but his inquiries always met with the same negative result.

Late one afternoon, however, when on the road between Wymondham and Diss, he suddenly shouted to the driver to stop, and jumping out, examined the track of wheels. The road, however, was hard at that spot, and it was some time before he could decide whether the car had travelled north or south.

"They've gone north!" he declared with satisfaction; therefore we continued to follow them towards Wymondham, where they had drawn up at the "Old Green Dragon," and gone forth again, striking into a by-road which led to Bracon Ash.

"Ha!" he cried, when he saw this, "so they're busy at work—that's plain!"

But by this time the light had faded, and much to our chagrin we were again compelled to give up the hunt, and find our way over by Hempnall, and so through Bungay back to Lowestoft.

Next day we were early back again at the spot, but heavy rain had unfortunately fallen all night, so the tracks had been obliterated.

After another week of unsuccessful journeying we were, one day, about half-way between Norwich going towards Aylsham, when my friend's keen eyes caught sight of a wheel-track coming out of a narrow by-road.

We halted, and descending he examined them minutely, declaring that they were what we were in search of, and quite fresh.

Therefore, considerably excited, we were soon upon the trail, following the car through Aylsham and North Walsham until, on the road that led towards the sea at Happisburgh, it suddenly turned into another byway.

Here Ray decided to pull up and follow on foot, which we did for nearly two miles, until we saw before us the railway line which runs between North Walsham and Yarmouth. We had left the road, for there, pulled up before us, was the car I had seen at Beccles, and on ahead were the two men, one of whom I recognised by his grey coat and white muffler.

They were beneath the railway bridge, carefully examining it.

"They're marking that down on their plan for destruction," remarked Ray between his teeth. "All these connections will be destroyed when they land. But, by heaven! we'll be even with them yet!"

We watched them in secret for a full half-hour, as they examined the railroad at several points, and when they had driven off we followed them along a road where ran six lines of telegraph into Happisburgh.

"Those wires," remarked Ray, "form one of the direct cables to Germany. They pass through Beccles, so you may rest assured that they've surveyed it well!"

At Happisburgh the tracks turned to the left, and thence again to the right to Walcot, but just as we were passing over a low hill we saw that the car on before us had stopped. The two men were photographing the country from Paston, inland towards Witton.

We drew up and watched their movements.

Then they went on, and we followed, parting company with their tracks at the cross-roads, they going westward, while we struck north, until we found ourselves once again in Cromer for the night.

That evening we made an amazing discovery at the hotel. Erna Stolberg was staying there alone under the name of Madame Hirsch! Ray first saw her seated in the reading-room, and called me. I peered in at the door and recognised her in a pale blue silk blouse and black net skirt, lying back in a chair reading an illustrated paper. She was evidently quite unsuspicious of our presence.

Ray was sorely puzzled. Next morning he sent a wire to Mrs. Hill-Mason's house in Charles Street, and before noon had received a reply from her at Bournemouth saying that Fräulein Stolberg had left her service a fortnight before.

"German spies are pretty active in East Anglia, old chap, as you've seen with your own eyes," he remarked to me.

In order that the woman should not notice us, we told the chauffeur to meet us out on the Norwich road, after which we travelled to quaint old Aylsham, where we idled away the day, spending the afternoon playing billiards at the "White Horse."

More than once during the day my companion examined the road outside for traces of wheel-tracks, but there were none like those of the car of those secret agents of Hermann Hartmann.

I noticed that Ray had brought with him a small brown brief-bag, an unusual thing for him to carry. But that morning he had placed it in the car with instructions to the chauffeur to move it on no account.

At four o'clock that afternoon he received a telegram, which he read through twice, and placed on the fire, remarking:

"From Vera. She's received the thanks of the Admiralty for her report. They promise to make inquiry. Probably they'll send somebody over who can't speak a word of German!"

We dined at half-past six off cold meat and pickles, but not until midnight did we set out upon the road, travelling north in the direction of Cromer, until we came to the cross roads at Hanworth, where we halted and Ray got down to examine the road. Wheel-tracks were there leading back to Roughton, and these we followed until, near the entrance to the village, now in complete darkness, we descended, Ray lifting out his precious bag.

"You've got your revolver?" he asked, when we had gone a hundred yards or so.

I replied in the affirmative, for nowadays I always carried it.

"Well, we are going to get into that house at Roughton I pointed out to you," he said. "I intend to have a look round."

"You mean to break in? Suppose we're caught!" I exclaimed.

"Bah! Spies are always cowards. Leave that to me."

So we went on until, having passed through the silent village, we entered a road where the bare trees met overhead, rendering it almost pitch-dark, and presently approached the house.

Not a light showed anywhere. Whoever were its occupants, they had retired.

For nearly half an hour we concealed ourselves in the bushes opposite, watching in patience, for the night was as yet young. In the distance we fancied we heard the sound of wheels, but they did not advance; therefore we agreed that it was only fancy.

After waiting what seemed to me hours, Ray switched on his electric lamp to see the time. It was then nearly two o'clock, so we decided to take another step forward.

We crossed the road and tried the iron gate. It was locked.

There was nothing for it but to scale it, and as I was in the act of clambering up I was startled by a strange voice behind me—a woman's voice raising an alarm!

Ray, who was standing behind me, closed with the unwelcome stranger in an instant, and placed his hand forcibly over her mouth while I sprang back to assist him. That moment was an exciting one.

"Put your handkerchief in her mouth, man!" he cried. "Don't you see who it is—the woman Stolberg!"

Quick as thought I took out my handkerchief and stuffed it into her mouth while he held her. Then I gripped her arms, while Ray produced the thin silk rope which he usually carried on such expeditions and with it bound her tightly hand and foot.

She struggled violently, cursing us in German the while, but all in vain. So at length we disposed of her comfortably against a tree-trunk in a field opposite, to which Ray very deftly secured her. She had evidently driven over from Cromer on some important errand to her friends and had stopped the cart some distance away from the house.

Cautiously we negotiated the high iron gate, and creeping noiselessly across the lawn, gained the window on the left of the entrance. Ray flashed his light upon it, and noting that the fastening was only an ordinary one, promptly commenced work upon it by inserting one of his burglarious tools between the sashes. In a few moments it sprang back with a click, and lifting the sash slowly and pushing aside the holland blind, he swung himself into a comfortably furnished sitting-room, I following quickly at his heels.

In that dead silence I could hear my heart throbbing.

We were actually in the house of the spies!

The room, which contained nothing of interest to us, smelt strongly of tobacco, while upon the table lay a big German pipe. Still gripping his leather bag Ray carefully opened the door, and crossing the wide old-fashioned hall, opened another door, when we found ourselves in an old-fashioned dining-room, the sideboard of which was decorated with some very nice antique blue china. From this apartment we visited the drawing-room and another smaller reception-room, and then, creeping on tiptoe, we ascended the old well staircase which once creaked horribly beneath me.

Here we were confronted with a serious problem. We knew not in which room the spies were sleeping.

Ray halted at the top of the stairs to take his bearings, and after some hesitation resolved to first investigate the room over the one by which we had entered. He tried the door. It was locked on the inside. Somebody was within.

So we crept across to the opposite side. Here the door was also locked, but a flash from the torch revealed that there was no key inside. It was a locked room, and Ray determined to see what lay beyond.

Therefore, with infinite care not to make a sound, he drew from his pocket some skeleton keys, one of which slid back the bolt, and in a moment we were within.

The torch, an instant later, revealed an amazing state of things. Pinned down to the large deal table before the window was a huge map of the district from Weybourne towards Yarmouth, about five feet square, made up of various sections of the six-inch ordnance map, and literally covered with annotations and amplifications in German, written in red ink. Upon strings stretched across one end of the room were a number of photographic films and prints in process of drying, while strewn about the place were rough military sketches—the result of the labours of many months—a couple of cameras, measuring tapes, a heliograph apparatus, a portfolio full of carefully drawn plans with German explanations beneath, and a tin box, which, when opened, we found to contain a number of neatly written reports and memoranda in German, all ready for transmission to Berlin!

Ray seized a whole handful of these papers—a translation of one of which is here reproduced—and stuffed them into his pocket, saying:

"These will prove interesting reading for us later on, no doubt."

EAST COAST OF ENGLAND—DISTRICT VI.

Memoranda by Captain Wilhelm Stolberg, 114th Regiment Westphalian Cuirassiers, on special duty February, 1906—December, 1908.

WEYBOURNE—Norfolk—England. (Section coloured red upon large scale map. Photographs Series B, 221 to 386.)

In Sheringham and Cromer comprised in this District are resident forty-six German subjects, mostly hotel servants, waiters, and tradesmen, who have each been allotted their task on "the Day."

Arms:—a store of arms is in a house at Kelling Heath, where on receipt of the signal all will secretly assemble, and at a given hour surprise and hold up the coastguard at all stations in their district, cut all telegraph and telephones shown upon the large map to be destroyed, wire in pre-arranged cipher to their comrades at Happisburgh to seize the German cable there, and take every precaution to prevent any fact whatsoever leaking out concerning the presence of our ships.

Men:—Every man is a trained soldier, and has taken the oath of loyalty to your Imperial Majesty. Their leader is Lieutenant Bischoffsheim, living in Tucker Street, Cromer, in the guise of a baker.

Explosives for Bridges:—These have been stored at Sandy Hill, close to Weybourne Station, marked on map.

Landing Place:—Weybourne is the easiest and safest along the whole coast. The coast-guard station, on the east, has a wire to Harwich, which will be cut before our ships are in sight. In Weybourne village there is a small telegraph office, but this will at the same time be seized by our people occupying an inn in the vicinity, a place which will be recognised by the display of a Union Jack.

Wires:—Eight important wires run through here, five of which must be cut, as well as the trunk telephone. Direct communication with Beccles is obtained.

Beach:—Hard, and an excellent road runs from the sea to the highway south. For soundings, see notes upon British soundings. Admiralty Chart No. 1630 accompanying.

Forge:—There is one at the end of the village.

Provisions:—Grocers' shops in village are small, therefore do not contain much stock. There are plenty of sheep and oxen in the district towards Gunton. (See accompanying lists of amount of live stock upon each farm.)

Motor-Cars:—(List of owners and addresses attached)...

A specimen of the notes of German spies.

But just at that moment in stepping back I unfortunately knocked over a frame containing some glass negatives, which fell from a shelf with a loud crash.

We both stood breathless. There was a quick movement in the room adjoining, and we heard men's voices shouting to each other in German.

"Stay here," Ray said firmly. "We must not show the white feather now."

Almost as the words left his mouth we were confronted by the two men whom we had seen surveying the railway line.

"Well!" cried Ray, gripping his precious bag and facing them boldly, "you see we've discovered your little game, gentlemen! Those notes on the map are particularly interesting."

"By what right, pray, do you enter here?" asked the bearded man, speaking in fairly good English.

"By the right of an Englishman, Herr Stolberg," was Ray's bold reply. "You'll find your clever wife tied up to a tree in the field opposite."

The younger man held a revolver, but from his face I saw that he was a coward.

"What do you mean?" demanded the other.

"I mean that I intend destroying all this excellent espionage work of yours. You've lived here for two years, and have been very busy travelling in your car and gathering information. But," he said, "you were a little unwise in putting upon your car the new Feldmarck non-skids, the only set, I believe, yet in England. They may be very good tyres, but scarcely adapted for spying purposes. I, for instance, noticed the difference in the tracks the wheels made one evening when you met your wife outside Metfield Park, and that is what led me to you."

"You'd destroy all my notes and plans!" he gasped, with a fierce oath in German. "You shall never do that—you English cur!"

"Then stand aside and watch!" he cried, withdrawing from the room on to the landing. "See, look here!" and he opened his bag. This caused both men to withdraw from the room to peer inside his bag.

With a quiet movement, however, Ray flung a small dark object into the centre of the room, and in an instant there was a bright blood-red flash, and the whole place was one mass of roaring flames, which, belching from the door, caused us all to beat a hasty retreat. In a moment the place was a furnace.

The spies shouted, cursed, and fired their revolvers at us through the thick smoke, but we were quickly downstairs and out in the road.

"That will soon drive out the rats," laughed Ray, as we watched the flames burst through the roof and saw the two men escape half dressed through the window we had opened.

And as, with the red glare behind us, we hurried back to the spot where we had left our car, Ray remarked, with a laugh of triumph:

"Stolberg bought that place two years ago with money, no doubt, supplied from Berlin, so he's scarcely likely to come upon us for incendiarism, I think. It was the only way—to make one big bonfire of the whole thing!"

CHAPTER IV
HOW THE GERMANS ARE PREPARING FOR INVASION

"We're going down to Maldon, in Essex," Ray Raymond explained as we drove along in a taxi-cab to Liverpool Street Station late one grey snowy afternoon soon after our return from Norfolk.

He had been away from London for three weeks, and I had no idea of his whereabouts, except that one night he rang me up on the telephone from the Cups Hotel, at Colchester.

An hour ago he had returned to New Stone Buildings in the guise of a respectable mechanic in his Sunday clothes, and, full of bustle and excitement, urged me to run across to Guilford Street and assume a similar disguise. Then, each with his modest bag, we had hailed a motor-cab and given the man instructions to drive to the Great Eastern terminus.

"You've read the affair in this evening's paper, I suppose?" my companion asked; "the mystery at Button's Hill?"

"Yes," I replied. "Are we about to investigate it?"

"That's my intention, my dear Jacox," was his quick reply, as he handed me his cigarette-case. Then, ten minutes later, when we were seated together alone in a third-class carriage slowly leaving London, he turned to me, and with a deep earnest look upon his face, said:

"There's much more behind what appears in the papers regarding this curious affair—depend upon it, old chap. I've wired to Vera to be prepared to come to Maldon on receipt of a telegram. The facts, as far as are at present known, are these," he went on as he slowly lit another cigarette: "At an early hour this morning a farm labourer, on his way to work between Latchingdon and Southminster, discovered, lying in a ditch, the body of James Pavely, aged forty-three, a well-known fisherman and pilot. His head had been crushed by savage blows, his clothes were soaked with blood, and he was nearly buried beneath the snow. The labourer alarmed the police, and the body was conveyed to Southminster. Pavely, who was very popular at the waterside at Maldon, was unmarried, and until recently had been rather well-to-do, but for the past few months bad luck is said to have persistently pursued him, and he had been left without a boat, even without a share in a boat, and more recently he had been out of a job altogether. Now," he added, with a keen look, "I want to fix that point in your mind. For months, ever since the summer, he has been known to be on the verge of starvation, yet the police have found in his trousers' pocket a handkerchief in which, carefully tied up, were forty-nine sovereigns!"

"His savings?" I suggested.

"No," declared my companion conclusively.

"But if he was murdered, why wasn't the money taken?" I queried.

Ray smiled, his face assuming that sphinx-like expression by which I knew that he had formed some theory—a theory he was about to put to the test.

"The reason we have to discover, Jacox," he said vaguely. "The dead man is a pilot," he added; "and in Maldon are many German spies."

"But I don't see that the fact of Pavely pursuing the honourable calling of pilot would arouse the enmity of any secret agent," I remarked.

"We shall see," was my friend's response; and he became immersed in his paper.

On reaching the prosperous little town of Maldon we left our bags in the cloak-room. The snow was lying thickly, but it was no longer falling. A sharp frost had set in, rendering the roads very slippery. In the darkness infrequent lights glimmered here and there in the quaint old streets and among the barges and coasting vessels which lay along the Hithe. The tide was nearly full, and the river covered with half-congealed snow and ice. Few passengers were abroad that wintry evening, but as we passed a small low-built public-house called the "Goat and Binnacle," at the waterside, we could hear that there were many customers within, all of whom seemed to be talking at once.

The red-curtained windows reflected a ruddy chequer upon the trampled snow, and men were coming up by twos and threes from the river craft, one and all wending their way to that low-browed house which seemed to be doing such a roaring trade.

"Let's take a look inside," Ray suggested in a whisper. "We might hear something."

So together we turned back, and entered the low-built, old-fashioned place.

Within, we found them all discussing the mysterious death of Jim Pavely.

Mostly English were the bronzed, weather-beaten men of the sea and the longshoremen who were smoking and drinking, and talking so earnestly, but a few foreigners were among them. There were two or three Frenchmen, dapper fellows in well-made pea-jackets and berets, who had rowed ashore from the big white yawl flying the tricolour, which had been lying off Heybridge waiting, so we heard, for a change from the present icy weather before going to sea again; and there were also a fair number of Swedes and Norwegians from the two timber-ships whose spars, we had noticed, towered above the rows of smaller and stumpier masts belonging to the local and coasting craft which lay alongside the Hithe. Then there was the first mate of one of the timber-ships, supposed by most of those present to be a German. At any rate, he seemed to be trying hard to carry on a conversation with the fair-haired landlord, an undoubted immigrant from the Fatherland.

From one of the seafaring customers with whom I began to chat, I learned that the keeper of the place was named Leopold Bramberger, and that he had been established in that little river-side hostelry rather more than a year, and was now a well-known and more or less respected inhabitant of the borough of Maldon. He had made a little money—so it was generally understood—in the course of some years' service at the Carlton Hotel in London as waiter. And a good waiter he certainly was, as many people living in that part of the country could testify; since he found time to go out as "an extra hand" to many a dinner-party; his services being much appreciated and bringing him in quite a comfortable little addition to what he made by the sale of drink down by the Blackwater. But he did not seem very anxious to talk with his compatriot; indeed, so frequent were the demands made for "another pot of four 'arf," "two of gin 'ot," "another glass of Scotch," and other delectable beverages, that he and his better half had all they could do to grapple with the wants of their customers.

From the conversation about us we gathered that the dead man, though previously somewhat abstemious, had lately become rather a constant frequenter of the "Goat and Binnacle," and though no one had seen him actually drunk, there were not a few who could testify to having seen him in a state very nearly approaching, in their opinion, to "half-seas-over."

"Well, I' give suthing to lay my 'ands on the blackguard as 'as done for pore Jim," remarked a burly longshoreman to his neighbour. "'E'd never done no one a bad turn, as I knows on, and a better feller there wasn't between 'ere an' 'Arwich."

"No there wasn't," came quite a chorus. Jim Pavely, whatever his misfortunes, was evidently a favourite.

"And no one wouldn't have any idea of robbin' pore Jim," interposed another customer; "every one knows that there's bin nothin' on 'im wuth stealin' this many a day—pore chap."

"Except that forty-nine pound," remarked the German landlord, in very good English.

"As for that," exclaimed a little man sitting in the chimney-corner, "I see Belton, the constable, as I were a-coming down here a quarter of an hour ago, an' he says as how there wasn't no signs of any attempt at robbery. Jim had his old five-bob watch in 'is pocket, not worth pawnin'; the sovereigns and some silver were in his trousers."

"Ah! That's the mystery!" exclaimed more than one in surprise. "Why no one wouldn't have thought as Jim 'ad seen the colour o' gold this three months past."

"Come on in and shut the door," cried some one, as a new-comer entered the tap-room, followed by an icy blast and a shower of snow, which was again falling.

"Why, it's Sergeant Newte!" exclaimed the publican, as a burly man in a dark overcoat entered, carefully closed the door, and moved ponderously towards the bar. A sudden hush fell upon the assembly, all eyes and ears being turned towards the representative of the law. All felt that the plain-clothes man bore news of the tragedy, and waited anxiously for the oracle to speak.

"Well, sir," asked Bramberger, "and what can I have the pleasure of serving you with? It isn't often we have the honour of your company down here."

"I won't have anything to-night, thanks," answered the man. "It isn't a drink I'm after, but just a little information that I fancy you, or some of these gentlemen here, may be able to give me. Every one knows that James Pavely was a pretty frequent customer of yours, and what I want to find out is, when he was last in here?"

"Let me see. Last night about seven, wasn't it, Molly?" returned the landlord, turning to his wife. "No, by the by, he came in and had something about a quarter to nine. That's the last we saw of him, poor fellow."

The sergeant in plain clothes produced his notebook. "Who else was in the bar with him?"

"Nobody in particular. Some of the hands from the barges, I fancy. He just had his drink and passed the time of day, as you may say, and was off in five or ten minutes."

"Eh, but you're making a mistake there, Mr. Bramberger," spoke up a voice near by; and the officer turned sharply in the direction of the speaker.

Urged on by those standing round him, Robert Rait, a big longshoreman, came slowly to the front. All eyes were upon him, which caused him to assume a somewhat sheepish aspect.

"Well, Sergeant, true as I'm standing 'ere, I see pore Jim come out of this 'ere bar just after twelve last night along with that young gent as is learnin' farming over Latchingdon way."

At this every one grew interested.

"Are you sure of what you say?" asked the officer sharply.

"Sartin sure. I were sittin' on my barge a-smokin' my pipe, an' I 'eard the clock over at the church, behind 'ere, strike twelve. I don't know why, but I remember I counted the strokes. Five minutes later out come Pavely with the young gent, who I've often seen in this bar afore, an' they walked off round by the Marine Lake. They never took no notice o' me. They was too busy a' talkin'."

As the policeman slowly rendered this into writing, most eyes sought Bramberger, who, feeling that he was the object of an attention perhaps not too favourable, remarked:

"Ah, yes. I believe I'm wrong, after all. It was twelve o'clock I meant— not nine."

"And what about this young gent?" queried the constable quickly. "Who is he, anyway? Was he here with Pavely?"

"He might have gone out with him, I didn't take particular notice of him," the German replied.

"But who is he?"

"Oh, you know him well enough. He's often in Maldon. It's young Mr. Freeman, who's learning estate work with Mr. Harris, near Southminster. He does drop in here now and again."

"Yes, I know him. A fellow-countryman of yours, ain't he?"

"No; he's English. I'd know a German well enough."

"Well, I've heard him speak. Mr. Jones, the schoolmaster, told me once he thought he spoke with a German accent," replied the officer.

"So he do, Sergeant," spoke up a sailorman, "now you mention it. I'm often in Hamburg, an' I know the German accent."

"You don't know anything about that forty-nine pounds, I suppose?" asked the blundering local sergeant of police, for, as is usually the case, the aid of New Scotland Yard had not been invoked. The police in our small country towns are always very loath to request assistance from London, as such action is admission of their own incompetence. Many a murder mystery could be solved and the criminal brought to justice by prompt investigation by competent detectives. But after blunt inquiries such as those now in progress, success is usually rendered impossible.

Raymond exchanged glances with me and smiled. How different, I reflected, were his careful, painstaking, and often mysterious methods of investigation.

"Those sovereigns in 'is 'andkerchief are a puzzle," declared the man Rait, "but somehow I fancy there's been a bit o' mystery about pore Jim of late. Teddy Owen told me a week ago 'e see 'im up in London, a-talkin' with a foreigner on the platform at Liverpool Street."

"Where is Owen?" asked the sergeant eagerly.

"Gone over to Malmö on a Swedish timber-ship," was Robert Rait's reply. "'E won't be back for a couple of months, I dare say."

This statement of the man Owen was to Raymond and myself very significant and suspicious. Could it be that the pilot Pavely had sold some secret to a foreign agent, and that the money he carried with him on the previous night was the price of his treason? It was distinctly curious that the assassin had not possessed himself of that handkerchief full of sovereigns.

We lingered in the low-pitched inn for yet another half-hour, my companion accounting for our visit by telling one of the men a fictitious story that we had been sent to install the electric light in some new premises at the back of the old church. We heard several more inquiries made by the sergeant, and many were the wild theories advanced by those seafaring loungers. Then, having listened attentively to all that passed, we retraced our steps to the station, obtained our bags, and drove to the King's Head Hotel, where we duly installed ourselves.

"There's something very big behind the cruel murder of the pilot—that's my belief!" declared Raymond before we parted for the night. "Nobody here dreams the truth—a truth that will be found as startling as it is strange."

I told him of my suspicions that the publican Bramberger was a spy. But he shook his head, saying:

"Don't form any immature conclusions, my dear Jacox. At present the truth is very cunningly concealed. It remains for us to lift the veil and expose the truth to the police and the public. Good-night."

Three days passed. Ray Raymond remained practically inactive, save that we both attended the inquest at Southminster as members of the public and listened to the evidence. The revelation that a man apparently in a state of great destitution carried forty-nine sovereigns upon him struck the coroner as unusual, and at his direction the jury adjourned the inquiry for a week, to allow the police to make further investigation.

As soon as this was decided my companion at once became all activity. He found the man Rait, a big, clumsy seafarer, and questioned him. But from him he obtained nothing further. With the publican Bramberger he contrived to strike up a friendship, loudly declaring his theory that the motive of the murder of poor Pavely was jealousy, it being now known that he had been courting the pretty daughter of an old boatman over at Burnham.

My position was, as usual, one of silent obedience. Hither and thither I went at his bidding, leaving to his, the master mind, the gradual solution of the mystery. He was one of those secretive men who delighted in retaining something up his sleeve. The expression upon his face was never indicative of what was passing within his mind.

The adjourned inquest was held at last, and again we were both present at the back of the room. The police practically admitted their inability to solve the mystery, and after a long deliberation the twelve tradesmen returned a verdict of "wilful murder," leaving the constabulary to further prosecute their inquiries.

Nearly a fortnight had passed since the sturdy North Sea pilot had been so cruelly done to death, and many were the new theories advanced nightly in the smoke-room of the "Goat and Binnacle."

I still remained at the "King's Head," but Raymond was often absent for whole days, and by his manner I knew the spy-seeker to be busy investigating some theory he had formed.

He had been absent a couple of days, staying over at the "White Hart" at Burnham-on-Crouch, that place so frequented by boating men in summer, when one afternoon I ran over to Chelmsford to call upon a man I knew. It was about ten o'clock at night when I left his house to walk to the station to catch the last train, when, to my surprise, I saw close to the Town Hall a smart female figure in a black tailor-made gown and big black hat, walking before me, accompanied by a tall, thin, rather well-dressed young man in breeches and gaiters, who seemed to be something of a dandy.

The girl's back struck me as familiar, and I crossed the road and went forward so as to get a glance at her face beneath the street-lamp.

Yes, I was not mistaken. It was Vera Vallance! Her companion, however, was a complete stranger to me—a well-set-up, rather good-looking young fellow, with a small black moustache, whose age I guessed to be about twenty-eight or so, and whose dark eyes were peculiarly bright and vivacious. He walked with swaggering gait, and seemed to be of a decidedly horsey type.

From their attitude it appeared that they were intimate friends, and as they walked towards the station, I watched his hand steal into her astrachan muff.

The incident was certainly puzzling. Was this man Vera's secret lover? It certainly seemed so.

Therefore, unseen by her, I kept close vigilance upon the pair, watching them gain the platform where stood the train by which I was to travel back to Maldon. He entered a first-class carriage, while she remained upon the platform. Therefore it was evident that she was not accompanying him.

The train moved off, and, with a laugh, she actually kissed her hand to the stranger. Then I sat back in my corner greatly puzzled and disturbed. Surely Ray Raymond could not know of these clandestine meetings?

I was well aware how devoted my friend was to her. Surely she was not now faithless to her vow!

It was not my place to speak, so I could only patiently watch the progress of events.

The dark-eyed man alighted with me at Witham, but did not enter the Maldon train. Therefore I lost sight of him.

Three days later I caught sight of him in the main street at Maldon, still in gaiters and riding-breeches, and wearing a black and white check coat and crimson knitted vest. Unnoticed, I watched him come forth from a saddler's shop, and after making several purchases, he strolled to my hotel, the "King's Head," where he was met by an elderly clean-shaven man of agricultural type, with whom he had luncheon in a corner of the coffee-room.

Ray was still absent. Would that he had been present, and that I dared to point out to him the man who had apparently usurped his place in Vera's heart!

At three o'clock, after his friend had left, the young man sat for some time writing a letter in the smoking-room, and afterwards called the boots and gave it to him, with orders to deliver it personally.

Then he left for the station apparently on his return to Witham.

After I got back to the "King's Head" I sought James, the boots, and inquired the addressee of the letter.

"I took it round to Mr. Bramberger at the 'Goat and Binnacle,' sir," was the servant's reply.

"You know the young gentleman—eh?"

"Oh yes, sir. He's Mr. Freeman, from Woodham Ferris. He's what they call a 'mud-pupil' of Mr. Harris, Lord Croyland's agent. He's learning estate-work."

"And he knows Mr. Bramberger?"

"I suppose so. I've often taken notes for him to the 'Goat and Binnacle.'"

I was silent, recollecting the curious allegation made by the man Rait, that he had seen the dead man in Freeman's company.

Some other questions I put to the boots, but he could tell me but little else, only that young Freeman was undoubtedly a gentleman, that he spent his money freely, and possessed a large circle of friends in the district.

I learned that he lived in a small furnished cottage outside the dull little town of Woodham Ferris, and that he had an elderly man-servant who generally "did" for him.

Had I been mistaken in Vera's motive? Had she become acquainted with him as part of a preconceived plan, some ingenious plan formed by that fearless hunter of the Kaiser's spies, who was my most intimate friend?

Yes, I could only think that I had sorely misjudged her.

Hearing nothing from Raymond on the following day, and noticing that the sensation caused by the death of the pilot had, by this time, quite subsided, I went again over to Chelmsford and lunched at the old-fashioned "Saracen's Head."

To my satisfaction, I learned that Vera had been staying there for the past ten days, and was still there. Whereupon I left the hotel and watched it during the remainder of that afternoon.

At dusk she came forth neat and pretty as usual, her face with its soft fair hair half concealed by her flimsy veil. At the door of the hotel she hesitated for a second, then she strolled to the other side of the town, where, at an unfrequented corner, she was joined by the dark-eyed man Freeman.

From the warm manner of his greeting it was apparent that he was charmed by her, and together they strolled along the quiet byways, she allowing him to link his arm in hers.

Knowing her ready self-sacrifice wherever the interests of her lover were concerned, I could only surmise that her present object was to watch this man, or to learn from him some important facts concerning the mystery which Ray was so silently investigating. Therefore, fearing to be observed if I followed the pair along those quiet thoroughfares, I turned on my heel, and half an hour later left Chelmsford for Maldon.

That same night, soon after eleven, Ray Raymond returned to the "King's Head," arriving by the last train from London.

"We must keep a wary eye upon that publican Bramberger, Jacox," he whispered when we were alone together in my bedroom. "You must deal with him. Frequent the 'Goat and Binnacle,' and see what's in progress there."

"Vera is at Chelmsford, I see," I remarked casually.

"Yes," he said, "she's already on friendly terms with Freeman. You've seen her, I suppose?"

I responded in the affirmative.

"Well, to-morrow I shall leave here again, to reappear in Maldon as a river-side labourer," he said. "You will retain your rôle of electrician, and patronise the homely comforts of our friend Bramberger's house."

He spoke with that clear decision which characterised all his actions, for in the investigation of any suspicion of the presence of spies, he first formed his theory, and then started straight away to prove it to his own satisfaction.

Next day soon after one o'clock I re-entered the low-built little river-side inn and found within a few bargemen and labourers gossiping, as such men will gossip. The landlord who served me eyed me up and down as though half inclined to recognise me, so I recalled the fact that I had been in his house a week or so ago.

Whereupon he immediately became communicative, and we had a friendly glass together. I told him that I had concluded my job—in order to account for my hours of idleness in the days that were to follow—and I then became a regular customer, seldom leaving before the house closed.

Bramberger was one day visited by the German mate of the timber-ship which had just come in, the man of his own nationality who had been in the bar on the night of our arrival at Maldon, and who seemed to be well known to his usual customers, for apparently he made regular visits from across the North Sea.

I noticed that during the afternoon they were closeted together in the landlord's private room, and during the evening they drank in company.

The return of this German at once aroused my suspicions, therefore at ten o'clock, instead of returning to the "King's Head," I concealed myself at the waterside and there waited. It was an intensely cold vigil, and as the time crept by, and the church clock struck hour after hour, I began to fear that my suspicions were unfounded.

At last, however, from the timber-craft lying in the Blackwater came a boat noiselessly into the deep shadow, and from it landed two men, each carrying a heavy box upon his shoulder. They walked straight over to the "Goat and Binnacle," the side door of which opened noiselessly, and having deposited their loads, they returned to the boat. This journey to and fro they repeated four times. Then they rowed away, and though I waited the greater part of the night, they did not return.

I reported this in a note I sent round to Ray at his lodging in the poorer quarter of the town, and in reply I received a message that he would meet me at the river-side at eleven that night.

Part of that evening I spent smoking in the inn, and an hour after closing-time I came upon my friend with whispered greeting at the appointed spot.

"Have you seen Freeman?" was his first question, and when I replied in the negative, he told me that he had just been admitted by Bramberger.

"You've got your revolver, I suppose?" he asked.

"I always carry it nowadays," was my reply.

"Well, old chap, to-night promises to be exciting."

"Why!" I exclaimed. "Look! There are three men lurking under that wall over yonder!"

"I know," he laughed. "They're our friends. To-night we shall avenge the death of the poor pilot Pavely. But remain silent, and you'll see!"

I noted that the three dark figures concealed near us were water-side labourers, fellows whose rough-looking exteriors were the reverse of reassuring. Yet I recollected that every man who worked on the Blackwater or the Crouch was a patriot, ready to tear the mask from the spies of England's enemies.

We must have waited in patience fully three hours, when again from the timber-ship lying in the Blackwater came the laden boat, and again were similar boxes landed and carried in the shadow up to the inn, the door of which opened silently to receive them. Wherever the Customs officers or police were, they noticed nothing amiss.

The two men had made their second journey to the "Goat and Binnacle," when Ray Raymond suddenly exclaimed:

"We're going to rush the place, Jacox. Have your gun ready"; and then he gave a low whistle.

In a moment fully a dozen men, some of whom I recognised as Customs officers in mufti and police in plain clothes, together with several longshoremen, emerged from the shadow, and in a moment we had surrounded the public-house.

The door had closed upon the two men who carried up the boxes, and a demand that it should be reopened met with no response. Therefore a long iron bar was procured from somewhere, and two policemen working with it soon prised the door from its hinges.

The lights within had all been suddenly extinguished, but finding myself in the little bar-parlour with two others of the party, I struck a vesta and relit the gas.

Two of the mysterious wooden cases brought from the ship were standing there.

We heard loud shouts in German, and a scuffle upon the stairs in the darkness, followed by a shot. Then a woman's scream mingled with the shouts and curses of my companions, and I found myself in the midst of a wild mêlée, in which furniture and bottles were being smashed about me. My friends were trying to secure Bramberger and Freeman, while both were fighting desperately for their lives.

Ray made a sudden spring upon the young man who had been so attracted by Vera Vallance, but for his pains received a savage cut in the arm from a knife.

The man stood at bay in the corner of the smoke-room with half a dozen of us before him. The fellow had set his jaws fiercely, and there was murder in his black eyes. Bramberger, however, had already been secured, and handcuffs had been slipped upon him by the police.

"Now," cried Ray Raymond, "tell your story, Richardson. These two blackguards must hear it before we hand them over." And I noticed that near me were two policemen, who had covered Freeman with their revolvers.

From among us a rough man in a shabby pea-jacket, whom I had seen once or twice in that inn, came forward, and without a word of preliminary exclaimed:

"Jim Pavely, the poor fellow whom these accursed foreigners murdered, was my brother-in-law. The night before he was killed he slept at my house. He was drunk, but he told me something that at first I didn't believe. He told me that on the previous day, spending so much time about this place, he had stumbled on the fact that a certain German timber-ship was in the habit of bringing up among its cargo a quantity of saccharine which was smuggled ashore at night and stored in the cellars below here. He had had words with the landlord Bramberger, but the latter had made him promise to keep his secret till next morning, when he would pay him a certain sum to say nothing to the Customs officers. Next afternoon at four o'clock he went to the 'Goat and Binnacle' to receive the money, and I entered after him, intending to assist him in getting all he could out of the German. But that fellow Freeman, yonder—whom I know to be also a German—was with his compatriot, and the three had consultation together in the back room. Half an hour later Jim Pavely came back to my house and showed me fifty pounds, and a written agreement signed by Bramberger to pay one hundred and fifty pounds more in gold in Calais, on condition that he remained abroad and held his tongue."

Then the informer paused.

"Go on," I urged. "What then?"

"Pavely told me something—something he had discovered. But I foolishly laughed his statement to scorn. He added that he was to sail in a French schooner that night, and that Freeman, who was in partnership with Bramberger, was to go over to Latchingdon with him that evening and introduce him to the skipper, who would land him at Calais. When he had gone, the story he had told me struck me as very astounding; therefore I resolved to follow him. I saw him come with Freeman out of this place just after midnight, and I followed them. When they got to Button's Hill, on that lonely stretch of road, I saw with my own eyes Freeman suddenly attack him with a life-preserver, and having smashed his skull before I could interfere, he stole the German's undertaking from his pocket."

At this, the man accused, standing in the corner covered by several revolvers, turned livid. He tried to protest, but his voice was only faint and hollow before the living witness of his crime.

He had collapsed.

"My first impulse was to denounce the assassin, but what the dead man had told me caused me to hesitate, and I resolved to first get at the truth, which I have done with Mr. Raymond's aid," Richardson went on. "The story of the schooner was true," he added, "except that it was a steam schooner-rigged yacht which was about to land some stuff for another depôt at Burnham."

"What stuff?" I asked quickly.

"Ammunition ready for the German army when it lands upon this coast. It was that fact which Pavely had discovered and told me. After agreeing to keep the secret of the saccharine, it seems that he discovered that the boxes really contained cartridges, a fact which he urged me to communicate to the War Office after he had secured the German's bribe."

"Yes," declared Raymond, "the extensive cellaring under this place is packed to the ceiling with ammunition ready for the Day of Invasion. See this, which has just been brought!"

After prising open one of the boxes, many rounds of German rifle-cartridges were revealed. "That man Freeman before you, though brought up in England and passing as an Englishman, is, I have discovered, a German agent, who, in the guise of estate-pupil, has been busy composing a voluminous report upon supplies, accommodation, forage, possible landing-places, and other information useful to the invader. His district has been the important country between the Blackwater and the Crouch, eastward of Maldon and Purleigh. Bramberger, who is also in the German Secret Service, has been accumulating this store of ammunition as well as forwarding his coadjutor's reports and plans to Berlin, for, being German, it excited no suspicion that he posted many bulky letters to Germany. He is often in direct communication with our friend in Pont Street. My secret investigations revealed all this, Jacox, hence I arranged this raid to-night."

"You'll never take me!" cried Freeman in defiance. But next moment these men, all of them constables in plain clothes, closed with him.

For a moment there was another desperate struggle, when with startling suddenness a shot rang out, and I saw Bramberger drop to the floor like a stone at my feet.

Freeman had wrested a weapon from one of his assailants and killed his fellow-spy; while, next instant, without reflection, he turned the revolver upon himself, and, before they could prevent him, had put a shot through his own brain, inflicting a wound that within half a minute proved mortal.

When we searched the cellars of the "Goat and Binnacle" we found no fewer than eighty-two cases of rifle cartridges; while next morning, in a small cottage within a stone's-throw of the "White Hart" at Burnham, we discovered sixty-odd cases of ammunition for various arms, together with ten cases of gun cotton and some other high explosives. Also we found six big cases full of proclamations, printed in English, threatening all who opposed the German advance with death. The document was a very remarkable one, and deeming it of sufficient interest, I have reproduced it in these pages.

DECREE CONCERNING THE POWER OF COUNCILS OF WAR.

WE, GOVERNOR-GENERAL OF EAST ANGLIA, by virtue of the powers conferred upon us by His Imperial Majesty the German Emperor, Commander-in-Chief of the German Armies, order, for the maintenance of the internal and external security of the counties of the Government-General: —

Article I.—Any individual guilty of incendiarism or of wilful inundation, of attack, or of resistance with violence, against the Government-General or the agents of the civil or military authorities, of sedition, of pillage, of theft with violence, of assisting prisoners to escape, or of inciting soldiers to treasonable acts, shall be PUNISHED BY DEATH.

In the case of any extenuating circumstances, the culprit may be sent to penal servitude with hard labour for twenty years.

Article II.—Any person provoking or inciting an individual to commit the crimes mentioned in Article I. will be sent to penal servitude with hard labour for ten years.

Article III.—Any person propagating false reports relative to the operations of war or political events will be imprisoned for one year, and fined up to £100.

In any case where the affirmation or propagation may cause prejudice against the German army, or against any authorities or functionaries established by it, the culprit will be sent to hard labour for ten years.

Article IV.—Any person usurping a public office, or who commits any act or issues any order in the name of a public functionary, will be imprisoned for five years, and fined £150.

Article V.—Any person who voluntarily destroys or abstracts any documents, registers, archives, or public documents deposited in public offices, or passing through their hands in virtue of their functions as government or civic officials, will be imprisoned for two years, and fined £150.

Article VI.—Any person obliterating, damaging, or tearing down official notices, orders, or proclamations of any sort issued by the German authorities will be imprisoned for six months, and fined £80.

Article VII.—Any resistance or disobedience of any order given in the interests of public security by military commanders and other authorities, or any provocation or incitement to commit such disobedience, will be punished by one year's imprisonment, or a fine of not less than £150.

Article VIII.—All offences enumerated in Articles I.—VII. are within the jurisdiction of the Councils of War.

Article IX.—It is within the competence of Councils of War to adjudicate upon all other crimes and offences against the internal and external security of the English provinces occupied by the German Army, and also upon all crimes against the military or civil authorities, or their agents, as well as murder, the fabrication of false money, of blackmail, and all other serious offences.

Article X.—Independent of the above, the military jurisdiction already proclaimed will remain in force regarding all actions tending to imperil the security of the German troops, to damage their interests, or to render assistance in the Army of the British Government.

Consequently, they will be PUNISHED BY DEATH, and we expressly repeat this, all persons who are not British soldiers and—

(*a*) Who serve the British Army or the Government as spies, or receive British spies, or give them assistance or asylum.

(*b*) Who serve as guides to British troops, or mislead the German troops when charged to act as guides.

(*c*) Who shoot, injure, or assault any German soldier or officer.

(*d*) Who destroy bridges or canals, interrupt railways or telegraph lines, render roads impassable, burn munitions of war, provisions, or quarters of the troops.

(*e*) Who take arms against the German troops.

Article XI.—The organisation of Councils of War mentioned in Articles VIII. and IX. of the Law of May 2,

1870, and their procedure are regulated by special laws which are the same as the summary jurisdiction of military tribunals. In the case of Article X. there remains in force the Law of July 21, 1867, concerning the military jurisdiction applicable to foreigners.

Article XII.—The present order is proclaimed and put into execution on the morrow of the day upon which it is affixed in the public places of each town and village.

THE GOVERNOR-GENERAL OF EAST ANGLIA.

Copy of the German Proclamation found in the Secret Store of Arms at Burnham-on-Crouch.

The affair caused the greatest consternation at the War Office, at whose instigation it was instantly hushed up by the police for fear of creating undue panic.

But the truth remains—a very bitter, serious, and significant truth—of Germany's hostile intentions at a not distant date, a date when an Englishman's home will, alas! no longer be his castle.

CHAPTER V
THE SECRET OF THE NEW
BRITISH AEROPLANE

"If we could only approach the Military Ballooning Department we might, perhaps, learn something," I remarked. "But I suppose that's quite out of the question?"

"Quite," declared Ray. "We should receive no information, and only be laughed at for our trouble."

"You don't think that the new Kershaw aeroplane can be the one now being tried by the Royal Engineers with so much secrecy on the Duke of Atholl's estate?"

"I think not," was his prompt reply. "My reason briefly is because I have discovered that two Germans stayed at the Blair Arms Hotel, at Blair Atholl, for six weeks last summer, and then suddenly disappeared— probably taking with them the plans of the airship about which there has been so much secrecy."

"I don't quite follow you," I said.

"No, there is still another fact. A month ago there arrived in England a man named Karl Straus, a lieutenant of the Military Ballooning Department of the German Army stationed at Düsseldorf. He paid several visits to our friend Hartmann in Pont Street, and then disappeared from London. Now, why did he come on a special mission to England? For one reason. Because of the failure of Germany's hope, the Zeppelin airship, combined with the report that our new Kershaw aeroplane is the most perfect of the many inventions, and destined to effect a revolution in warfare. The Kershaw, which was only completed at South Farnborough two months ago, is now being tried in strictest secrecy. Vera was told so by an engineer officer she met at a dance at Chatham a short time ago."

"And it is being tried here in the north somewhere," I added, as together, seated in a "forty-eight Daimler," we ascended Glen Garry from Blair Atholl—which we had left a couple of hours before—and sped along over the wild, treeless Grampians towards Dalwhinnie. The March morning was bitterly cold, and snow covered the ground, rendering the Highland scenery more picturesque and imposing. And as we preferred an open car to a closed one, the journey was very cold.

Our inquiries in Blair Atholl had had a negative result. In the long, old-fashioned Blair Arms Hotel Ray had made a number of searching inquiries, for though two officers of the Ballooning Department lived there, and had been conducting the experiments in Blair Park, it was plain that the machine had never yet taken flight. So the pair of mysterious Germans, whose names we discovered in the visitors' book, had either obtained the details they wanted or had left the neighbourhood in disgust.

It was at my friend's suggestion that we had hired the car from Perth, and had now set out upon a tour of discovery in the wildest and least frequented districts of the Highlands—some of which are in winter the most unfrequented in all Great Britain. Something—what I know not—had apparently convinced him that the tests were still in progress.

"And where the trials are taking place we shall, I feel certain, find this inquisitive person Karl Straus," he declared. "From Berlin, through a confidential source, I hear that it was he who obtained the German General Staff photographs and plan of the new French aeroplane that was tried down in the Basque country last May. He's an expert aeronaut and engineer, and speaks English well; our object is to discover his whereabouts."

In pursuance of this quest we visited the various hotels on our way north. The "Loch Ericht" at Dalwhinnie we found closed, therefore we went on to Newtonmore, and by taking luncheon at the hotel there ascertained that there were no visitors who might be either British military officers or German spies.

In the gloomy, frosty afternoon we, a month after the affair down at Maldon, sped up the Speyside through dark pine forests and snow-covered moorland till we found ourselves in the long grey street of Kingussie, where we halted at the Star Hotel, a small place with a verandah, very popular in summer, but in winter deserted.

Leaving me to warm myself at the fire, Ray crossed to the telegraph office to despatch a message, and afterwards I saw him enter a small shop where picture post-cards were sold. For a quarter of an hour he remained inside, and then went to another shop a few doors further down.

Afterwards he rejoined me, and as we remounted into the car I saw that his face wore a dark, puzzled expression.

"Anything wrong?" I inquired, as we sped away through the firs towards Loch Alvie and Aviemore.

"No," he replied. Then, after a pause, he asked, "You once used to ride a motor-cycle, didn't you, Jack?"

I replied in the affirmative; whereupon he said that it would be necessary for me to hire one, an observation which somewhat mystified me. And for the next hour we roared along over the loose, uneven road through Aviemore, where the chief hotel was, of course, closed, and on over Dulnan Bridge, that paradise of the summer tourist; then turning to the right past the post office, until we were soon "honk-honking" up the wide main street of Grantown.

Here in summer and autumn the place is alive with tourists; but in winter, with its tearing winds and gusty snowstorms, the little place presents a very different appearance. The excellent "Grant Arms," standing back from the road at the further end of the town, is, however, one of the few first-class hotels in the Highlands open all the year round. And here we put up, both of us glad to obtain shelter from the sleet which, since the twilight had faded, had been cutting our faces.

While I sat before the big smoking-room fire with a cigarette, after we had been to our rooms to remove the mud from our faces, Ray was bustling about the hotel, eagerly scanning the visitors' book, among other things.

Our quest was a decidedly vague one, and as I sat staring into the flames I confess I entertained serious misgivings.

When I went forth into the hall to find my friend, I was told that he had gone out.

A quarter of an hour later he returned, saying:

"I've seen a garage along the street; come with me and hire a motor-cycle. You'll probably want it."

"Why?" I asked.

"Wait and see," was his response; therefore I put on my hat and coat and walked with him to the garage, about half-way along the street, where I picked out a good strong machine which was duly wheeled back to the hotel.

That night, among the eight or nine guests assembled for dinner, there was not one who had any resemblance either to a German spy or an officer of the Military Balloon Factory at South Farnborough.

In the days following we used our map well, scouring the whole of the Spey side to the Bridge of Avon, and on to Rothes, while westward we drove by Carrbridge, over the Slochd Mor to Loch Moy and across to Daviot. We explored the steep hills of Cromdale and Glen Tulchan, surveyed the rugged country from the summit of Carn Glas, and made judicious inquiry in all quarters, both among village people, shepherds, and others. Nowhere however could we gather any information that any trials of an airship were in progress.

Sometimes in leggings, mackintosh, and goggles, I went forth alone on my motor-cycle, negotiating the rougher byways and making confidential inquiry. But the result was ever a negative one and always disheartening.

On one occasion I had been out alone and reached the hotel, when, some hours later, our chauffeur returned with the car empty, and handed me a hastily scribbled note to explain that Ray had left suddenly for the south and instructing me to remain at Grantown till his return.

By that I imagined that he had made some discovery. Or had he gone south to see Vera, his well-beloved?

Curiously enough, next day a foreigner—probably a German—arrived at the hotel, and, as may be imagined, I at once took steps to keep him under the strictest observation. He was a quiet, apparently inoffensive person about thirty-five, who, among his impedimenta, brought a motor-cycle and box camera. Before he had been in the place twenty-four hours I had convinced myself that he was the spy Straus.

This fact I wired to Bruton Street in the code we had long ago arranged, hoping that the message would find my friend.

To my surprise, all the reply I got was: "Be careful that you have made no mistake."

What could he mean? I read and re-read the message, but remained much puzzled, while my excitement increased.

Each day the new arrival, who had written the name of "F. Goldstein" in the visitors' book, went forth on his cycle to explore the beauties of the Highlands, the thaw having now cleared the roads, and on each occasion I managed by dint of many subterfuges to watch his proceedings. His gaze was ever in the distance, and each time he gained high ground he swept the surrounding country with a pair of powerful prismatic field-glasses.

I confess I was rather annoyed at Ray's conduct in thus abandoning me at the very moment of my discovery, for here was the ballooning expert Straus bent upon seeing and photographing our newest arm of defence.

As the days passed I exerted every precaution, yet I followed him everywhere, sometimes using the car, and at others the motor-cycle.

The spy, a bespectacled, round-faced Teuton who spoke with a strong accent, was ever active, ever eager to discover something in the air. Yet, to my intense satisfaction, he seemed to be utterly unaware that I was keeping so strict a watch upon his movements. Purposely I avoided speaking to him in the hotel, for fear of arousing his suspicions.

One day Mr. Goldstein did not appear, and in response to my inquiry the waiter informed me that he had caught cold and was confined to his room.

A spy with a cold! I laughed within myself, and the afternoon being bright, I took a run south through the Abernethy Forest down to Loch Pityoulish. On my return I crossed Dulnan Bridge, where the turbulent Dulnan River hurtles along over the stones on its way down to the Spey. I dismounted, hot and tired, and propped up my cycle against the parapet to rest and admire the dark pine-clad gorge which opened to the north.

My reflections were suddenly cut short by a loud humming sound which seemed to come from the road which I had just traversed. Instinctively I looked round for the approaching motor-car. The sound came nearer, but instead of a car, I saw in the air, above the tops of the firs against the distant hill in the background, a splendid aeroplane with two men aboard. Swiftly it swept over the stream with the ease and majesty of an enormous albatross!

Next instant it had disappeared from my gaze. Yet in that brief moment I had had ocular demonstration that the secret trials were in progress in the neighbourhood.

I waited on tiptoe with excitement. Again the whirring sound came nearer, the occupants of the neighbouring cottages being undisturbed, believing it to be a motor-car. Once again I saw the new aeroplane circling above the tree-tops to the north, after which it turned suddenly and made off in a bee-line south, in the direction whence I had travelled.

I had actually seen the new invention!

Scarcely, however, had I recovered from my surprise when I heard, coming from the direction of Grantown, the "pop-pop-pop" of a motor-cycle, and across the bridge like a flash, in the direction the aerial machine had taken, came the spy whom I had only that morning left an invalid in bed.

That evening, while writing a letter in the hotel, I had a surprise; I was called to the telephone, and heard Ray's voice asking me to send the car to him.

He told me that he was staying as Mr. Charles Black at the Star Hotel in Kingussie, about twenty-eight miles distant, and promised to come over to see me shortly.

I told him what I had seen that afternoon, and how the spy had been on the alert, but to my surprise he only replied:

"Good! Keep on the watch. If what I expect is true, then we're on a big thing. Keep in touch with me on the 'phone, and have a continuous eye on your Mr. Goldstein."

I replied that I would, and that our friend had just returned.

Then he rang off.

Why was he at Kingussie, instead of assisting me?

Next day I was early astir, and before luncheon had covered many miles on the motor-cycle. Ray had not asked me over to Kingussie. If he wanted me, he would have said so.

Goldstein had not appeared downstairs, therefore after luncheon, I went forth again, taking the road northward from Grantown, and just as I was passing beneath the castellated railway-bridge about a mile and a half from the hotel, I again suddenly saw straight before me the wonderful Kershaw aeroplane. The car looked like a long, thin cylinder of bright silvery metal, which I took to be aluminium, and in it I discerned two men.

It travelled in a circle several times over the tree-tops, and then, just as at Dulnan Bridge, it dived straight away over the dark pine forest towards the lonely moors of Cromdale. Without a second's hesitation I mounted and rode full speed after her, keeping her well in sight as I went towards Deva.

Yet scarcely had I gone half a mile when I again heard behind me the "pop-pop-pop" of another cycle, and turning, saw to my satisfaction the man Goldstein, who had evidently seen the aeroplane, and was now bent upon obtaining all details of it.

Going up the hill I drew away from him, but as we descended he passed me, and in order to pose as an excited onlooker, I shouted to him my surprise in seeing such an apparatus in the air.

He evidently knew more of the new invention than I did. And yet Ray held aloof from me.

Next day, having been out for a stroll, I returned to the hotel about noon, when a few moments later my friend entered the reading-room.

"Let's go to your room," he suggested; therefore we ascended the stairs, and I opened the door with my key.

As soon as I had done so, he made a swift tour of the apartment, examining both the carpet and the red plush-covered chairs without uttering a word.

Then he stood in the centre of the room for a moment, and slowly selected a cigarette from his case. Ray Raymond was thinking—thinking deeply.

"Your friend Goldstein has a visitor," he remarked at last.

"Not to my knowledge," I said.

"He occupies room No. 11 in this hotel," he went on. "This is 16, therefore he must be quite near you."

"But who's the visitor?"

"A friend of Goldstein's. Downstairs you can discover his name."

I descended and found that on the previous evening there had certainly arrived at the hotel a Mr. William Smith, who occupied room No. 11.

But how was Ray aware of it?

I returned to my room, and found him staring out of the window into the roadway below. I saw that he was unusually agitated.

"My dear Jack," he said, turning to me when I told him the name of the occupant of No. 11, "how horribly stuffy this room is! Do you never have the window open?"

"Of course," I said, crossing to open it as usual. But I found that it had been jammed down tightly, and that felt had been placed in the crevices by the hotel people to exclude the draught.

Ray noticed it, and a curious smile crossed his aquiline countenance.

"I'd remove all that, if I were you," he exclaimed. "And I'd also pull out all that stuffing I see up the chimney. You never have a fire here, I suppose."

"I hate a fire in my bedroom," I answered. "But what has that to do with our friend Goldstein?"

"A good deal," was his reply. "Take my advice and have a fire here;" and by his look I saw that he had discovered more than he wished at that juncture to tell me. Had I known the astounding truth, I certainly should not have taken his words so calmly.

He appeared to evince an interest in my room, its position and its contents, but when I remarked upon it he pretended unconcern. He rang the bell and inquired of the waiter for Mr. Goldstein and Mr. William Smith, but the man informed him that both gentlemen were out. "I believe," added the waiter, "that Mr. Goldstein is leaving us this evening or to-morrow, sir."

"Leaving!" I echoed as soon as the man had closed the door. "Shall I follow?"

"No. It really isn't worth while," Ray replied, "at least not just at present. Remain here and have a care of yourself, Jack."

What did he mean? We ate a hasty lunch, and then, mounting into the car, my companion ordered the chauffeur to drive south again past Dulnan Bridge to Duthil, where we turned up to the right and ascended the thickly wooded hill of Lochgorm on that stony road that leads out upon the desolate Muirs of Cromdale. After we had cleared the wood he ordered the man to pull up, for the road was so bad. Descending, we climbed the steep ascent to the summit of a hill, where, after sweeping the surrounding country with a small pair of powerful glasses I carried, I at last discerned the aeroplane heading westward some ten miles distant.

Unfortunately, however, the clouds came down upon us, and we quickly found ourselves enveloped in a gradually thickening Scotch mist, while the aeroplane, soon but a faint grey shadow, quickly faded from our gaze.

Ray Raymond was ever a dogged person. He decided to descend, and this we did, passing over the other side of the hill for half an hour, progress of course being slow on account of the clouds.

Presently a puff of cold wind came up out of the east, and patches of dun-coloured moorland began to appear below through the rents of the fast-breaking clouds; when presently our watchful eyes caught the dull leaden gleam of a sheet of water about three miles ahead, which a look at my map enabled me to recognise as Lochindorb.

And just as we were able to locate the spot we again saw the big white-winged aeroplane as she swooped down to the surface of the loch, upon which she floated swanlike and majestic.

"Well?" I asked, turning and looking him in the face.

"Well, Jack, I've seen it in flight just as you have," he said, "but I've never yet approached it. I've had reasons for keeping away. After to-day, however, there is no longer much necessity for hesitation."

"I hardly follow you, old chap," I declared, my eyes still fixed through the glasses upon the aeroplane sailing along the surface of the distant lake.

"Probably not," he laughed, "but you'll see the motive of my actions before a few days are over, I hope. Let's go back." And returning to the car he carried me as far as the entrance to Grantown, where he deposited me, and then turning, ordered the man to drive with all speed back to Kingussie.

When I re-entered my comfortable hotel I learnt that Goldstein had left by the afternoon train for the south. My interest therefore lay in the new arrival in No. 11, but though I waited up till midnight, he did not return.

Just as I was returning to bed I made a curious discovery in my room. Running from the top of the high, old-fashioned mahogany wardrobe, with its heavily ornamented cornice, was a long piece of strong, black cord, which, passing down the side panel, was placed close to the wainscoting, so as to avoid notice, the end being placed beneath the mat outside the door.

At once I suspected a practical joke, but on mounting one of the old-fashioned chairs, I looked along the top of the wardrobe, but discerned nothing.

So I gathered up the piece of cord, held it in my hand with curiosity for a few moments, and then wondering who had any object in playing such a prank, turned in and slept soundly till morning.

I had scarcely sat down to breakfast in the small upstairs coffee-room—which is used in winter—when I was summoned to the telephone, where Ray predicted that the mysterious Mr. Smith would soon return, and if he did, I was to betray no interest in him whatsoever, and above all, avoid any friendship.

Such instructions mystified me. But I had not long to wait for the return of the man who called himself Smith, for he arrived just as it was growing dusk.

After dinner I was seated in front of the blazing fire in my room, smoking and reading the *Courier*, when I heard a man in heavy boots pass my door, and recognised his low, hacking cough as that of the occupant of No. 11.

I opened the door, and peering forth saw that he was dressed in his loose mackintosh and cap and carried a stout stick. He was going forth for a night walk!

Therefore I slipped on my thick boots and coat and followed. He had turned to the right on leaving the hotel, but in the silence of the night it was difficult, nay, almost impossible, to watch his movements unobserved.

For about two miles I went forward, following the sound of his footsteps in the dark night in the direction of Dava Moor, until we entered the forest of Glaschoile, where the footsteps suddenly ceased.

I halted to listen. There was a dead silence. The man had realised that he was being followed, and had plunged into the forest.

So, disappointed, I was compelled to retrace my steps to the hotel.

I tried to telephone to Ray, but was told that late the previous night he had gone out on the car and had not returned.

Therefore I remained there, impatient and helpless, the mysterious Smith being still absent.

At three o'clock that afternoon the car pulled up before the door and Ray descended.

"Put on your coat and come with me," he said briefly. And a few minutes later we were tearing along over the same road which the mysterious Smith had taken in the darkness—the direct road which leads north by way of Dava, away to Forres.

Just past the little school house of Dava we left the main road, and striking across the wide, bleak, snow-covered moor for about a mile, suddenly came into view of a wide and lonely expanse of dark water in the centre of the desolate landscape. It was Lochindorb, where, in the distance, we had seen the Kershaw aeroplane alight and sail along the surface.

As we reached the edge of the loch I saw out upon a small islet in the centre a ruined castle, a long, almost unbroken, grey wall of uniform height, without turrets or battlements, occupying the whole of the islet. Below the walls a few bushes grew from the water's edge, but it was as dreary and isolated a spot as I had ever seen. Beyond stretched the big, dull sheet of water, backed only by the low, uninteresting moorland, the only break in the all-pervading flatness and monotony being afforded by a few wind-stunted trees on the right of the road, and a small dark plantation ahead.

When the car had stopped and we had got out and walked a few yards, Ray said:

"Yonder is the old castle of Lochindorb, Jack. Behind those walls is the shed which shelters the Kershaw aeroplane. Look!"

And gazing in the direction he indicated, I saw a skiff with three occupants coming across from the shadows on the left towards the island. The man steering was a corporal of engineers in khaki.

"It appears," Ray went on, "that the machine takes her flight from the open surface of the loch, which, as you see, is about two miles long. She enters and leaves the shed by water."

As we were speaking, a bearded gillie of gigantic stature came up from nowhere and promptly ordered us away, an order which we were very reluctantly compelled to obey.

At last, however, we had discovered the obscure spot where the secret trials were in progress.

"I knew from the first that the tests must be in progress in this district," Ray said, "for a month ago that motor engineer in Grantown of whom you hired your cycle made a small part of a new motor for a man who was a stranger. The part was broken, and the stranger ordered another to be made. I learnt that the first night we were in Grantown."

He resolved to spend that night at Grantown, therefore we dined together, and when we rose from table he went to his room in order to obtain his pipe.

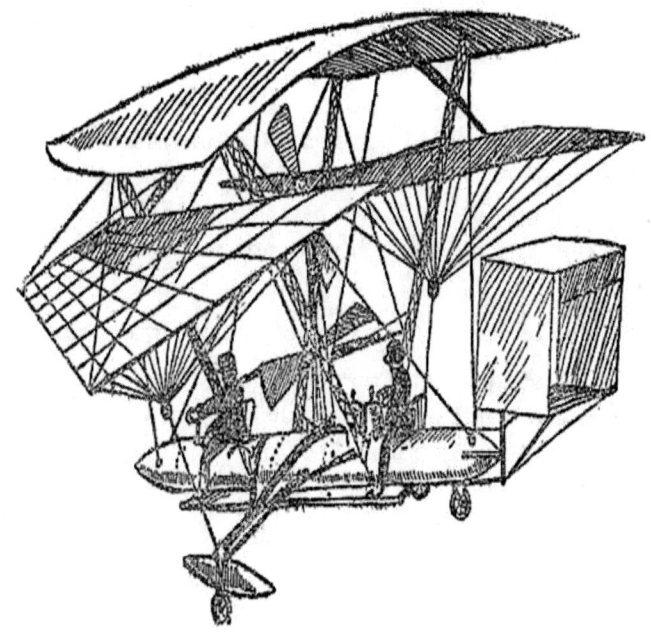

THE NEW BRITISH ARMY AEROPLANE: ROUGH SKETCH DRAWN BY LIEUT. KARL STRAUS, OF THE GERMAN SECRET SERVICE.

Ten minutes later he returned, saying:

"Just come with me for a moment, Jack."

I rose and followed.

We ascended the stairs, and passing along the corridor he halted before the door of No. 11 and tapped at it quietly.

It opened, and Smith stood upon the threshold.

"I wish to speak with you a moment," Ray said, facing him determinedly.

The man's face fell. We both entered, but so surprised was he that he could utter no protest.

We saw that on the table beneath the lamp was spread a number of photographs and papers.

He had been writing upon a sheet of foolscap and the writing was in German.

"Yes," exclaimed Ray in a tone of satisfaction as he bent over to glance at the first few lines. "I see. You report: 'The upper plane is somewhat curved, with an——'"

"What's my business to do with you, pray?" the man asked defiantly in excellent English.

"Well, your business has interested me greatly, Herr Straus," calmly replied my companion, "and I congratulate you upon the ingenious method by which you got a sight of the Kershaw aeroplane at an early hour this morning. I was at Lochindorb with you—and rather cold waiting, wasn't it?"

The man now recognised gave vent to a quick imprecation.

"I see you've just developed that photograph you took in secret as she sailed within twenty yards of you! But I shall trouble you to give it over to me, together with the rough sketch I see, and your written description of our new military invention," he said, with mock politeness.

"I don't know you—and I shall do nothing of the sort."

"I know you, Karl Straus, as a spy of Germany," exclaimed my friend, with a grin. "Your reputation for ingenuity and cunning reached us from France"; and snatching up the sheet of foolscap he turned to me, saying, "Listen to this, Jack," and while the German agent stood biting his lips in chagrin at being discovered at the eleventh hour, my friend read aloud the spy's report, as follows:

> "The upper plane of the Kershaw aeroplane is somewhat
> curved, with an upward curve at the front. The side planes
> are composed of a light framework covered with a number
> of small squares of some light material, each stretched
> on a light frame hinged to the main frame at the rear end
> of each. To the front end is fastened a strong silken cord.
> These cords are all fastened at their lower ends to a large
> ring. To this is attached a wire rope, which passes over

a pulley-wheel at the end of a species of outrigger, and thence into the cigar-like body of the car. From what I have observed when the machine is in flight, it is evident to me that the steersman (who sits at the fore part of the car) is able to manipulate these by means of levers, so that the numerous flaps forming the surface of the side planes can be opened and closed at will.

"Thus suppose the machine to be diving; slackening these ropes, the pressure of the air underneath causes the flaps to open. As soon as this happens their inclination upwards tends to make the machine rise so long as the propellers are driving her forward, the angle of ascent being controlled by the angle to which they are allowed to open. If the machine inclines to lean over to right or left, the opening and closing of the flaps on one side or the other can be used to counteract it and restore the balance. With all kept tightly closed she can go forward or dive. With them open, and engines stopped, she dives quickly. The rudder is of box-kite form, and fastened to the after end of the cigar-like car, which apparently contains the engines, petrol tanks, etc., and enough air space to render the machine buoyant when water-borne. The propellers, which are placed on hollow shafts, whose bearings are supported on horizontal braces between the two V-shaped aluminium lattice girders attaching the planes to the car, are driven by separate endless chains, which come up out of the centre of the cylinder. They seem to be made either of aluminium, or more probably magnalium.

"My drawing has rather exaggerated the diameter of the cylindrical car. There is a light wooden foot-board at either side, which also helps to steady the machine when on the water and two small floats at the end of the outriggers for the same purpose. There are also three small wheels fitted, I presume for facilitating ascent from dry ground.

"Karl Straus."

The spy laughed a low, hollow laugh of defiance. What could he say? He had been outwitted just at the supreme moment of his success.

"I admit, my friend, that you were extremely clever in putting forward Goldstein as the spy, and thus misleading my friend Jacox," Ray said in triumph, as he laid his hand upon the rough sketch of the Kershaw invention. "But for a very timely discovery, too, my friend would have met with the terrible fate which you and your accomplice planned with such devilish ingenuity. So if you don't wish to be arrested for conspiracy and murder you'd better make yourself scarce out of England quickly."

"What do you mean, Ray?" I cried.

"I'll show you," he answered as he gathered up the whole of the spy's papers while the German stood helpless. "Come along to your room with me."

When inside he pointed to the old red-plush-covered chairs, and said:

"Do you recollect my arrival after Straus's visit? I examined those chairs, and saw upon one the traces of chalk. The shoes of the occupant of room No. 11 had been chalked by the boots with his number, and upon the chair I saw traces, and knew that he had stood there to gain the top of your wardrobe."

"For what reason?" I asked.

For answer he turned up the gas and pointed to the cornice of the ceiling behind the wardrobe, where I saw that upon the leaden gas-pipe running along it was a long, narrow strip of what looked like paper which had been pasted.

"Those men meant to kill you, Jack," he said. "On the morning I came here Straus had entered, climbed up to the gas-pipe, and with his clasp-knife cut a hole in it. Over that he, as you see, placed several thicknesses of medical plaster, attaching to it a piece of strong black cord, and carrying it outside the door. After that they plugged up your window and chimney, so that when you were asleep all they had to do was to just pull the string, which would strip off the plaster, allow the gas to escape into the room, and thus asphyxiate you. The plaster could be dragged beneath the door into the passage outside."

"Great heavens!" I gasped, staring astounded at the white medical plaster on the gas-pipe along the cornice. "What a narrow escape I've had!"

"Yes. While I was in London, Vera went up with her maid and stayed at the 'Star' at Kingussie, where she overheard the two men in conversation, and learnt the clever trick they were playing with Goldstein as the spy. She suspected that they intended to rid themselves of your unwelcome surveillance, and returned at once to me in London. Fortunately I discovered the dastardly plot, and that morning I cut the cord."

"That fellow Straus is a much more desperate character than he looks."

"Yes. But we'll just go back and you can tell him your opinion of him," he laughed.

We went together along to No. 11. The spy had already left, but ascending the stairs was Vera, in a long travelling-coat, her maid following with the wraps.

She had just arrived from London, and after she had greeted us in her usual merry manner, told us that she was the bearer of very important news—news of the activity of spies in another quarter.

We quickly told her how we had managed to outwit Straus, while I, on my part, thanked her warmly for having made that startling discovery which had, no doubt, saved me from falling a victim to that dastardly plot formed by one of the most ingenious of the many unscrupulous spies of the Kaiser.

CHAPTER VI
THE SECRET OF THE NEW ARMOUR-PLATES

"I wonder if that fellow is aware of his danger?" remarked Ray, speaking to himself behind the paper he was reading before the fire in New Stone Buildings, one afternoon not long after we had returned from Scotland.

"What fellow?" I inquired.

"Why Professor Emden," he replied. "It seems that in a lecture at the London Institution last night, he announced that he had discovered a new process for the hardening of steel, which gives it no less than eight times the resisting power of the present English steel!"

"Well!" I asked, looking across at my friend, and then glancing at Vera, who had called and was seated with us, her hat still on, and a charming figure to boot.

"My dear fellow, can't you see that such an invention would be of the utmost value to our friends the Germans? They'd use it for the armour-plates of their new navy."

"H'm! And you suspect they'll try and obtain Emden's secret—eh?"

"I don't suspect, I'm confident of it," he declared, throwing aside the paper. "I suppose he's a bespectacled, unsuspicious man, like all scientists. *The Times* is enthusiastic over the discovery—declaring that the Admiralty should secure it at once, if they have not already done so. It's being made experimentally at Sheffield, it seems, and has been tried in secret somewhere out near the Orkneys. Admiralty experts are astounded at the results."

"Who is Emden?" I asked. "Just look at 'Who's Who?' It's by your elbow, old chap."

Ray proceeded to search the fat red book of reference, and presently exclaimed:

"It seems he's a Fellow of the Royal Society, a very distinguished chemist, and a leading authority on electro-metallurgy and ferro-alloys. He has improved upon the Kjellin furnace as installed at Krupp's at Essen, and at Vickers, Sons, and Maxim's at Sheffield, and by this improvement, it seems, has been able to invent the new steel-making process."

"If he has improved upon any of the machinery or processes at the Krupp works," remarked Vera, glancing across at me, "then, no doubt, our friends across the North Sea will endeavour to filch the secret from him."

"Yes," I agreed, "he certainly ought to be warned of his danger. As soon as Hartmann sees the announcement in the papers, there's certain to be a desperate attempt to get hold of the secret."

"That mustn't be allowed, my dear fellow," Ray exclaimed. "With such steel as this the British Navy will have a splendid and distinct advantage over that of our friend 'William the Sudden.' This is a great and important secret which England must keep at all hazards."

"Certainly," declared Vera. "Really, Ray, you ought to see Professor Emden and have a chat with him."

"His address is given at Richmond," was my friend's reply, "but I have to go up to Selkirk early to-morrow, and shall be away nearly a week."

"Then shall I run down and see him this evening?" I suggested. And agreeing with my idea, he wrote the address for me. Then we made a cup of tea for Vera, who always delighted in the rough-and-ready bachelordom of a barrister's chambers. Afterwards Ray took his fiancée home to her aunt's, while I went back to my rather dismal lodgings in Guilford Street, Russell Square.

At nine o'clock that evening I rang at a pleasant, good-sized, modern house, which overlooked the beautiful Terrace Gardens and the river lying deep below at Richmond—a house which, perhaps, commanded the finest view within twenty miles of London.

The door was upon that main road which leads from the town up to the "Star and Garter," but the frontage faced the Gardens. The dark-eyed maid who opened the door informed me that the Professor was at home, and took my card upstairs. Then, a few moments later, I was ushered up to a cosy den, the study of a studious man, where I found the distinguished scientist standing in expectation, with his back to the fire.

He was a strange-looking man of sixty-five, his hair unusually white and slightly bald on top. Tall beyond the average, he wore a moustache and slight pointed beard, while his countenance seemed very broad in the forehead tapering to a point. His face was, indeed, almost grotesque.

I commenced by apologising for my intrusion, but explained that I had called on a purely confidential matter. When the door was closed, and we were alone, I said:

"My mission, Professor, is a somewhat curious one"; and I went on to explain our fears that German secret agents might obtain knowledge of the new process to which he had referred at the London Institution on the previous night.

For a moment he stroked his pointed white beard thoughtfully. I detected that he was as eccentric as he was curious-looking. Then, with a light laugh, he replied:

"Really Mr.—Mr. Jacox, I can't see your motive, or that of your friends, in thus interfering in my private affairs!"

"But is not this splendid discovery of yours of national importance?" I protested. "Will it not give us an enormous advantage over our enemies? Therefore, is it not more than probable that you have already attracted the attention of these spies of Germany?"

"My dear sir," he laughed, "I tell you quite frankly that I don't believe in all these stories about German spies. What is there in England for Germany to discover? Nothing; they know everything. No, Mr. Jacox, I'm an Englishman, a patriot, and I still believe in England's power. We have nothing whatever to fear from Germany."

"Your theory is hardly borne out by facts, Professor," I said, proceeding to tell him of our discovery at Rosyth, and how we had outwitted the spies regarding the new submarine, and also the airship at Lochindorb.

But the strange-looking old scientist, distinguished as he was, only laughed my fears to scorn.

"I'd like to see any German trying to learn my secret," he said defiantly.

"Then I would urge you to take every precaution. These agents employed by the German Secret Police on behalf of the General Staff are bold and unscrupulous."

"And do you allege that there are actually German spies in England?" asked the strange man.

"Most certainly. We have in England and Scotland more than five thousand fixed agents, men of almost every nationality except German, and in every walk of life, from humble labourers to men and women in good positions, all of whom are collecting information at the order of the German travelling agents, who visit them from time to time, collect their reports, and pay them their salaries. French, Swiss, and Italians are mostly employed,"

I said. "At the present time my friend Raymond has under observation a German band, seven young fellows all army officers, who are playing in the streets of Leeds, and at the same time making a secret map of the water-mains of that city, in order that when 'the Day' of invasion comes, the enemy will be able to suddenly deprive a densely populated area of water."

"But have you any actual proof of this?" he inquired.

As he spoke the door opened, and there entered a pretty dark-haired girl of twenty-two, wearing a light skirt and a pale pink evening blouse.

"Oh, dad!" she exclaimed, halting suddenly, "I'm sorry I didn't know you had a visitor."

"I shan't be a moment, Nella dear," the curious-looking old man said, and after a quick, inquisitive glance at me the girl withdrew.

"Well," exclaimed the Professor, with a smile, "I'm really very obliged to you for troubling to come here to warn me, but I think, my dear sir, that warnings are quite unnecessary. I haven't the slightest fear that any attempt will ever be made to secure my secret"; and he rose impatiently.

"Very well," I replied, shrugging my shoulders. "I have warned you, Professor Emden. The Government will not admit the presence of spies amongst us, and for that reason we are now collecting indisputable evidence."

"Ah!" he laughed, "and you want me to help you, eh? Well, sir, I don't believe in a word of this scare—so I must decline that honour."

"And you will take no unusual precaution to keep the truth out of the hands of our enemies, eh?"

"I leave it to Joynson's of Sheffield," he said. "They've paid me a large sum down and a royalty for the secret of my process, and it is scarcely likely that they'll allow it to fall into other hands, is it?"

"They will not, but you, a private individual, may," I said.

"I think not," he laughed, and a moment later I descended the stairs, passing his pretty daughter Nella on the way out.

That night I called on Ray at Bruton Street, but he was out at the theatre with Vera. At half-past eleven they called as they went back to the girl's aunt's, and as they sat before the fire, Vera with her opera-cloak thrown back revealing a pretty pale blue corsage a trifle décolleté, I reported the non-success of my mission.

"He's a pig-headed old ass!" I declared. "One of millions of others in England. They close their eyes to the dangers of this horde of spies among us, and will only open them when the Germans come marching up the street and billet themselves in their houses. But he's a strange man, Ray, a very strange man," I added.

"You're right, Mr. Jacox," the girl declared. "Instead of teaching boys how to scout and instructing young men in the use of popguns, we should strike first at the root of all things. Cut off the source of this secret information which daily goes across the North Sea. Such hidebound patriots as the Professor are a peril to the nation!"

"If he refuses to help himself, Jacox, we must protect him ourselves," Ray declared. "I leave it to you and Vera to keep an open eye until I return from Selkirk next Monday. I'm bound to go down and see my sister. She seems very ill indeed."

And so a very important and delicate affair was thus placed in my hands.

Vera Vallance announced herself ready and eager to assist me, and that night I walked back to Bloomsbury much puzzled how next to act.

That the Germans would attempt to secure the secret of the new steel was absolutely certain. But to us, success meant the keeping of it to Britain, and the armouring of our new *Dreadnoughts* with a resisting power eight times that of our enemies.

Next day I journeyed down to Sheffield and called upon the manager of Messrs. Joynson and Mackinder, the great steel-makers, who, as you know, hold the contracts for making the armour-plates of our improved *Dreadnoughts*. He told me how the firm had just constructed six of the new Emden electrical furnaces, and had also taken over the wonderful new process which the Professor had invented.

He then courteously took me across to that portion of the great grimy works, with its wonderful steel melting and refining furnaces, to where the Emden process was about to be carried out.

"I suppose you have no fear of the new method being learnt by any of your rivals—by any German firm, for instance?" I asked.

"Not in the least," laughed the manager, a bluff, grey-bearded man, speaking in his broad Hallamshire dialect; "we take good care of that. Each workman only does a part, the whole of the process being only known to myself. It wouldn't do for us to give Professor Emden forty thousand pounds for the secret and then allow it to fall into foreign hands. The Germans would, of course, give anything for it," he added. "Emden is a patriotic Englishman even though he is very eccentric, and if he liked he could have got almost anything he cared to ask from Krupp's."

"That's just the point," I said; and then, as we walked back to the office, I explained my fears. But, like the Professor himself, he only laughed them to scorn. So that evening I again returned to London filled with anxiety and disappointment.

Just before eleven that same night I strolled past the house of Hermann Hartmann, in Pont Street, vaguely wondering what I could do to prevent a theft which must, I knew, shortly be committed. In all probability the ingenious Hartmann already had a secret agent in Joynson's works, but even if he had, he would certainly not be able to discover the secret. I had quite satisfied myself upon that point.

No, the peril lay in the Professor himself—the strange old pig-headed patriot.

Scarcely had I passed Hartmann's house, the exterior of which I knew so well, when I heard the front door close and saw a man coming down the steps. As he walked in my direction I halted beneath a lamp to light a cigarette, and by so doing I obtained a glimpse of his face as he passed.

He was a young, good-looking, smartly dressed man, with dark eyes and hair and a rather sallow complexion. I put him down to be an Italian, but I had never set eyes upon him before. No doubt he was one of Hartmann's travelling agents—a man who went up and down England visiting the fixed spies of Germany, or "letter-boxes," as they are known in the bureau of secret police in Berlin—collecting their reports and making payments for information or services rendered.

Knowing so much of the ways of the German secret agent, curiosity prompted me to follow him. He strolled as far as the corner of Sloane Street and Knightsbridge, and then boarded a motor-bus as far as Piccadilly Circus. Thence he walked to the German beer-hall, the Gambrinus, just off Coventry Street, where he joined a tall, thin, grey-moustached man, an Italian like himself, who was seated awaiting him. I idled across to a table close by, called for beer, and sat smoking a cigarette and straining my ears to catch their conversation, which was in Italian, a language I know fairly well.

I discovered the following facts. The thin-faced man was called Giovanni, while the elegant young fellow was Uberto, and they were discussing the arrival of somebody. Giovanni seemed dubious about something, while the man who had left Hartmann's seemed enthusiastic.

After a quarter of an hour Uberto glanced at his watch, made some remark to his companion, and they rose and went out together, driving in a taxicab westward, I following in another, which I fortunately found just in time. Through Kensington we went, over Hammersmith Bridge, through Barnes, and across the Common.

Then I realised we were going to Richmond.

The chase grew exciting. Before me I could see the red back-lamp of the taxi as it sped forward, and half an hour later we were crossing Richmond Bridge, where, a short distance along the road to Twickenham, they suddenly swung round to the left into St. Margaret's and pulled up before a good-sized detached house which stood back in its own grounds, in which were several big trees. The thoroughfare was, I noted, called Brunswick road.

My taxi-driver proved himself no fool. I had told him to follow; therefore, unable to pull up sharply, he swept past, and did not stop until we were round the bend in the quiet suburban road and thus out of sight.

I ordered him to remain, and, alighting, strolled back past the house in question. About its dark exterior was a distinct air of mystery. The pair had entered, and the taxi was awaiting them. The house was an old-fashioned one, solid and substantial in character, and apparently the residence of some prosperous City man; yet I wondered why its owner should have visitors at that hour. Surely great urgency had compelled the pair to come all the way from Piccadilly Circus to consult him.

But a surprise was in store for me.

After lurking about in the shadows with that expert evasiveness which I had now acquired, I presently saw the pair make their exit, but, to my surprise, they were accompanied out to the kerb by a woman—apparently a lady in black evening dress, the bodice of which was cut low.

About her shoulders she had wrapped a pale blue shawl, and as the young Uberto entered the taxi I heard her exclaim in Italian:

"*Addio!* To-morrow at one then, at Prince's."

As she moved I saw her countenance by the light of the cab lamp, a handsome, well-cut face, typical of a woman of Piedmont, for she had spoken in a dialect unmistakably that of Turin. The Turinese are more French than Italian, and are as different in both temperament and language from those of the south as the people of the Ardennes differ from those of Paris.

Both men shook hands with her warmly, bade her "*Addio,*" and entering the taxi, drove away back to London, while I stood still watching.

And as I gazed I saw as she walked back to the house, in the doorway, silhouetted against the light, an old man coming forward towards her.

"*Dio!*" she cried, half in alarm at seeing him. Then in Italian, she added, "Why do you risk being seen, you imbecile? Why didn't you keep where you were?"

Then the door closed, and seeking my taxi I also returned to Bloomsbury.

But that incident had aroused a good deal of doubt and suspicion within me. Who was that handsome young Italian woman whom the spies had visited at that late hour? And, above all, who was that man with whom she had been annoyed for showing himself?

Next day proved conclusively that some crooked business was in progress, for while I sat alone eating my lunch in a corner of the big room at Prince's Restaurant in Piccadilly, I was amazed to see the well-dressed young Italian—the man whom I had seen emerge from Hartmann's in Pont Street, enter with no other person than Nella Emden.

Surely the spies had already made considerable progress! My indignation was such that I could have walked over to the table where the pair had seated themselves, and denounced that elegant Italian as a spy of the Kaiser. But I foresaw that by patience I might yet discover more that would be of interest.

From my corner I watched the pair unnoticed. The girl was certainly extremely good-looking, young, and by her manner I could see that she was shy at being with a male companion alone in a public restaurant. He, on his part, was exercising over her all the fascination of his nation. Once or twice I saw him smile covertly across behind me, and when I had an opportunity to glance round I realised, to my surprise, that the man whom he had called Giovanni was lunching with the handsome Italian woman from St. Margaret's.

It seemed that they were watching the young pair. For what reason, I wondered?

I remained on the alert, but that day discovered nothing more, though I followed the young pair back to Richmond and saw the Italian part affectionately from Nella Emden near her father's house.

For some days I prosecuted an unceasing vigil, for already I had recognised the seriousness of a secret falling into the enemies' hands which would undoubtedly give them the advantage in the coming struggle.

One afternoon Vera Vallance met me at Waterloo Station, and together we went down to Richmond, where I showed her the Professor's house, and together we waited for the coming of Nella. Vera, enthusiastic as ever, and ingenious at keeping observation, followed the girl, while in fear of being recognised I went back to London.

Next day she called at New Stone Buildings, smart, neat, and altogether sweet and winning.

"Well, Mr. Jacox," she said, seating herself by my fire, "I had a curious experience after I left you yesterday afternoon. Nella went first by tram to Twickenham, and near the Town Hall there met the young Italian, who had a companion—Hartmann himself!"

"Hartmann!" I gasped. "Then our suspicions are surely well grounded!"

"Of course they are," she said. "I at once drew back, fearing that our clever friend of Pont Street should notice me. Fortunately he did not, therefore I was able to watch and ascertain where they went—to the house in St. Margaret's where you saw that Italian woman. They apparently stayed there to tea, for about half-past five the young man came out and walked in the direction of Richmond Bridge. I, however, remained behind, and though I waited for hours, until long after dark, neither Hartmann nor the girl made their reappearance. But at nine a very remarkable incident occurred."

"What?" I inquired eagerly.

"Three men came along the road in the darkness carrying something. When they drew near me and turned into the gate of the house, I stood aghast. Upon their shoulders was a coffin!"

"A coffin!" I echoed, staring at her.

"Yes. And though I waited until midnight, Hartmann did not come forth, neither did the Professor's daughter. What do you make of it?" she asked, looking into my eyes.

I admitted that the affair was a mystery, and suggested that we might ascertain whether Nella had returned to her home.

"Yes," she said. "Go down to Richmond and see."

This I did without delay. I watched the house during that afternoon, and just at dusk saw the dark-eyed maid-servant emerge to post a letter. I followed her up the hill to the pillar-box, and by the application of a couple of half-crowns obtained some information.

"No, sir," replied the girl, "Miss Nella's not come home. The master's in a great state about her. She went out for a walk yesterday afternoon, and though he's been to the police, nobody seems to have seen her."

"She was her father's assistant in his experiments, I've heard?"

"Yes, sir, she was. Ever since poor Mrs. Emden died, two years ago, she's been her father's right hand."

"Had she a lover?"

"Well"—and the girl hesitated. "We in the kitchen have our suspicions. Davis the cook saw her last Sunday walking over in Teddington with a dark young man, who looked like a foreigner. But," she added, "why do you want to know all this?"

"I'm trying to trace the young lady," I said, in the hope that she would believe me to be a detective. "Tell me," I urged; "does the Professor make any experiments at home?"

"Oh yes, sir; his laboratory is up on the top floor—fitted up with an electric furnace and lots of funny appliances."

"Has he any friends who are foreigners?" I inquired.

"Not that I know of," was the girl's reply. And I thought she regarded me rather strangely. Why, I could not conceive. Her name was Annie Whybrow, she told me, and then, unable to detain her longer I allowed her to re-enter the house.

Vera's story of the coffin being taken into that mysterious house in Brunswick Road, combined with the non-return of the pretty Nella, was certainly mystifying.

I returned to London, saw Vera, and we resolved to wire to Ray at Selkirk asking him to return to London as soon as possible.

That night, and the next, I haunted the usual resorts of foreigners in the West End, the underground Café de l'Europe, the Spaten beer-hall in Leicester Square, the Café Monico, the Gambrinus, and other places, in order to discover the young Italian. On the second evening I was successful, for I saw him in the Monico, and on inquiring of a man I knew, I learnt that his name was Uberto Mellini, that until recently he had lived in Paris, and that at the present moment he was staying in a house in Dean Street, Soho.

At midnight, when I returned to Bloomsbury, I found Vera and Ray anxiously awaiting me. The latter had only arrived in London from Scotland an hour before, and his fiancée had evidently told him of the curious events which had transpired and the sinister mystery surrounding the young girl's disappearance.

"I can see no reason for it at all," he declared, when we commenced to discuss the situation. "It's quite plain that our friends the enemy are actively at work, but surely the fact that Nella is missing would put the Professor upon his guard. This young Italian Mellini is evidently a new importation, and has pretended to form an attachment for Nella for some ulterior object."

"Certainly," I said. "But what do you make of the incident of the coffin?"

"There has been no funeral from that house in Brunswick Road?"

"Not as far as I can gather."

"The Registrar of Deaths would be able to inform us," he said reflectively. "We must inquire."

Next day all three of us returned to Richmond, and while Ray and Vera crossed the bridge to the opposite side of the Thames to find the Registrar's office, I lingered and watched in the vicinity of the Professor's house.

I waited for many weary hours in the wet—for rain fell the whole day—but Ray did not return, which caused me considerable misgivings. I was compelled to resort to all sorts of subterfuges in order not to attract attention; but as my friend had directed me to remain and watch, I waited patiently at my post.

Just after the street lamps were lit, a telegraph messenger arrived, and ten minutes after he had gone the girl Annie came out with hat and jacket on, and turning to the left hurried in my direction.

As she passed I spoke to her, and, recognising me, she explained that she was going for a cab to convey the Professor to the station.

"Miss Nella is at Liverpool," she added excitedly. "The master has had a wire from her, asking him to go there at once. She's very ill, it seems. The poor master is greatly excited. He's just telephoned to the police saying that Miss Nella has been found."

And then the girl hurried away, down the hill to the foot of the bridge, where there was a cab-stand.

Nella at Liverpool! What could possibly have occurred?

Later on I watched the Professor, carrying only a handbag, enter a cab and drive rapidly to the station, while Annie returned to the house and closed the front door.

It was then about six o'clock, and I had been watching there for nearly eight hours. Therefore I decided to go in search of Ray, who was over at St. Margaret's, and who, I thought, would most probably be watching the house to which the coffin had been taken.

In this I was not mistaken, for I found him idling at the end of that quiet, dark suburban road. He was on the alert the instant he recognised me, and in a few rapid sentences I told him what had occurred.

It puzzled him greatly.

"I've ascertained that Hartmann is back at Pont Street," he said. "But why the coffin should be in yonder house is still a mystery. The Registrar has had no intimation of any death in Brunswick Road for the past eight months. I've, however, found the local undertaker, who says that a plain coffin was ordered for a gentleman and that they duly delivered it. They did not see the body, being told that the funeral was to be undertaken by a big West End firm, and that the body was to be conveyed for burial somewhere near Leicester."

"Have you found out anything further regarding the occupants of the house?"

"No, only that it was taken furnished by a gentleman a month ago—a foreigner whose description exactly tallies with that of Hartmann—for an old man and his daughter—both Italians. They've kept themselves very much to themselves, therefore the neighbours know practically nothing about their business."

"Well, Nella Emden was enticed in there. I'm certain of that," I said. "Yet the fact that she's in Liverpool rather negatives my first theory of foul play," I added.

"Yes. But we must still remain watchful. Vera has gone to make some inquiries for me over at Mortlake. I expect her back in half an hour. You return and keep a watchful eye upon the Professor's place. One never knows what crooked business may be on hand!"

So back I went, and through the whole evening waited there, chilled to the bone, in vain expectancy.

I had noticed from Ray's manner that he had become very suspicious. He somehow scented the presence of spies at times when, I confess, I felt calm and reassured. And his natural intuition was seldom, if ever, wrong.

The church bells across the river had chimed midnight, the Professor's servants had put out the lights and retired, and the thoroughfare was now deserted. Hungry and tired out, I was contemplating relaxing my vigil when Ray suddenly turned a corner and joined me, saying breathlessly:

"Uberto and his friend are coming up the hill with another man. Vera and I have seen them call at Brunswick Road, and they are now on their way here. We must keep a strict watch. Something is up!"

We separated, and concealing ourselves in the basements of the houses opposite, we witnessed that which caused our heart-beats to quicken.

The three men came along in silence in the night, for they evidently wore rubber heels on their boots. The constable was then some distance down the hill, therefore they passed him.

As they approached the house, the man whom I had heard addressed as Giovanni hurried forward, and slipping suddenly into the narrow front garden, approached the kitchen window. Inserting something between the sashes, he pushed back the latch, carefully drew back the blind, and was within the house almost before the two others had entered the garden.

Then, without a sound, the pair followed him. Indeed, the three spies had entered the premises so quickly that we could scarcely believe our own eyes.

"The police!" whispered Ray. "We must get the constable. Slip down the hill and tell him. We'll make a fine capture this time!"

Down the hill I sped, and five minutes later was back with the constable, having briefly explained to him our suspicions.

"I don't know anything about German spies, sir, but whoever's inside is liable for burglariously entering, and we'll have 'em," whispered the officer.

Silently we entered just as the spies had done, passing through the kitchen, and up the stairs. The laboratory was at the top of the house I knew, and was always kept locked. Therefore we crept forward, without the slightest sound.

Once or twice, we listened. The spies were absolutely silent—well trained to that sort of nocturnal investigation, no doubt.

As Ray and I got to the door of the big room, which, by the light of the flash-lamp used by the intruders, we could see was fitted with all sorts of appliances, we witnessed through the crack that they had secured a number of specimens of metals and were all three at that moment engaged in drilling a hole in the big dark green safe standing in the corner.

"Now," whispered the constable, "let's rush them." And with a loud shout we dashed in upon them, revolvers in hand.

In an instant we were in total darkness. Deep curses in Italian sounded, and I heard a desperate struggle taking place. Somebody grabbed at me, but it was our friend the constable. Then, by the red flash of a revolver which somebody fired, I distinguished the flying form of one of the intruders through the doorway.

Next second, in the darkness, I felt a man brush past me, and instantly I closed with him. We fell together, and as I gripped the fellow's throat he ejaculated a loud imprecation in Italian. Then we rolled over in desperate embrace, but as I forced him beneath me, shouting to the constable, whose lantern had been knocked from his hand and broken, I suddenly felt a crushing blow upon the skull. I saw a thousand stars, and then the blackness of unconsciousness fell upon me.

When I again grew cognisant of what was going on about me, I found myself lying in bed in the Richmond Cottage Hospital with a pleasant-faced nurse bending eagerly over me. It was still night, for the gas was burning.

She asked how I felt, remarking that I had received a nasty crack, and had lain there unconscious for three whole days.

Presently I felt the presence of some one else near me, and gradually made them out to be Ray and Vera.

At first they would tell me nothing, but after the doctor had seen me, Ray in his cheery way said:

"Yours was a bit of hard luck, old fellow. The blackguards all got away—all three of them. But we were just in time, for in that safe were the memoranda of the Professor's experiments which, together with the specimens of the new metal that could have been analysed, would have undoubtedly placed the secret of the new steel in the hands of the German Admiralty!"

"Then we really prevented them?" I said eagerly, feeling the bandages about my head.

"Just in the very nick of time, old man," he replied. "And we did more. We managed to save Miss Nella."

"How?" I inquired eagerly.

"She's here. She'll tell you herself." And next moment I saw her standing before me with the Professor.

"Yes, Mr. Jacox," the girl said. "I have come to thank you. I was first approached by the young Italian while crossing Richmond Bridge one day, and later on he introduced me to his sister, who lived in St. Margaret's. On the afternoon when I was induced to go there I was given something in my tea which at once rendered me unconscious. When I recovered, I found myself lying in a coffin secured to rings inside, while a villainous old man, a bearded German, and an Italian woman were about to screw down the lid. I screamed, but they took no notice, until in fear I fainted. Ah! shall I ever forget those horrible moments? I was alone, helpless in the hands of those fiends, all because I had allowed myself to become attracted by a stranger! They held me there for days, trying to learn from me the secret of my father's discovery. But I would tell them nothing. Ah! how I suffered, believing every hour that they would close down that lid. Then the brutes, finding me defiant, and believing that no one was aware of their existence, hit upon another device—sending a false telegram to my father from Liverpool, and thus taking him away from the house in order to be afforded a clear field for their investigations. Of this I, of course, knew nothing until your friends entered the house forcibly with the police and found me still imprisoned—ah! yes! ready for death and burial."

And then the strange old Professor, stepping forward, seized my hand warmly in his, saying:

"To you and your two good friends, Mr. Jacox, the country owes a great and deep debt of gratitude. I was foolish in disregarding your timely warning, for my dear daughter very nearly lost her life, because the blackguards knew she had assisted me in my experiments and had made the notes at my dictation, while Britain very nearly lost the secret upon which, in the near future, will depend her supremacy at sea."

CHAPTER VII
THE SECRET OF THE IMPROVED "DREADNOUGHT"

The road was crooked and narrow, and the car was a nondescript "ninety," full of knocks and noise.

By appointment I had, for certain reasons that will afterwards be apparent, met, in the American Bar of the "Savoy," two hours before, the Honourable Robert Brackenbury, the dark, clean-shaven young man now driving, and he had engaged me, at a salary of two pounds ten per week, to be his chauffeur. I had driven him out through the London traffic, until, satisfied with my skill, he had taken the wheel himself, and we were now out upon the Great North Road, where he had a pressing engagement to meet a friend.

Beyond Hatfield we passed through Ayot Green, and were on our way to Welwyn, when suddenly he swung the powerful car into a narrow stony by-road, where, after several sharp turns, he pulled up before a pleasant, old-fashioned, red-roofed cottage standing back in a large garden and covered with ivy and climbing roses.

A big, stout, clean-shaven, merry-faced man, with slightly curly fair hair, standing in the rustic porch, waved his hand in welcome as we both descended.

I was invited into the clean cottage parlour, and there introduced to the stout man, who, I found, was named Charles Shand, and by whose speech I instantly recognised an American.

"Good!" he exclaimed. "So this is the new chauffeur, eh?" he asked, looking me up and down with his large blue eyes. "Say, young man," he added, "you've got a good berth if you can drive well—and what's more important, keep a still tongue."

I glanced from one to the other in surprise. What did he mean?

Both saw that I was puzzled, whereupon he hastened to allay my surprise by explaining.

"My friend and I run a car each. He has a six-cylinder 'sixty' here, and we want you to look after both. No cleaning. You are engineer, and will drive occasionally. Come and see the other car." And taking me to the rear of the premises, they showed me, standing in a newly built shed, one of the latest pattern six-cylinder "Napiers" fitted with every modern improvement. It was painted cream, and upon the panels an imposing crest. A big searchlight was set over the splash-board. It was fitted with the latest lubrication, and seemed almost new. To me, motor enthusiast as I am, it was a delight to have such a splendid car under my control, and my heart leapt within me.

"My friend, Mr. Brackenbury, will be liberal in the matter of wages," remarked Shand, "provided that you simply do as you are bid and ask no questions. Blind obedience is all that we require. Our private business does not concern you in the least—you understand that?"

"Perfectly," I said.

"Then if you make a promise of faithful and silent service, we shall pay you three pounds ten a week instead of the two ten which we arranged this morning," said Brackenbury.

I thanked them both, and returning to the house Shand produced some whisky and a syphon, gave me a drink and a cigar, and told me that if I wished to stroll about for an hour I was at liberty to do so.

The afternoon was a warm one in July, therefore I passed out into a field, and beneath the shade of a tree threw myself down to smoke and reflect. For nearly four months, though Ray and I had been ever watchful, we had discovered but little. We had had our suspicions aroused, however, and I had resolved to follow them up. Both men seemed good fellows enough, yet the glances they had exchanged were meaning, and thereby increased my suspicions.

When, an hour later, I re-entered the house and knocked at the door of the room, I found the pair with a map spread out on the table. They had evidently been in earnest consultation.

"Fortunately for you you are not married, Nye," exclaimed the Honourable Robert, whom I strongly suspected to be of German birth, though he spoke English perfectly and had appeared to have many friends among the habitués of the "Savoy." Nye was the name I had given. "You'll have two places of residence—here with Shand, and with me at my little place over at Barnes. You know the main roads pretty well, you told me?"

"I did a lot of touring when I was with Mr. Michelreid, the novelist," I said. "He used to be always in search of fresh places to write about. We always went to the Continent a lot."

"Well," he laughed, "you'll soon have an opportunity of putting your knowledge of the road to the test. To be of any real service to us, you'll have to be able to find your way, say, from here to Harwich in the night without taking one wrong turning."

"I've been touring England for nearly five years, off and on," I said, with confidence; "therefore few people know the roads, perhaps, better than myself."

"Very well, we shall see," remarked Shand; "only not a word—not even to your sweetheart. My friend and I are engaged in some purely private affairs—in fact, I think there is no harm in telling you—now that you are to be our confidential servant—that we are secret agents of the Government, and as such are compelled on occasions to act in a manner that any one unacquainted with the truth might consider somewhat peculiar. Do you understand?"

"Perfectly," I said.

"And not a word must pass your lips—not to a soul," he urged. "For each success we gain in the various missions entrusted to us you will receive from the Secret Service fund a handsome honorarium as acknowledgment of your faithful services."

Then he walked away, gaily singing the gay chanson of Magda at the Ambassadeurs:

"Sous le ciel pur ou le ciel gris
Dès que les joyeux gazouillis
Des oiselets se font entendre,
Une voix amoureuse et tendre
Par la fenêtre au blanc rideau
Lance les couplets d'un rondeau;
C'est la voix d'une midinette
Qui fait, en chantant, sa toilette.
Ah! le joli réveil-matin,
Quand il faut partir au turbin!
Bientôt, de la chambre voisine,
Répond une voix masculine.
Paris! Paris! Gai paradis!
Voilà les chansons de Paris!"

Much gratified at securing such a post, I drove the Honourable Robert back to London and waited for him in the courtyard of the Hotel Cecil while he was inside for a quarter of an hour. Then, getting up beside me he directed me to drive to Hammersmith Bridge, where, at a big block of red-brick flats overlooking the river, called Lonsdale Mansions, we pulled up, and he took me up to his small cosily furnished flat, where William, the clean-shaven and highly-respectable valet, awaited him.

The "ninety" was garaged, I found, almost opposite, and when I returned to the flat the Honourable Robert was at the telephone in the dining-room talking to the man we had left near Welwyn.

The elderly woman who acted as cook showed me my room, gave me my dinner, and I sat smoking with William for an hour or so afterwards.

The valet was a very inquisitive person, and I could not fail to notice how cleverly he tried to pump me concerning my post. He, however, failed to obtain much from me.

"The guv'nor is one of the best fellows alive—a thorough sportsman," he informed me. "Respect his confidence, and don't breathe a word to any one as to his doings, and you'll find your place worth hundreds a year."

"But why these strict injunctions regarding silence?" I inquired, in the hope of learning something.

"Well—because he's compelled to mix himself up with queer affairs and queer people sometimes, and in his position as the younger son of a peer it wouldn't do if it leaked out. I simply act as he bids, and seek no explanation. You'll have to do the same."

Hardly had he ceased speaking when "the guv'nor," in dinner-jacket and black tie, entered, and said:

"William, I want you to take a letter for me to Raven at Nottingham by the next train. It leaves St. Pancras at 10.45. You'll be there at 2.30 in the morning. He's at the 'Black Boy.' Get an answer and take the 5.50 back. You'll be here again soon after nine in the morning."

"Very well, sir," answered the valet, taking the letter from his master's hand; and ten minutes later he went downstairs to catch his train.

This incident showed that Robert Brackenbury was essentially a man of action. His keen, dark aquiline face, bright, sharp eyes, and quick, almost electric movements combined to show him to be a man of nerve, resource, and rapid decision. The square lower jaw betokened hard determination, while at the same time his manner was easy, nonchalant, and essentially that of a born gentleman.

William returned next morning, and a few days passed uneventfully. Both morning and evening each day, at hours prearranged, he "got on" to Shand, but their conversations were very enigmatical. Several times I happened to be in the room, but could learn nothing from the talk, which seemed, in the main, to refer to the rise and fall of certain mining shares.

Each day I drove him out in the "ninety." The car, a four-cylinder, had no flexibility, and was a perfect terror in traffic. The noise it caused was as though it had no silencer, while the police everywhere looked askance as we crept through the Strand, dodged the motor-buses in Oxford Street, or put on a move down Kensington Gore.

While Bob Brackenbury—as he was known to his friends of the "Savoy"—was out one day, I was in his bedroom with William, when the latter opened one of the huge wardrobes there. Inside I saw hanging a collection of at least fifty coats of all kinds, some smart and of latest style, others old-fashioned and dingy, while more than one was greasy, out-at-elbow, and ragged. I made no remark. Never in my life had I seen such an extensive collection of clothes belonging to one man. Surely those ragged coats were kept there for purposes of disguise! Yet would it not be highly necessary for a member of the Secret Service to possess certain disguises, I reflected!

William noticed my interest, and shut the doors hurriedly.

I drove Brackenbury hither and thither to various parts of London, for he seemed to possess many friends. Once we took two pretty young ladies from Hampstead down to the "Mitre" at Hampton Court, and on another afternoon we took a young French girl and her mother from the "Carlton" down to the "Old Bridge House" at Windsor.

To me it was apparent that Bob Brackenbury was very popular with a certain set at the Motor Club, at the Automobile Club, and at other resorts.

My duties were not at all arduous, and such a thoroughgoing sportsman was my master that he treated me almost as an equal. When out in the country he compelled me to have lunch at his table "for company," he said. My people, I told him, had been wealthy before the South African War, but had been ruined by it, and though I had been at Rugby and had done one year at Balliol College, Oxford, I hid the fact now that I was compelled to earn my living as a mere chauffeur. He had no idea that I was a barrister, with chambers in New Stone Buildings.

One morning after breakfast Mr. Brackenbury called me into the little dining-room, wherein stood his capacious roll-top desk against the wall, with the telephone upon it, and inviting me to a seat opposite the fireplace, said in a voice which betrayed just the faintest accent:

"Nye, I want to speak confidentially to you for a few minutes. You recollect that the day before yesterday when down at Windsor I was speaking with a police-inspector in uniform, who called at the hotel to see me, eh?"

"Yes. He looked round the car and spoke to me. I thought he'd come to take our name for exceeding the limit on the Staines road."

"You'd remember him again if you saw him?"

"Certainly," was my prompt reply.

"Well, don't forget him," he urged, "because you may, before long, be required to meet him. And if you should chance to mistake the man, a very serious *contretemps* would ensue."

"I'd recognise him again among a thousand!" I declared.

"Good. Now listen attentively to me for a few minutes," he said, lighting a fresh cigarette and fixing his dark, penetrating eyes upon mine. "I and my friend Shand have a very difficult task. A certain Colonel von Rausch, of the German Intelligence Department, is, we have discovered, in England on a secret mission. It is suspected that he is here controlling a number of spies who had been engaged in staff-rides in the eastern counties, and to receive their reports. My object is to learn the truth, and it can only be done by great tact and caution. I tell you this so that any orders I give you may not surprise you. Obey, and do not seek motive. Am I clear?"

"Certainly," I answered, interested in what he told me. It was curious that he, undoubtedly a German, was at the same time antagonistic to the colonel of the Kaiser's army.

"Well, I'm leaving London in an hour. Await orders from me, and obey them promptly," he said, dismissing me.

Through that day and the next I waited. He had taken William with him into the country, and left me alone in the flat. Once or twice the telephone rang, but to the various inquirers I replied that my master was absent.

Inactivity there was tantalising. I was naturally fond of adventure, and I had taken on the guise of chauffeur surely for the unmasking of a foreign spy.

On the third day, about two in the afternoon, I received a trunk call on the 'phone. The post office at Market Harborough called me up, and the voice which I heard was that of my master.

"Oh! that's you, Nye!" he said. "Well, I want you to start in the car in an hour, and run her up to Peterborough. When in the Market Place, inquire the road to Edgcott Hall. It's about six miles out on the Leicester road. Inquire for me there as Captain Kinghorne—remember the name now. Do you hear distinctly?"

I replied in the affirmative.

"Recollect what I told you before I left. I shall expect you about six. Good-bye," he said, and then rang off.

Full of excitement, I got out the car from the garage, filled the petrol tank, saw to the carbide, and then set out across the suspension bridge at Hammersmith, and went through Kensal Green and Hampstead over to Highgate, where I got upon the North Road.

It had been raining, and there was plenty of mud about, but the big, powerful car ran well notwithstanding the terrific noise it created. Indeed, she was such a terror and possessed so many defects that little wonder its maker had not placed his name upon her. As a hill-climber, however, she was excellent, and though being compelled constantly to change my "speeds," I did an average of thirty miles an hour after getting into the open country beyond Codicote.

Through crooked old Hitchin I slowed up, then away again through Henlow and Eton Socon up Alconbury Hill and down the broad road with its many telegraph lines, I went with my exhaust open, roaring and throbbing, through Stilton village into the quiet old cathedral town of Peterborough. Inquiry in the Market Place led me across a level crossing near the station and down a long hill, then out again into a flat agricultural district until I came to the handsome lodge-gates of Edgcott Hall.

Up a fine elm avenue I went for nearly a mile, until I saw before me in the crimson sunset a long, old Elizabethan mansion with high twisted chimneys and many latticed windows. The door was open, and as I pulled up I saw within a great high wall with stained windows like a church and stands of armour ranged down either side.

A footman in yellow waistcoat answered my ring, and my inquiry for Captain Kinghorne brought forth my master, smartly dressed in a brown flannel suit and smiling.

"Hulloa, Nye!" he exclaimed. "Got here all right, then. Newton will show the way to the garage," and he indicated the footman. "When you've put her up, I want to see you in my room."

The footman, mounted beside me, directed me across the park to the kennels of the celebrated Edgcott hounds, and behind these I found a well-appointed garage, in which were two other cars, a "sixteen" Fiat of a type three years ago, and a "forty" Charron with a limousine body, a very heavy, ponderous affair.

A quarter of an hour later I found myself with the Honourable Bob in a big, old-fashioned bedroom overlooking the park.

"You understood me on the 'phone, Nye?" he asked when I had closed the door and we were alone. "Shand is guest here with me under the name of Pawson, while, as you know, I'm Captain Kinghorne, D.S.O. This is necessary," he laughed. "The name of Bob Brackenbury would, in an instant, frighten away our friend the German. The people here, the Edgcotts, don't know our real names," he added. "All you have to do is to remain here and act as I direct."

A moment later the stout American entered and greeting me, turned to his friend, saying:

"I suppose Nye knows that Charles Shand is off the map at present, eh?"

"I've just been explaining," my master replied.

"And you'd better spread a picturesque story among the servants, too, Nye," the American went on—"the bravery of Captain Kinghorne at Ladysmith, and the wide circle of financial friends possessed by Archibald Pawson, of Goldfields, Nevada. The Edgcotts must be filled up with us, and that infernal Dutchman mustn't suspect that we have anything to do with Whitehall."

At that moment William, the valet, came in.

"Von Rausch met a strange man this afternoon in a little thatched inn called the 'Fitzwilliam Arms,' over at Castor. They were nearly half an hour together. One of the grooms pulled up there for a drink and saw them."

"Suppose he met one of his secret agents," remarked my master, with a glance at his friend. "We've got to have our eyes open, and there mustn't be any moss on us in this affair. To expose this man and his spying crowd will be to teach Germany a lesson which she's long wanted. We shall receive the private thanks of the Cabinet for our services, which would be to us, patriotic Englishmen as we all are, something to be proud of."

"Guess two heads are better than one, as the hatter said when twins entered his shop," laughed the broad-faced American.

We both agreed, and a few moments later I left the room.

The Edgcotts seemed to be entertaining quite a large house-party, all of them smart people, for that evening after dinner I caught sight of pretty women in handsome dresses and flashing jewels. Being a warm night, bridge was played in the fine old hall, where the vaulted roof echoed back the well-bred laughter and gay chatter of the party, which included Mr. Henry Seymour, Civil Lord of the Admiralty, and several well-known politicians.

Essentially a sporting crowd, many of them were men and women who hunted in winter with the Cottesmore, the Woodland Pytchley and the Edgcott packs. William and I peeped in through the crack of one of the doors, and he pointed out to me a tall, fair-haired, middle-aged man whose soft-pleated shirt-front and the cut of whose dress-coat betrayed him to be a foreigner. At that moment he was leaning over the chair of a pretty little dark-haired woman in pale blue, who struck me as a foreigner also, and who wore twisted twice around her neck a magnificent rope of large pearls.

"That's von Rausch," William explained. "And look at the guv'nor!" he added. "He seems to be having a good time with the thin woman over there. He's talking in French to her."

My eyes wandered in search of Pawson, and I saw that he was seated at one of the bridge-tables silently contemplating his hand.

The German spy was evidently a great favourite with the ladies. Perhaps his popularity with the fair sex had gained for him entry to that little circle of the elegant world. Two young girls approached him, laughing gaily and slowly fanning themselves. He then chatted with all three in English which had only a slight trace of Teutonic accent.

And that man was, I reflected, the head of a horde of secret agents which the German War Office had flung upon our eastern coast. To expose and crush them all was surely the patriotic duty of any Englishman.

The magnificent old mansion with its splendid paintings, its antique furniture, its armour, its bric-à-brac, old silver, and splendid heirlooms of the Edgcotts rang with the laughter of the assembly as two young subalterns indulged in humorous horse-play.

The appearance of the old sphinx-like family butler, however, compelled us to leave our point of observation, and for an hour I strolled with William out in the park in the balmy moonlight of the summer night.

"There'll be a sensation before long," declared the valet to me. "You watch."

"In what way?" I inquired, with curiosity.

"Wait and see," he laughed, as though he possessed knowledge of what was intended.

Next day I drove my master and the German Colonel over to Nottingham, where we put up for an hour at the Black Boy Hotel. This struck me as curious, for I recollected that William had been sent down from London with a message to some person named Raven staying at that hotel.

All the way from Edgcott, through Oakham, Melton Mowbray, and Trent, I had endeavoured to catch some of the conversation between the pair in the car behind me. The noise and rattle, however, prevented me from overhearing much, but the stray sentences which did reach me when I slowed down to change my speeds showed them to be on the most friendly terms.

Evidently the spy was entirely unsuspicious of his friend.

At the hotel, after I had put up the car, I saw my master and the German speaking with a tall, thin, consumptive-looking man in black, whose white tie showed him to be a dissenting minister. He was clean-shaven, aged fifty, and had an unusually protruding chin.

All three went out together and walked along the street chatting. When they had gone I went back into the yard, and on inquiry found that the minister was the Reverend Richard Raven, of the Baptist Missionary Society.

He had been a missionary in China, and had addressed several meetings in Nottingham and the neighbourhood on behalf of the society.

Why, I wondered, had Bob Brackenbury, so essentially a man about town, come there to consult a Baptist missionary, and accompanied, too, by the man he was scheming to unmask?

But the ways of the Secret Service were devious and crooked, I argued. There was method in it all. Had Ray and I been mistaken after all? So I, too, lit a cigarette, and strolled out into the bustling provincial street awaiting my master and his friend.

After an hour and a half the trio came back and had a drink together in the smoking-room—the missionary taking lemonade—and then I brought round the car, and we began the return journey of about sixty-five miles.

"What do you think of it now?" asked my master of his companion as soon as we were away from the hotel.

"Excellent!" was the German's reply. "It only now lies with her, eh?" And he laughed lightly.

Dinner was over when we returned, and Captain Kinghorne was profuse in his apologies to his host. I had previously been warned to say nothing of where we had been, and I heard my master explain that we had passed through Huntingdon, where a tyre-burst had delayed us.

I became puzzled. Yes, it was certainly both interesting and exciting. Little did the gallant German Colonel dream of the sword of England's wrath suspended above his head.

Nearly a week passed. Captain Kinghorne, D.S.O., and Mr. Pawson, of Goldfields, Nevada, shared, I saw, with the Colonel the highest popularity among members of the house-party. With Mr. Henry Seymour they had become on particularly friendly terms. There were picnics, tennis, and a couple of dances to which all the local notabilities were bidden. At them all Kinghorne was the life and soul of the general merriment. A good many quiet flirtations were in progress too. Kinghorne seemed to be particularly attracted by the pretty little widow whom I had first seen in pale blue, and who I discovered was French, her name being the Baronne de Bourbriac. She seemed to divide her attentions between Mr. Seymour and the German Colonel.

From mademoiselle, her maid, I learned that Madame la Baronne had lost her husband after only four months of matrimony, and now found herself in possession of a great fortune, a house in the Avenue des Champs Elysées, a villa at Roquebrune, and the great mediæval château of Bourbriac, in the great wine-lands along the Saône.

Was she, I wondered, contemplating matrimony again? One evening before the dressing-bell sounded, I met them quite accidentally strolling together across the park, and the earnestness of their conversation caused my wonder to increase.

Careful observation, however, showed me that Colonel von Rausch was almost as much a favourite with the little widow as was the Honourable Bob. Indeed, in the three days which followed I recognised plainly that the skittish little widow, so charming, so chic, and dressed with that perfection only possible with the true Parisienne, was playing a double game.

I felt inclined to tell my master, yet on due reflection saw that his love affairs were no concern of mine, while to speak would be only to betray myself as spying upon him.

So I held silence, but nevertheless continued to watch.

Several times I took out Brackenbury, Shand, von Rausch, and others in the car. Twice the widow went for a run alone with my master and myself. Life was, to say the least, extremely pleasant in those warm summer days at Edgcott.

Late one afternoon the Honourable Bob found me in the garage, and in a low voice said:

"You must pretend to be unwell, Nye. I want to take von Rausch out by myself, so go back to the house and pretend you're queer."

This I did without question, and he and the Colonel were out together in an unknown direction until nearly midnight. Had they, I wondered, gone again to meet the consumptive converter of the Chinese to Christianity?

I took William into my confidence, but he was silent. He would express no opinion.

"There's no moss on the guv'nor, you bet," was all he would vouchsafe.

Thus for yet another four days things progressed merrily at Edgcott Hall. William had been sent away on a message up to Manchester, and I was taking his place, when one evening, while I was getting out "the guv'nor's" dress clothes, he entered the room, and closing the door carefully, said:

"Be ready for something to happen to-night, Nye. We're going to hold up the spy and make him disgorge all the secret reports supplied by his agents. Listen to my instructions, for all must be done without any fuss. We don't want to upset the good people here. You see that small dressing-case of mine over there?"—and he indicated a square crocodile-skin case with silver fittings. "Well, at ten o'clock go and get the car out on the excuse that you have to go into Peterborough for me. You will find Shand's bag already in it, so put your own in also, but don't let anybody see you. Run her down the road about a mile from the lodge-gates and into that by-road just beyond the finger-posts where I showed you the other day. Then pull up, put out the lights, and leave her as though you've had a breakdown. Walk back here, get my dressing-case, and carry it back to the car. Then wait for us. Only recollect, don't return to get my bag until half-past ten. You see those two candles on the dressing-table? Now if any hitch occurs, I shall light them. So if I do, leave my bag here and bring my car back. You understand?"

"Quite," I said, full of excitement. And then I helped him to dress hurriedly, and he went downstairs.

We were about to "hold up" the spy. But how?

Those hours dragged slowly by. I peeped into the hall after dinner and saw the Honourable Bob seated in a corner with the Baronne, away from the others, chatting with her. The spy, all unsuspicious, was talking to his hostess, while Shand was playing poker.

Just before ten I crept out with my small bag, unseen by any one, and walked across the park to the garage. The night was stormy, the moon was hidden behind a cloud-bank. There was nobody about, so I got out the "ninety," started her, and mounting at the wheel was soon gliding down the avenue, out of the lodge-gates, and into the by-road which the Honourable Bob had indicated. Descending, I looked inside the car and saw that Shand's bag had already been placed there by an unknown hand.

In that short run I noticed I had lost the screw cap of the radiator. This surprised me, for I recollected how that evening when filling up with water I had screwed it down tightly. Somebody must have tampered with it— some stable lad, perhaps.

Having extinguished the head-lights, I walked back to the Hall by the stile and footpath, avoiding the lodge-gates, and managed to slip up to my master's room, just as the stable-clock was chiming the half hour.

The candles were unlit. All was therefore in order. The dressing-bag was, however, not there. I searched for it in vain. Then stealing out again I sped by the footpath back to the car.

Somebody hailed me in the darkness as I approached the spot where I had left her.

I recognized the spy's voice.

"Have you see Herr Brackenbury?" he asked in his broken English.

I halted, amazed. The spy had, it seemed, outwitted us and upset all our plans!

Scarcely could I reply, however, before I heard a movement behind me, and two figures loomed up. They were my master and Shand.

"All right?" inquired the American in a low voice, to which the spy gave an affirmative answer.

"Light those lamps, Nye," ordered my master quickly. "We must get away this instant."

"But——" I exclaimed.

"Quick, my dear fellow! There's not a moment to lose. Jump in, boys," he urged.

And a couple of minutes later, with our lamps glaring, we had turned out upon the broad highway and were travelling at a full forty miles an hour upon the high road to Leicester.

What could it all mean? My master and his companion seemed on the most friendly terms with the spy.

Ten miles from the lodge-gates of Edgcott at a cross-road we picked up an ill-dressed man whom I recognised as the Baptist missionary, Richard

Raven, and with the Honourable Bob at my side directing me we tore on through the night, traversing numberless by-roads, until at dawn I suddenly recognised that we were on the North Road, close to Codicote.

A quarter of an hour later we had run the car round to the rear of Shand's pretty rose-embowered cottage, and all descended.

I made excuse to the Honourable Bob that the screw top of the radiator was missing, whereupon von Rausch laughed heartily, and picking up a piece of wire from the bench he bent it so as to form a hook, and with it fished down in the hot water inside.

His companions stood watching, but judge my surprise when I saw him of a sudden draw forth a small aluminium cylinder, the top of which he screwed off and from it took out a piece of tracing-linen tightly folded.

This he spread out, and my quick eyes saw that it was a carefully drawn tracing of a portion of the new type of battleship of the *Neptune* class (the improved *Dreadnought* type), with many marginal notes in German in a feminine hand.

In an instant the astounding truth became plain to me. The Baronne, who was in von Rausch's employ, had no doubt surreptitiously obtained the original from Mr. Henry Seymour's despatch-box, it having been sent down to him to Edgcott for his approval.

A most important British naval secret was, I saw, in the hands of the clever spies of the Kaiser!

I made no remark, for in presence of those men was I not helpless?

They took the tracing in the house, and for half an hour held carousal in celebration of their success.

Presently Brackenbury came forth to me and said:

"The Colonel is going to Harwich this evening, and you must drive him. The boat for the 'Hook' leaves at half-past ten, I think."

"Very well, sir," I replied, with apparent indifference. "I shall be quite ready."

At seven we started, von Rausch and I, and until darkness fell I drove eastward, when at last we found ourselves in Ipswich.

Suddenly, close to the White Horse Hotel and within hailing distance of a police-constable, I brought the car to a dead stop, and turning to the German, who was seated beside me, said in as quiet a tone as I could:

"Colonel von Rausch, I'll just trouble you to hand over to me the tracing you and your friends have stolen from Mr. Henry Seymour—the details of the new battleship about to be built at Chatham."

"What do you mean?" cried the spy. "Drive on, you fool. I have no time to lose."

"I wish for that tracing," I said, whipping out the revolver I always carried. "Give it to me."

"What next!" he laughed, in open defiance. "Who are you, a mere servant, that you should dictate to me?"

"I'm an Englishman!" I replied. "And I'll not allow you to take that secret to your employers in Berlin."

The Colonel glanced round in some confusion. He was evidently averse to a scene in that open street.

"Come into the hotel yonder," he said. "We can discuss the matter there."

"It admits of no discussion," I said firmly. "You will hand me the tracing over which you have so ingeniously deceived me, or I shall call the constable yonder and have you detained while we communicate with the Admiralty."

"Drive on, I tell you," he cried in anger. "Don't be an ass!"

"I am not a fool," I answered. "Give me that tracing."

"Never."

I turned and whistled to the constable, who had already noticed us in heated discussion.

The officer approached, but von Rausch, finding himself in a corner, quickly produced an envelope containing the tracing and handed it to me, urging:

"Remain silent, Nye. Say nothing. You have promised."

I broke open the envelope, and after satisfying myself he had not deceived me, I placed it safely in my breast-pocket, as further evidence of the work of the Kaiser's spies amongst us.

Then, with excuses to the constable, I swung the car into the yard of the White Horse Hotel, where the spy descended, and with a fierce imprecation in German he hurried out, and I saw him no more.

At midnight I was in Ray's chambers, in Bruton Street, and we rang up Mr. Henry Seymour, who had, we found, returned to his house in Curzon Street from Edgcott only a couple of hours before.

In ignorance that spies had obtained the secret of the *Neptune* or improved *Dreadnought*, he would not at first believe the story we told him.

But when in his own library half an hour later we handed him back the tracing, he was compelled to admit the existence of German espionage in England, though in the House of Commons only a week before he had scorned the very idea.

CHAPTER VIII
THE GERMAN PLOT AGAINST ENGLAND

"When last I had the pleasure of meeting mademoiselle, both her nationality and her name were—well—slightly different, eh?" I remarked, bending forward with a smile.

From her pretty lips rang out a merry ripple of laughter, and over her sweet face spread a mischievous look.

"I admit the allegation, M'sieur Jacox," was her rather saucy response in French. "But I had no idea you would again recognise me."

"Ah, mademoiselle, beauty such as yours is not universal, and is always to be remembered," I said, with an expression of mock reproval.

"Now, why do you flatter me—you?" she asked, "especially after what passed at Caux."

"Surely I may be permitted to admire you, Suzette? Especially as I am now aware of the truth."

She started, and stared at me for a moment, a neat little figure in black. Then she gave her shoulders a slight shrug, pouting like a spoiled child.

There were none to overhear us. It was out of the season in Paris, and on that afternoon, the 15th of August, 1908, to be exact, we had driven by "auto" into the Bois, and were taking our "five o'clock" under the trees at Pré Catalan, that well-known restaurant in the centre of the beautiful pleasure wood of the Parisians.

I had serious business with Suzette Darbour.

After our success in preventing the plans of the improved *Dreadnoughts* falling into German hands, I had, at Ray's suggestion, left Charing Cross in search of the dainty little divinity before me, the neat-waisted girl with the big dark eyes, the tiny mouth, and the cheeks that still bore the bloom of youth upon them—the girl who, at the Hôtel d'Angleterre, in Copenhagen, had been known as Vera Yermoloff, of Riga, and who had afterwards lived in the gay little watering-place of Caux under the same name, and had so entirely deceived me—the girl whom I now knew to be the catspaw of others—in a word, a decoy!

Yet how sweet, how modest her manner, how demure she looked as she sat there before me at the little table beneath the trees, sipping her tea and lifting her smiling eyes to mine. Even though I had told her plainly that I was aware of the truth, she remained quite unconcerned. She had no fear of me apparently. For her, exposure and the police had no terrors. She seemed rather amused than otherwise.

I lit a cigarette, and by so doing obtained time for reflection.

My search had led me first to the Midi, thence into Italy, across to Sebenico in Dalmatia, to Venice, and back to Paris, where only that morning, with the assistance of my old friend of my student days in the French capital, Gaston Bernard, of the Prefecture of Police, I had succeeded in running her to earth. I had only that morning found her residing with a girl friend—a seamstress at Duclerc's—in a tiny flat *au cinquième* in a frowsy old house at the top of the Rue Pigalle, and living in her own name, that of Suzette Darbour.

And as I sat smoking I wondered if I dared request her assistance.

In the course of my efforts to combat the work of German spies in England I had been forced to make many queer friendships, but none perhaps so strange as the one I was now cultivating. Suzette Darbour was, I had learned from Ray Raymond a few months ago, a decoy in association with a very prince of swindlers, an American who made his head-quarters in Paris, and who had in the past year or two effected amazing *coups*, financial and otherwise, in the various capitals of Europe.

Her age was perhaps twenty-two, though certainly she did not look more than eighteen. She spoke both English and Russian quite well, for, as she had told me long ago, she had spent her early days in Petersburg. And probably in those twenty years of her life she had learnt more than many women had learned in forty.

Hers was an angelic face, with big, wide-open, truthful eyes, but her heart was, I knew, cold and callous.

Could I—dare I—take her into my service—to assist me in a matter of the most vital importance to British interests? The mission upon which I was engaged at that moment was both delicate and difficult. A single false move would mean exposure.

I was playing a deep game, and it surely behoved me to exercise every precaution. During the years I had been endeavouring to prove the peril to which England was exposed from foreign invasion, I had never been nearer failure than now. Indeed, I held my breath each time I recollected all that depended upon my success.

Ray Raymond, Vera Vallance, and myself had constituted ourselves into a little band with the object of combating the activity of the ingenious spies of the Kaiser. Little does the average Englishman dream of the work of the secret agent, or how his success or failure is reflected in our diplomatic negotiations with the Powers. Ambassadors and ministers may wear smart uniforms with glittering decorations, and move in their splendid embassies surrounded by their brilliant staffs; attachés may flirt, and first secretaries may take tea with duchesses, yet to the spy is left the real work of diplomacy, for, after all, it is upon the knowledge he obtains that His Excellency the Ambassador frames his despatch to his Government, or the Minister for Foreign Affairs presents a "Note" to the Powers.

We had for months been working on without publicity, unheeded, unrecognised, unprotected, unknown. A thankless though dangerous task, our only reward had been a kind word from the silent, sad-faced Prime Minister himself. For months our whereabouts had been unknown, even to each other. Ray generally scented the presence of spies, and it was for me to carry through the inquiry in the manner which I considered best and safest for myself.

"Suzette," I said at length, looking at her across the rising smoke from my cigarette, "when we last met you had the advantage of me. To-day we stand upon even ground."

"Pardon! I don't quite understand?" asked the little lady in the sheath costume with just a slight tremor of the eyelids.

"Well—I have discovered that you and Henry Banfield are friends—that to you he owes much of his success, and that to you is the credit of a little affair in Marienbad, which ended rather unpleasantly for a certain hosiery manufacturer from Chemnitz named Müller."

Her faced blanched, her eyes grew terrified, and her nails clenched themselves into her white palms.

"Ah! Then you—you have found me, m'sieur, for purposes of revenge—you—you intend to give me over to the police because of the fraud I practised upon you! But I ask you to have pity for me," she begged in French. "I am a woman—and—and I swear to you that I was forced to act towards you as I did."

"You forced open my despatch-box, believing that I carried valuables there, and found, to your dismay, only a few papers."

"I was compelled to do so by Banfield," she said simply. "He mistook you for another man, a diplomat, and believed that you had certain important documents with you."

"Then he made a very great mistake," I laughed. "And after your clever love-making with me you only got some extracts from a Government report, together with a few old letters."

"From those letters we discovered who you really were," mademoiselle said. "And then we were afraid."

I smiled.

"Afraid that I would pay Banfield back in his own coin, eh?"

"I was afraid. He was not, for he told me that if you attempted any reprisal, he would at once denounce you to the Germans."

"Thanks. I'm glad you've told me that," I said, with feigned unconcern. Truth to tell, however, I was much upset by the knowledge that the cunning American who so cleverly evaded the police had discovered my present vocation.

Yet, after all, had not the explanation of the pretty girl before me rather strengthened my hand?

"Well, Suzette," I said, with a moment's reflection, "I have not sought you in order to threaten you. On the contrary, I am extremely anxious that we should be friends. Indeed, I want you, if you will, to do me a service."

She looked me straight in the face, apparently much puzzled.

"I thought you were my enemy," she remarked.

"That I am not. If you will only allow me, I will be your friend."

Her fine eyes were downcast, and I fancied I detected in them the light of unshed tears. How strange it was that upon her attitude towards me should depend a nation's welfare!

"First, you must forgive me for my action at Caux," she said in a low, earnest voice, scarce above a whisper. "You know my position, alas! I dare not disobey that man who holds my future so irrevocably in his hands."

"He threatens you, then?"

"Yes. If I disobeyed any single one of his commands, he would deliver me over at once to the police for a serious affair—a crime, however, of which I swear to you that I am innocent—the crime of murder!"

"He holds threats over you," I said, tossing away my cigarette. "Describe the affair to me."

"It is the crime of the Rue de Royat, two years ago. You no doubt recollect it," she faltered, after some hesitation. "A Russian lady, named Levitsky, was found strangled in her flat and all her jewellery taken."

"And Banfield charges you with the crime?"

"I admit that I was in the apartment when the crime was committed—decoyed there for that purpose—but I am not the culprit."

"But surely you could prove the identity of the assassin?"

"I saw him for an instant. But I had no knowledge of who he was."

"Then why do you fear this American crook? Why not dissociate yourself from him?"

"Because it would mean my betrayal and ruin. I have no means of disproving this dastardly allegation. I am in his power."

"You love him, perhaps?" I remarked, my gaze full upon her.

"Love him!" she protested, with flashing eyes. "I hate him!" And she went on to explain how she was held powerless in the hands of the scoundrel.

"You have a lover, I understand, mademoiselle?" I remarked presently.

She was silent, but about the corners of her pretty mouth there played a slight smile which told the truth.

"Why not cut yourself adrift from this life of yours?" I urged. "Let me be your friend and assist you against this fellow Banfield."

"How could you assist me? He knows what you are, and would denounce you instantly!"

What she said was certainly a very awkward truth. Banfield was one of the cleverest scoundrels in Europe, an unscrupulous man who, by reason of certain sharp deals, had become possessed of very considerable wealth, his criminal methods being always most carefully concealed. The police knew him to be a swindler, but there was never sufficient evidence to convict.

To obtain Suzette's services I would, I saw, be compelled to propitiate him.

Alone there, beneath the softly murmuring trees, I stretched forth my hand across the table and took her neatly gloved fingers in mine, saying:

"Suzette, what I am you already know. I am a cosmopolitan, perhaps unscrupulous, as a man occupied as I am must needs be. I am an Englishman and, I hope, a patriot. Yet I trust I have always been chivalrous towards a woman. You are, I see, oppressed—held in a bondage that is hateful——"

At my words she burst into tears, holding my hand convulsively in hers.

"No," I said in a voice of sympathy. "The professions of neither of us are—well, exactly honourable, are they? Nevertheless, let us be friends. I want your assistance, and in return I will assist you. Let us be frank and open with each other. I will explain the truth and rely upon your secrecy. Listen. In Berlin certain negotiations are at this moment in active progress with St. Petersburg and New York, with the object of forming an offensive alliance against England. This would mean that in the coming war, which is inevitable, my country must meet not only her fiercest enemy, Germany, but also the United States and Russia. I have reason to believe that matters have secretly progressed until they are very near a settlement. What I desire to know is the actual inducement held out by the Kaiser's Foreign Office. Do you follow?"

"Perfectly," she said, at once attentive. "I quite recognise the danger to your country."

"The danger is to France also," I pointed out. "For the past six months an active exchange of despatches has been in progress, but so carefully has the truth been concealed that only by sheer accident—a word let drop in a drawing-room in London—I scented what was in the wind. Then I at once saw that you, Suzette, was the only person who could assist us."

"How?"

"You are an expert in the art of prying into despatch-boxes," I laughed.

"Well?"

"In Berlin, at the Kaiserhof Hotel, there is staying a certain Charles Pierron. If any one is aware of the truth that man is. I want you to go to Berlin, make his acquaintance, and learn what he knows. If what I suspect be true, he possesses copies of the despatches emanating from the German Foreign Office. And of these I must obtain a glimpse at all hazards."

"Who is this Pierron?"

"He was at the 'Angleterre,' in Copenhagen, when you were there, but I do not think you saw him. The reason of my presence there was because I chanced to be interested in his movements."

"What is he—an undesirable?"

"As undesirable as I am myself, mademoiselle," I laughed. "He is a French secret agent—an Anglophobe to his finger-tips."

She laughed.

"I see, m'sieur," she exclaimed; "you desire me to adopt the profession of the spy with the kid glove, eh?"

I nodded in the affirmative.

"Pierron knows me. Indeed, he already has good cause to remember me in England, where he acted as a spy of Germany," I remarked. "He is always impressionable where the fair sex is concerned, and you will, I feel confident, quickly be successful if you lived for a few days at the 'Kaiserhof' as Vera Yermoloff."

She was silent, apparently reflecting deeply.

"I am prepared, of course, to offer you a monetary consideration," I added in a low voice.

"No monetary consideration is needed, m'sieur," was her quick response. "In return for the fraud I practised upon you, it is only just that I should render you this service. Yet without Banfield's knowledge it would be utterly impossible."

"Why?"

"Because I dare not leave Paris without his permission."

"Then you must go with his knowledge—make up some story—a relative ill or something—to account for your journey to Berlin."

She seemed undecided. Therefore I repeated my suggestion, well knowing that the sweet-faced girl could, if she wished, obtain for us the knowledge which would place power in the hands of Great Britain—power to upset the machinations of our enemies.

Mine was becoming a profession full of subterfuge.

Her breast heaved and fell in a long-drawn sigh. I saw that she was wavering.

She sipped her tea in silence, her eyes fixed upon the shady trees opposite.

"Suzette," I exclaimed at last, "your lover's name is Armand Thomas, clerk at the head office of the Compte d'Escompte. He believes you to be the niece of the rich American, Henry Banfield, little dreaming of your real position."

"How do you know that?"

I smiled, telling her that I had made it my business to discover the facts.

"You love him?" I asked, looking her straight in the face.

"Yes," was her serious response.

"And you have kept this love affair secret from Banfield?"

"Of course. If he knew the truth he would be enraged. He has always forbidden me to fall in love."

"Because he fears that your lover may act as your protector and shield you from his evil influence," I remarked. "Well, Suzette," I added, "you are a very clever girl. If you are successful on this mission I will, I promise, find a means of uniting you with your lover."

She shook her head sadly, replying:

"Remember Banfield's threat. Disobedience of any of his commands will mean my ruin. Besides, he knows who and what you are. Therefore how can you assist me?"

"Mademoiselle," I said, again extending my hand to my dainty little friend, "I make you this promise not only on my own behalf—but also on behalf of my country, England. Is it a compact?"

"Do you really believe you can help me to free myself of my hateful bond?" she cried, bending towards me with eager anticipation.

"I tell you, Suzette, that in return for this service you shall be free."

Tears again stood in those fine dark eyes. I knew of her secret affection for young Thomas, the hard-working bank clerk, who dared not aspire to the hand of the niece of the great American financier.

What a narrative of subterfuge and adventure the delightful little girl seated there before me could write! The small amount I knew was amazingly romantic. Some of Banfield's smartest financial *coups* had been accomplished owing to her clever manœuvring and to the information she had gained by her almost childish artlessness. Surely the British Government could have no more ingenious seeker after political secrets than she. Women are always more successful as spies than men. That is why so many are employed by both Germany and France.

In all the varied adventures in my search after spies I had never met a girl with a stranger history than Suzette Darbour. That she had actually imposed upon me was in itself, I think, sufficient evidence of her wit, cunning, and innate ability.

When I rose from the table and strolled back to where we had left the "auto," it was with the knowledge that my long search had not been in vain. She had taken my hand in promise to go to the "Kaiserhof" in Berlin and pry into the papers of that foremost of secret agents, Charles Pierron.

At five o'clock next morning I was back again in London, and at ten I was seated in conference with Ray Raymond in his cosy flat in Bruton Street.

"We must get at the terms offered by the Germans, Jacox," he declared, snapping his fingers impatiently. "It is imperative that the Foreign Office should know them. At present our hands are utterly tied. We are unable to act, and our diplomacy is at a complete standstill. The situation is dangerous—distinctly dangerous. The guv'nor was only saying so last night. Once the agreement is signed, then good-bye for ever to Britain's power and prestige."

I explained that so carefully was the secret preserved that I had been unable to discover anything. Yet I had hopes.

"My dear Jack, England relies entirely upon you," he exclaimed. "We must know the plans of our enemies if we are successfully to combat them. In the past you've often done marvels. I can only hope that you will be equally successful in this critical moment."

Then after a long and confidential chat we parted and a couple of hours later I was again in the boat train, bound for the Continent. I recognised how urgent was the matter, and how each hour's delay increased our peril.

The public, or rather the omnivorous readers of the halfpenny press, little dream how near we were at that moment to disaster. The completion of the cleverly laid plans of Germany would mean a sudden blow aimed at us, not only at our own shores, but also at our colonies at the same moment—and such a blow, with our weakened army and neglected navy, we could not possibly ward off.

Well I remember how that night I sat in the corner of the *wagon-lit* of the Simplon Express and reflected deeply. I was on my way to Milan to join a friend. At Boulogne I had received a wire from Suzette, who had already departed on her mission to Berlin.

My chief difficulty lay in the unfortunate fact that I was well known to Pierron, who had now forsaken his original employers the Germans, hence I dare not go to the German capital, lest he should recognise me. I knew that in the pay of the French Secret Service was a clerk in the Treaty department of the German Foreign Office, and without doubt he was furnishing Pierron with copies of all the correspondence in progress. Both the French and German Governments spend six times the amount annually upon secret service that we do, hence they are always well and accurately informed.

At Milan next day the porter at the "Métropole," the small hotel in the Piazza del Duomo where I always stay, handed me a telegram, a cipher message from Ray, which announced that his father had discovered that, according to a despatch just received from His Majesty's Ambassador at St. Petersburg, there was now no doubt whatever that the terms offered by Germany were extremely advantageous to both Russia and the United States, and that it was believed that the agreement was on the actual point of being concluded.

That decided me. I felt that at all hazards, even though Pierron might detect my presence, I must be in Berlin.

I was, however, unable to leave Milan at once, for Ford, whom I was awaiting, was on his way from Corfu and had telegraphed saying that he had missed the mail train at Brindisi, and would not arrive before the morrow.

So all that day I was compelled to hang about Milan, drinking vermouth and bitter at Biffi's café in the Galleria, and dining alone at Salvini's. I always hate Milan, for it is the noisiest and most uninteresting city in all Italy.

Next afternoon I met Ford at the station and compelled him to scramble into the Bâle express with me, directly after he had alighted.

"I go to Berlin. You come with me, and go on to St. Petersburg," I said in reply to his questions.

He was a middle-aged man, a retired army officer and a perfect linguist, who was a secret agent of the British Government and a great friend of Ray's.

All the way on that long, tedious run to Berlin we discussed the situation. I was the first to explain to him our imminent peril, and with what craft and cunning the German Chancellor had formed his plans for the defeat and downfall of our Empire.

As soon as he knew, all trace of fatigue vanished from him. He went along the corridor, washed, put on a fresh collar, brushed his well-worn suit of navy serge, and returned spruce and smart, ready for any adventure.

I told him nothing of Suzette. Her existence I had resolved to keep to myself. In going to Berlin I knew well that I was playing both a dangerous and desperate game. Pierron hated me, and if he detected me, he might very easily denounce me to the police as a spy. Such a *contretemps* would, I reflected, mean for me ten years' confinement in a fortress. The German authorities would certainly not forget how for the past two years I had hunted their agents up and down Great Britain, and been the means of deporting several as undesirable aliens.

Nevertheless, I felt, somehow, that my place was near Suzette, so that I could prompt her, and if she were successful I could read with my own eyes the copies of the diplomatic correspondence from the German Foreign Office.

On arrival at Berlin I bade Ford farewell, having given him certain instructions how to act on arrival in Petersburg. During our journey we had made up a special telegraph code, and when I grasped his hand he said:

"Well, good luck, Jacox. Be careful. *Au revoir!*"

And he hurried along the platform to catch the Nord Express to bear him to the Russian capital.

At the "Kaiserhof" I took a sitting room and bed-room adjoining. It was then about ten o'clock at night; therefore I sat down and wrote a note to "Mdlle. Vera Yermoloff," which I gave a waiter to deliver.

Ten minutes later I received a scribbled reply, requesting me to meet her at half-past ten at a certain café near the Lehrte Station.

I was awaiting her when she arrived. After she had greeted me and expressed surprise at my sudden appearance, she informed me she had not yet met Pierron, for he was absent—in Hamburg it was said.

"I hear he returns to-night," she added. "Therefore, I hope to meet him to-morrow."

I explained the extreme urgency of the matter, and then drove her back to the hotel, alighting from the cab a few hundred yards away. To another café I strolled to rest and have a smoke, and it was near midnight when I re-entered the "Kaiserhof."

As I crossed the great hall a *contretemps* occurred. I came face to face with Pierron, a tall, sallow-faced, red-bearded man with eyes set close together, elegantly dressed, and wearing a big diamond in his cravat.

In an instant he recognised me, whereupon I bowed, saying:

"Ah, m'sieur! It is really quite a long time since we met—in Denmark last, was it not?"

He raised his eyebrows slightly, and replied in a withering tone:

"I do not know by what right m'sieur presumes to address me!"

That moment required all my courage and self-possession. I had not expected to meet him so suddenly. He had evidently just come from his journey, for he wore a light travelling-coat and soft felt hat.

"Well," I said, "I have something to say to you—something to tell you in private, if you could grant me a few minutes." I merely said this in order to gain time.

"*Bien!* to-morrow, then—at whatever hour m'sieur may name."

To-morrow. It would then be too late. In an hour he might inform the police, and I would find myself under arrest. The German police would be only too pleased to have an opportunity of retaliating.

"No," I exclaimed. "To-night. Now. Our business will only take a few moments. Come to my sitting-room. The matter I want to explain brooks no delay. Every moment is of consequence."

"Very well," laughed the Frenchman, with a distinct air of bravado. "You believe yourself extremely clever, no doubt, M'sieur Jacox. Let me hear what you have to say."

Together we ascended the broad marble steps to the first floor, and I held open the door of my sitting-room. When he had entered, I closed it, and offering him a chair, commenced in a resolute tone:

"Now, M'sieur Pierron, I am here to offer terms to you."

"Terms!" he laughed. "*Diable!* What do you mean?"

"I mean that I foresee your evil intention against myself, because of my success in the Brest affair," was my quick reply. "You will denounce me here in Germany as a British agent, eh?"

"You are perfectly correct in your surmise, m'sieur. Here they have an unpleasant habit in their treatment of foreign spies."

"And does it not usually take two persons to play a game?" I asked, perfectly cool. "Are you not a spy also?"

"Go to the police, *mon cher ami*, and tell them what you will," he laughed defiantly. "Straus, the chief of police here, is my friend. You would not be the first person who has tried to secure my arrest and failed."

His words confounded me. I saw that I alone was in peril, and that he, by reason of his personal friendship with the chief of police, was immune from arrest.

I had walked deliberately, and with eyes wide open, into the trap!

"You see," he laughed, pointing to the telephone instrument on the little writing-table, "I have only to take that and call up the police office, and your British Government will lose the services of one of its shrewdest agents."

"So that is your revenge, eh?" I asked, realising how utterly helpless I now was in the hands of my bitterest enemy—the man who had turned a traitor. I could see no way out.

"Bah!" he laughed in my face. "The power of your wonderful old country—so old that it has become worm-eaten—is already at an end. In a month you will have German soldiers swarming upon your shores, while America will seize Canada and Australia, and Russia will advance into India. You will be crushed, beaten, humiliated—and the German eagle will fly over your proud London. The John Bull bladder is to be pricked!" he laughed.

"That is not exactly news to me, M'sieur Pierron," I answered quite coolly. "The danger of my country is equally a danger to yours. With England crushed, France, too, must fall."

"We have an army—a brave army—while you have only the skeleton that your great Haldane has left to you," he sneered. "But enough! I have long desired this interview, and am pleased that it has taken place here in Berlin," and he deliberately walked across to the telephone.

I tried to snatch the transmitter from his hand, but though we struggled, he succeeded in inquiring for a number—the number of the police headquarters.

I was caught like a rat in a trap, fool that I was to have come there at risk of my liberty—I who was always so wary and so circumspect!

I sprang at his throat, to prevent him speaking further.

"You shall not do this!" I cried.

But his reply was only a hoarse laugh of triumph.

He was asking for somebody—his friend, the chief of police! Then turning to me with a laugh, he said:

"Straus will undoubtedly be pleased to arrest such big game as yourself."

As he uttered the words there sounded a low tap upon the door, and next second it opened, revealing the neat figure in pale blue.

Pierron turned quickly, but in an instant his face was blanched.

"*Dieu! Suzette!*" he gasped, staring at her, while she stood upon the threshold, a strange look overspreading her countenance as she recognised him.

"Ah! Look, M'sieur Jacox!" she shrieked a second later. "Yes—yes, it is that man!" she went on, pointing her finger at him. "At last! Thank God! I have found him!"

"What do you mean?" I demanded. "This is M'sieur Pierron."

"I tell you," she cried, "that is the man whom I saw at the Rue de Royat—the man who strangled poor Madame Levitsky!"

"You lie!" he cried, stepping towards her. "I—I've never seen you before!"

"And yet you have just uttered mademoiselle's name, m'sieur," I remarked quietly.

"He knows that I was present at the time of the tragedy," exclaimed Suzette quickly, "and that he was the paid assassin of Henry Banfield. He killed the unfortunate woman for two reasons: first, in order to obtain her husband's papers, which had both political and financial importance; and secondly, to obtain her jewellery, which was of very considerable value. And upon me, because I was defenceless, the guilt was placed. They said I was jealous of her."

"Suzette," I said slowly, "leave this man to me."

Then, glancing towards him, I saw what a terrible effect her denunciation had had upon him. Pale to the lips, he stood cowed, even trembling, for before him was the living witness of his crime.

I stood with my back to the door, barring his escape.

"Now," I said, "what is your defence?"

He was silent.

I repeated my question in a hard, distinct voice.

"Let's cry quits," he said in a low, hoarse tone. "I will preserve your secret—if you will keep mine. Will you not accept terms?"

"Not those," I replied promptly. "Suzette has been accused by Banfield, and by you, of the crime which you committed. She shall therefore name her own terms."

Realising that, by the fortunate discovery of the assassin of Madame Levitsky, she had at once freed herself from the trammels cast about her by Banfield, it was not surprising that the girl should stipulate as a condition of allowing the spy his freedom that he should hand over to me all the copies of the secret diplomatic correspondence which he possessed.

At first he loudly protested that he had none, but I compelled him to hand me the key of his despatch-box, and accompanying him to his room at the further end of the corridor, we searched and there found within the steel box a file of papers which he held ready to hand over to the Quai d'Orsay— the actual information of which I had been in such active search.

The German inducements were all set out clearly and concisely, the copies being in the neat hand of the traitorous clerk in the Treaty Department.

Pierron, the tables thus turned upon him, begged me to allow him at least to have copies. This I refused, triumphantly taking possession of the whole file and bidding him good-night.

In an hour we had both left the German capital, and next day I had the satisfaction of handing the copy of the German proposals and the whole correspondence to the Minister for Foreign Affairs at Downing Street.

An extraordinary meeting of the Cabinet was held, and cipher instructions at once sent to each of His Majesty's Ambassadors abroad— instructions which had the result of successfully combating the intrigue at Berlin, and for the time being breaking up the proposed powerful combination against us.

The bitter chagrin of the German Chancellor is well known in diplomatic circles, yet to Suzette Darbour our kid-gloved *coup* meant her freedom.

In my presence she openly defied Henry Banfield and cut herself adrift from him, while Charles Pierron, after his ignominious failure in Berlin, and possibly on account of certain allegations made by the rich American, who wished to get rid of him, was dismissed from the French Secret Service and disappeared, while the pretty Suzette, three months afterwards, married Armand Thomas.

I was present at the quiet wedding out at Melun in the first days of 1909, being the bearer of a costly present in the form of a pretty diamond pendant, as well as a dozen pairs of sixteen-button-length kid gloves from an anonymous donor.

She alone knew that the pendant had been sent to her as a mark of gratitude by the grave-faced old peer, the confirmed woman-hater, who was Minister for Foreign Affairs of His Majesty King Edward the Seventh.

More than once lately I have been a welcome visitor at the bright little apartment within a stone's-throw of the Étoile.

CHAPTER IX
THE SECRET OF OUR NEW GUN

Ray and I were in Newcastle-on-Tyne a few weeks after our success in frustrating the German plot against England.

Certain observations we had kept had led us to believe that a frantic endeavour was being made to obtain certain details of a new type of gun, of enormous power and range, which at that moment was under construction at the Armstrong Works at Elswick.

The Tyne and Tees have long ago been surveyed by Germany, and no doubt the accurate and detailed information pigeon-holed in the Intelligence Bureau at Berlin would, if seen by the good people of Newcastle, cause them a *mauvais quart d'heure*, as well as considerable alarm.

Yet there are one or two secrets of the Tyne and its defences which are fortunately not yet the property of our friends the enemy.

Vera was in Switzerland with her father.

But from our quarters at the Station Hotel in Newcastle we made many careful and confidential inquiries. We discovered, among other things, the existence of a secret German club in a back street off Grainger Street, and the members of this institution we watched narrowly.

Now no British workman will willingly give away any secret to a foreign Power, and we did not suspect that any one employed at the great Elswick Works would be guilty of treachery. In these days of socialistic, fire-brand oratory there is always, however, the danger of a discharged workman making revelations with objects of private vengeance, never realising that it is a nation's secrets that he may be betraying. Yet in the course of a fortnight's inquiry we learned nothing to lead us to suspect that our enemies would obtain the information they sought.

Among the members of the secret German club—which, by the way, included in its membership several Swiss and Belgians—was a middle-aged man who went by the name of John Barker, but who was either a German or a Swede, and whose real name most probably ended in "burger."

He was, we found, employed as foreign-correspondence clerk in the offices of a well-known shipping firm, and amateur photography seemed his chief hobby. He had a number of friends, one of whom was a man named Charles Rosser, a highly respectable, hardworking man, who was a foreman fitter at Elswick.

We watched the pair closely, for our suspicions were at last aroused.

Rosser often spent the evening with his friend Barker at theatres and music-halls, and it was evident that the shipping clerk paid for everything. Once or twice Barker went out to Rosser's house in Dilston Road, close to the Nun's Moor Recreation Ground, and there spent the evening with his wife and family.

We took turns at keeping observation, but one night Ray, who had been out following the pair, entered my room at the hotel, saying:

"Barker is persuading his friend to buy a new house in the Bentinck Road. It's a small, neat little red-brick villa, just completed, and the price is three hundred and fifty pounds."

"Well?" I asked.

"Well, to-night I overheard part of their conversation. Barker actually offers to lend his friend half the money."

"Ah!" I cried. "On certain conditions, I suppose?"

"No conditions were mentioned, but, no doubt, he intends to get poor Rosser into his toils, that he'll be compelled to supply some information in order to save himself and his family from ruin. The spies of Germany are quite unscrupulous, remember!"

"Yes," I remarked. "The truth is quite clear. We must protect Rosser from this. He's no doubt tempting the unsuspecting fellow, and posing as a man of means. Rosser doesn't know that his generous friend is a spy."

For the next few days it fell to my lot to watch Barker. I followed him on Saturday afternoon to Tynemouth, where it seemed his hobby was to snap-shot incoming and outgoing ships at the estuary, at the same time asking of seafaring men in the vicinity how far the boat would be from the shore where he was standing.

Both part of that afternoon and part of Sunday he was engaged in taking some measurements near the Ridges Reservoir, North Shields, afterwards going on to Tynemouth again, and snap-shotting the castle from various positions, the railway and its tunnels, the various slips, the jetty, the fish quay, the harbour, and the Narrows. Indeed, he seemed to be making a most careful photographic survey of the whole town.

He carried with him a memorandum book, in which he made many notes. All this he did openly, in full presence of passers-by, and even of the police, for who suspects German spies in Tynemouth?

About six o'clock on Sunday afternoon he entered the Royal Station Hotel, took off his light overcoat, and, hanging it in the hall, went into the coffee-room to order tea.

I had followed him in order to have tea myself, and I took off my own overcoat and hung it up next to his.

But I did not enter the coffee-room; instead, I went into the smoking-room. There I called for a drink, and, having swallowed it, returned to the pegs where our coats were hanging.

Swiftly I placed my hand in the breast pocket of his coat, and there felt some papers which, in a second, I had seized and transferred to my own pocket. Then I put on my coat leisurely, and strolled across to the station.

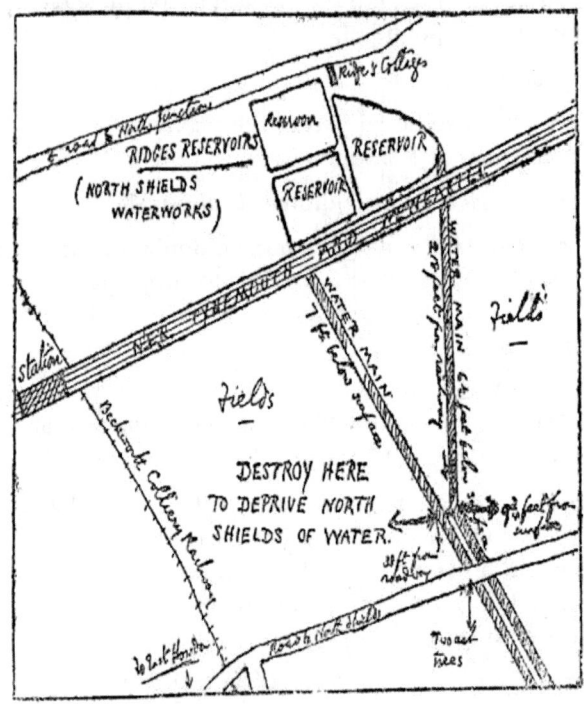

**MAP OF THE NORTH SHIELDS RESERVOIRS,
AND HOW TO CUT OFF THE WATER SUPPLY,
PREPARED BY THE SPY JOHN BARKER.**

A train was fortunately just about to leave for Newcastle, and I jumped in. Then when we had moved away from the platform I eagerly examined what I had secured.

It consisted of a tipster's circular, some newspaper cuttings concerning football, a rough sketch of how the water supply of North Shields could be cut off, and a private letter from a business man which may be of interest if I reproduce it. It read as follows:

"Berkeley Chambers, "Cannon Street, "London, E.C., "*May 3rd*, 1908.

"My dear John,

"I herewith enclose the interest in advance—four five-pound notes.

"Continue to act as you have done, and obtain orders wherever possible.

"Business just now, I am glad to say, leaves but little to be desired, and we hope that next year your share of profits may be increased.

"We have every confidence in this, you understand.

"Write to us oftener and give us news of your doings, as we are always interested in your welfare.

"It is unwise of you, I think, to doubt Uncle Charles, for I have always found him to be a man in whom one can repose the utmost confidence. He is, I believe, taking a house near Tynemouth.

"Every one is at present well, but the spring in London is always trying. However, we are hoping for warmer weather.

"My wife and the children, especially little Charlie, Frederick, and Charlotte—who is growing quite a big girl—send their love to you.

"Your affectionate cousin,

"Henry Lewis."

That letter, innocent enough upon the face of it, contained certain instructions to the spy, besides enclosing his monthly payment of £20.

Read by the alphabetical instructions with which every German secret agent is supplied and which vary in various districts, the message it contained was as follows:

(Phrase I) I send you your monthly payment.

(Phrase 2) Your informations during the past month are satisfactory.

(Phrase 3) Your service in general is giving satisfaction, and if it continues so, we shall at the next inspection augment your monthly payment.

(Phrase 4) We wish you, however, to send us more detailed notes, and report oftener.

(Phrase 5) Cease your observations upon Charles. We have what we require. Turn your attention to defences at Tynemouth.

(Phrase 6) As you know, the chief (spring) is very difficult to please, for at the last inspection we were given increased work.

(Phrase 7) Remain in negotiation with your three correspondents—Charles (meaning the foreman, Rosser), Charlotte, and Frederick—until you hear further. You may make them offers for the information.

Thus it will be seen that any one into whose hands this letter from "Henry Lewis" fell would be unable to ascertain its real meaning.

The fictitious Lewis, we afterwards discovered, occupied a small office in Berkeley Chambers in the guise of a commission agent, but was no doubt the travelling agent whose actions were controllable by Hermann Hartmann, but who in turn controlled the fixed agents of that district lying between the Humber and the Tweed.

Most of these travelling agents visit their fixed agents—the men who do the real work of espionage—in the guise of a commercial traveller if the agent is a shopkeeper, or if he is not, he will represent himself as a client or an insurance agent, an auctioneer or a house agent. This last *métier* is greatly recommended by the German Secret Police as the best mode of concealing espionage, and is adopted by the most dangerous and ingenious of the spies.

When I returned I showed my treasures to Ray, who at once became excited.

"The fellow is a fixed agent here in Newcastle, no doubt," he declared. "We must watch him well."

We continued our observations. The spy and Rosser were inseparable. They met each evening, and more than once the whole Rosser family went out to entertainments at Mr. Barker's expense. He would allow the foreman fitter to pay for nothing.

Judicious inquiries at Elswick revealed the fact that Charles Rosser was one of the most skilful fitters in the employ of the firm, and that such was the confidence placed in him, that he was at present engaged in the finishing of the new gun which was to be a triumph of the British Navy—a weapon which was far and away in advance of any possessed by any other nation, or anything ever turned out from Krupp's.

It was ticklish and exciting work, watching the two men and observing the subtle craftiness of the German, who was trying to get the honest Englishman into his power. But in our self-imposed campaign of contra-espionage we had had many stirring adventures, and after all, our life in Newcastle was not unpleasant. Barker was engaged at his office all day, and we were then free. It was only at evening when we were compelled to adopt those hundred and one subterfuges, and whenever the watching was wearisome and chill we always recollected that we were performing a patriotic duty, even though it be silent, unknown, and unrecognised.

One night the pair were together in a bar in Westgate Road, when, from their conversation, it was made very clear to me that Barker had advanced his friend one hundred and seventy-five pounds, and that the deeds of the new house were to be signed next day. Rosser was extremely grateful to his friend. Half the purchase-money was to remain on mortgage—a mortgage made over to Barker himself—just as we had expected.

The men clinked glasses, and it was plain that Rosser had not the least suspicion of the abyss opened before him. There are some men who are entirely unsuspecting, and perhaps the British workman is most of all.

When I reported this to Ray and we had consulted together, we decided that the time was ripe to approach Rosser and expose his generous friend.

It was now quite plain to us that Barker would quickly bring pressure to bear upon the foreman fitter to either supply a drawing and rough specifications of the new gun, or else come face to face with ruin. We had ascertained that, though an honest workman, Rosser only lived upon his weekly wages, and had nothing put by for the support of his wife and four children. The patriotic scruples of a man are not difficult to overcome when he sees his wife and family in danger of starvation.

On the next evening we followed Rosser from his work up to Dilston Road and called at his clean and humble home.

At first he greatly resented our intrusion, and was most indignant at our suggestion that he was about to be made a cat's-paw by the Kaiser's spies.

But on production of the letter, which we deciphered, the plan of the Ridges Waterworks, and our allegations concerning his generous friend, he began to reflect.

"Has he ever asked you about the new gun now being made at Elswick?" I asked.

"Well"—he hesitated—"now I recall the fact, he has on several occasions."

"Ah!" I said. "He intended to either ruin you, Rosser, or compel you to become a traitor."

"He'd never do that!" declared the stout-hearted Briton. "By God! If what you tell me is true," he cried fiercely, "I'll wring the blackguard's neck."

"No," I said, "don't do that. He's paid the purchase money for a new house for you, hasn't he?"

"Yes."

"Then leave him to us. We'll compel him to hand back the mortgage, and your revenge shall be a new house at the expense of the German Government," whereat both Ray and he laughed heartily.

Next night we faced the spy at his own rooms, and on pain of exposure and the police compelled him to hand over the new little villa to his intended victim unconditionally, a fact which caused him the most intense chagrin, and induced him to utter the most fearful threats of vengeance against us.

But we had already had many such threats. So we only laughed at them.

We had, however, the satisfaction of exposing the spy to the firm which employed him, and we were present on the platform of the Central Station when, two days later, having given up his rooms and packed his belongings, he left the Tyne-side for London, evidently to consult his travelling-inspector, "Henry Lewis."

Several months passed. The attempt to obtain details of our new gun had passed completely from my mind.

An inquiry which Ray and I had been actively prosecuting into an attempt to learn the secrets of the "transmitting-room" of our new *Dreadnoughts* had led me to the south of Germany. I had had a rather exciting experience in Dresden and was now on my way back to London.

"Ah! Your London is such a strange place. So dull, so *triste*—so very damp and foggy," remarked the girl seated in the train before me.

"Not always, mademoiselle," I replied. "You have been there in winter. You should go in June. In the season it is as pleasant as anywhere else in the world."

"I have no desire to return. And yet——"

"Well?"

"And yet I have decided to go straight on from the Gare du Nord."

"The midday service! I shall cross by that also. We shall be fellow-travellers," I said.

We were together in the night *rapide* from Berlin to Paris, and had just left the great echoing station of Cologne, with few stops between there and Paris. Day was breaking.

I had met Julie Granier under curious circumstances only a few hours before.

At Berlin, being known to the controller of the Wagon-lit Company, I was at once given a two-berth compartment in the long, dusty sleeping-car, those big carriages in which I so often spent days, and nights too, for the matter of that.

"M'sieur is for Paris?" asked the brown-uniformed conductor as I entered, and after flinging in my traps, I descended, went to the buffet and had a mazagran and cigarette until our departure.

I had not sat there more than five minutes when the conductor, a man with whom I had travelled a dozen times, put his head in at the door, and, seeing me, withdrew. Then, a few moments later, he entered with a tall, dark-haired, good-looking girl, who stood aside as he approached me, cap in hand.

"Excuse me, m'sieur, but a lady wishes to ask a great favour of you."

"Of me? What is it?" I inquired, rising.

Glancing at the tall figure in black, I saw that she was not more than twenty-two at the outside, and that she had the bearing and manner of a lady.

"Well, m'sieur, she will explain herself," the man said, whereupon the fair stranger approached bowing, and exclaimed:

"I trust m'sieur will pardon me for what I am about to ask," she said in French. "I know it is great presumption on my part, a total stranger, but the fact is that I am bound to get to Paris to-morrow. It is imperative—most imperative—that I should be there and keep an appointment. I find, however, that all the berths are taken, and that the only vacant one is in your compartment. I thought——" and she hesitated, with downcast eyes.

"You mean that you want me to allow you to travel here, mademoiselle?" I said, with a smile.

"Ah, m'sieur! If you would; if you only would! It would be an act of friendship that I would never forget."

She saw my hesitation, and I detected how anxious she became. Her gloved hands were trembling, and she seemed agitated and pale to the lips.

Again I scrutinised her. There was nothing of the spy or adventuress about her. On the contrary, she seemed a very charmingly modest young woman, for in continuation of her request she suggested that she could sit in the conductor's seat in the corridor.

"But surely that would be rather wearisome, mademoiselle?" I said.

"No, no, not at all. I must get to Paris at all costs. Ah, m'sieur! You will allow me to do as I ask, will you not? Do. I implore you."

I made no reply, for truth to tell, although I was not suspicious, I hesitated to allow the fair stranger to be my travelling companion. It was against my principle. Yet reading disinclination in my silence, she continued:

"Ah, m'sieur! If you only knew in what deadly peril I am! By granting this favour to me you can" — and she broke off short. "Well," she went on, "I may as well tell you the truth, m'sieur," and in her eyes there was a strange look that I had never seen in those of any woman before, "you can save my life."

"Your life!" I echoed, but at that moment the sleeping-car conductor, standing at the buffet-door, called:

"*En voiture*, m'sieur. The train is just starting."

"Do take me," implored the girl. "Do, m'sieur. Do."

There was no time for further discussion, therefore I did as she requested, and a few moments later, with a dressing-case, which was all the baggage she had, she mounted into the *wagon-lit*, and we moved off to the French capital.

I offered her the sleeping-compartment to herself, but she steadily refused to accept it.

"No, m'sieur, certainly not," was her reply. "I shall sit in the corridor all night, as I have already said."

And so, hour after hour, while all the passengers had retired to rest, we sat at the end of the car and chatted. I asked her if she liked a cigarette, and she gladly accepted. So we smoked together, while she told me something of herself. She was a native of Orleans, where her people had been wealthy landowners, she said, but some unfortunate speculation on her father's part brought ruin to them, and she was now governess in the family of a certain Baron de Moret, of the Château de Moret, near Paris.

A governess! I had believed from her dress and manner that she was at least the daughter of some French aristocrat, and I confess I was disappointed to find that she was only a superior servant.

"I have just come from Breslau," she explained. "On very urgent business—business that concerns my own self. If I am not in Paris this morning I shall, in all probability, pay the penalty with my life."

"How? What do you mean?"

In the grey dawn as the express roared on towards Paris I saw that her countenance was that of a woman who held a secret. At first I had been conscious that there was something unusual about her, and suspected her to be an adventuress, but now, on further acquaintance, I became convinced that she held possession of some knowledge that she was yearning to betray, yet feared to do so.

One fact that struck me as curious was that, in the course of our conversation, she showed that she knew my destination was London. At first this puzzled me, but on reflection I saw that the conductor, knowing me, had told her.

At Erquelinnes we had descended and had our early *café complet*, and now as we rushed onward to the capital she had suddenly made up her mind to go through to London.

"When we arrive in Paris I must leave you to keep my appointments," she said. "We will meet again at the Gare du Nord—at the Calais train, eh?"

"Most certainly," was the reply.

"Ah!" she sighed, looking straight into my face with those dark eyes that were so luminous. "You do not know—you can never guess what a great service you have rendered me by allowing me to travel here with you. My peril is the gravest that—well, that ever threatened a woman— yet now, by your aid, I shall be able to save myself. Otherwise, to-morrow my body would have been exposed in the Morgue—the corpse of a woman unknown."

"These words of yours interest me."

"Ah, m'sieur! You do not know. And I cannot tell you. It is a secret—ah! if I only dare speak you would help me, I know," and I saw in her face a look full of apprehension and distress.

As she raised her hand to push the dark hair from her brow, as though it oppressed her, my eyes caught sight of something glistening upon her wrist, half concealed by the lace on her sleeve. It was a magnificent diamond bangle.

Surely such an ornament would not be worn by a mere governess! I looked again into her handsome face, and wondered if she were deceiving me.

"If it be in my power to assist you, mademoiselle, I will do so with the greatest pleasure. But, of course, I cannot without knowing the circumstances."

"And I regret that my lips are closed concerning them," she sighed, looking straight before her despairingly.

"Do you fear to go alone?"

"I fear my enemies no longer," was her reply as she glanced at the little gold watch in her belt. "I shall be in Paris before noon—thanks to you, m'sieur."

"Well, when you first made the request I had no idea of the urgency of your journey," I remarked. "But I'm glad, very glad, that I've had an opportunity of rendering you some slight service."

"Slight, m'sieur? Why, you have saved me! I owe you a debt which I can never repay—never." And the laces at her throat rose and fell as she sighed, her wonderful eyes still fixed upon me.

Gradually the wintry sun rose over the bare, frozen wine-lands over which we were speeding, when with a sudden application of the brakes we pulled up at a little station for a change of engine.

Then, after three minutes, we were off again, until at nine o'clock we ran slowly into the huge terminus in Paris.

She had tidied her hair, washed, brushed her dress, and, as I assisted her to alight, she bore no trace of her long journey across Germany and France. Strange how well French women travel! English women are always tousled and tumbled after a night journey, but a French or Italian woman never.

"*Au revoir*, m'sieur, till twelve at the Gare du Nord," she exclaimed, with a merry smile and a bow as she drove away in a cab, leaving me upon the kerb gazing after her and wondering.

Was she really a governess, as she pretended?

Her clothes, her manner, her smart chatter, her exquisite *chic*, all revealed good breeding and a high station in life. There was no touch of cheap shabbiness—or at least I could not detect it.

A few moments before twelve she alighted at the Gare du Nord and greeted me merrily. Her face was slightly flushed, and I thought her hand trembled as I took it. But together we walked to the train, wherein I had already secured seats and places in the *wagon-restaurant*.

The railway officials, the controller of the train, the chief of the restaurant, and other officials, recognising me, saluted, whereupon she said:

"You seem very well known in Paris, m'sieur."

"I'm a constant traveller," I replied, with a laugh. "A little too constant, perhaps. One gets wearied with such continual travel as I am forced to undertake. I never know to-morrow where I may be, and I move swiftly from one capital to another, never spending more than a day or two in the same place."

"But it must be very pleasant to travel so much," she declared. "I would love to be able to do so. I'm passionately fond of constant change."

Together we travelled to Calais, crossed to Dover, and that same evening alighted at Victoria.

On our journey to London she gave me an address in the Vauxhall Bridge Road, where, she said, a letter would find her. She refused to tell me her destination, or to allow me to see her into a hansom. This latter fact caused me considerable reflection. Why had she so suddenly made up her mind to come to London, and why should I not know whither she went when she had told me so many details concerning herself?

Of one fact I felt quite convinced, namely, that she had lied to me. She was not a governess, as she pretended. Besides, I had been seized by suspicion that a tall, thin-faced, elderly man, rather shabbily dressed, whom I had noticed on the platform in Paris, had followed us. He had travelled second-class, and, on alighting at Victoria, had quickly made his way through the crowd until he lingered quite close to us as I wished her farewell.

His reappearance there recalled to me that he had watched us as we had walked up and down the platform of the Gare du Nord, and had appeared intensely interested in all our movements. Whether my pretty travelling companion noticed him I do not know. I, however, followed her as she walked out of the station carrying her dressing-bag, and saw the tall man striding after her. Adventurer was written upon the fellow's face. His grey moustache was upturned, and his keen grey eyes looked out from beneath shaggy brows, while his dark, thread-bare overcoat was tightly buttoned across his chest for greater warmth.

Without approaching her he stood back in the shadow and saw her enter a hansom in the station-yard and drive out into Buckingham Palace Road. It was clear that she was not going to the address she had given me, for she was driving in the opposite direction.

My duty was to drive direct to Bruton Street to see Ray and report what I had discovered, but so interested was I in the thin-faced watcher that I gave over my wraps to a porter who knew me, exchanged my heavy travelling-coat for a lighter one I happened to have, and walked out to keep further observation upon the stranger.

Had not mademoiselle declared herself to be in danger of her life? If so, was it not possible that this fellow, whoever he was, was a secret assassin?

I did not like the aspect of the affair at all. I ought to have warned her against him, and I now became filled with regret. She was a complete mystery, and as I dogged the footsteps of the unknown foreigner—for that he undoubtedly was—I became more deeply interested in what was in progress.

He walked to Trafalgar Square, where he hesitated in such a manner as to show that he was not well acquainted with London. He did not know which of the converging thoroughfares to take. At last he inquired of the constable on point-duty, and then went up St. Martin's Lane.

As soon as he had turned I approached the policeman, and asked what the stranger wanted, explaining that he was a suspicious character whom I was following.

"'E's a Frenchman, sir. 'E wants Burton Crescent."

"Where's that?"

"Why, just off the Euston Road—close to Judd Street. I've told 'im the way."

I entered a hansom and drove to the place in question, a semicircle of dark-looking, old-fashioned houses of the Bloomsbury type—most of them let out in apartments. Then alighting, I loitered for half an hour up and down to await the arrival of the stranger.

He came at last, his tall, meagre figure looming dark in the lamp-light. Very eagerly he walked round the Crescent, examining the numbers of the houses, until he came to one rather cleaner than the others, of which he took careful observation.

I, too, took note of the number.

Afterwards the stranger turned into the Euston Road, crossed to King's Cross Station, where he sent a telegram, and then went to one of the small uninviting private hotels in the neighbourhood. Having seen him there, I returned to Burton Crescent, and for an hour watched the house, wondering whether Julie Granier had taken up her abode there. To me it seemed as though the stranger had overheard the directions she had given the cabman.

The windows of the house were closed by green Venetian blinds. I could see that there were lights in most of the rooms, while over the fanlight of the front door was a small transparent square of glass. The front steps were well kept, and in the deep basement was a well-lighted kitchen.

I had been there about half an hour when the door opened, and a middle-aged man in evening dress, and wearing a black overcoat and crush hat, emerged. His dark face was an aristocratic one, and as he descended the steps he drew on his white gloves, for he was evidently on his way to the theatre. I took good notice of his face, for it was a striking countenance, one which once seen could never be forgotten.

A man-servant behind him blew a cab-whistle, a hansom drew up, and he drove away. Then I walked up and down in the vicinity, keeping a weary vigil, for my curiosity was now much excited. The stranger meant mischief. Of that I was certain.

The one point I wished to clear up was whether Julie Granier was actually within that house. But though I watched until I became half frozen in the drizzling rain, all was in vain. So I took a cab and drove to Bruton Street.

That same night, when I got to my rooms, I wrote a line to the address that Julie had given me, asking whether she would make an appointment to meet me, as I wished to give her some very important information concerning herself, and to this, on the following day, I received a reply asking me to call at the house in Burton Crescent that evening at nine o'clock.

Naturally I went. My surmise was correct that the house watched by the stranger was her abode. The fellow was keeping observation upon it with some evil intent.

The man-servant, on admitting me, showed me into a well-furnished drawing-room on the first floor, where sat my pretty travelling companion ready to receive me.

In French she greeted me very warmly, bade me be seated, and after some preliminaries inquired the nature of the information which I wished to impart to her.

Very briefly I told her of the shabby watcher, whereupon she sprang to her feet with a cry of mingled terror and surprise.

"Describe him—quickly!" she urged in breathless agitation.

I did so, and she sat back again in her chair, staring straight before her.

"Ah!" she gasped, her countenance pale as death. "Then they mean revenge, after all. Very well! Now that I am forewarned I shall know how to act."

She rose, and pacing the room in agitation pushed back the dark hair from her brow. Then her hands clenched themselves, and her teeth were set, for she was desperate.

The shabby man was an emissary of her enemies. She told me as much. Yet in all she said was mystery. At one moment I was convinced that she had told the truth when she said she was a governess, and at the next I suspected her of trying to deceive.

Presently, after she had handed me a cigarette, the servant tapped the door, and a well-dressed man entered—the same man I had seen leave the house two nights previously.

"May I introduce you?" mademoiselle asked. "M'sieur Jacox—M'sieur le Baron de Moret."

"Charmed to make your acquaintance, sir," the Baron said, grasping my hand. "Mademoiselle here has already spoken of you."

"The satisfaction is mutual, I assure you, Baron," was my reply, and then we reseated ourselves and began to chat.

Suddenly mademoiselle made some remark in a language—some Slav language—which I did not understand. The effect it had upon the newcomer was almost electrical. He started from his seat, glaring at her. Then he began to question her rapidly in the unknown tongue.

He was a flashily dressed man of overbearing manner, with a thick neck and square, determined chin. It was quite evident that the warning I had given them aroused their apprehension, for they held a rapid consultation, and then Julie went out, returning with another man, a dark-haired, low-bred looking foreigner, who spoke the same tongue as his companions.

They disregarded my presence altogether in their eager consultation; therefore I rose to go, for I saw that I was not wanted.

Julie held my hand and looked into my eyes in mute appeal. She appeared anxious to say something to me in private. At least that was my impression.

When I left the house I passed, at the end of the Crescent, a shabby man idly smoking. Was he one of the watchers?

Four days went by.

One evening I was passing through the red-carpeted hall of the Savoy Hotel when a neatly dressed figure in black rose and greeted me. It was Julie, who seemed to have been awaiting me.

"May I speak to you?" she asked breathlessly, when we had exchanged greetings. "I wish to apologise for the manner in which I treated you the other evening."

I assured her that no apologies were needed, and together we seated ourselves in a corner.

"I really ought not to trouble you with my affairs," she said presently, in an apologetic tone. "But you remember what I told you when you so kindly allowed me to travel by the *wagon-lit*—I mean of my peril?"

"Certainly. But I thought it was all over."

"I foolishly believed that it was. But I am watched—I—I'm a marked woman." Then, after some hesitation, she added, "I wonder if you would do me another favour. You could save my life, M'sieur Jacox, if you only would."

"Well, if I can render you such a service, mademoiselle, I shall be only too delighted."

"At present my plans are immature," she answered after a pause. "But why not dine with me to-morrow night? We have some friends, but we shall be able to escape them and discuss the matter alone. Do come!"

I accepted, and she, taking a taxi in the Strand, drove off.

On the following night at eight I entered the comfortable drawing-room in Burton Crescent, where three well-dressed men and three rather smart ladies were assembled, including my hostess. They were all foreigners, and among them was the Baron, who appeared to be the most honoured guest. It was now quite plain that, instead of being a governess as she had asserted, my friend was a lady of good family, and the Baron's social equal.

The party was a very pleasant one, and there was considerable merriment at table. My hostess's apprehension of the previous day had all disappeared, while the Baron's demeanour was one of calm security.

I sat at her left hand, and she was particularly gracious to me, the whole conversation at table being in French.

At last, after dessert, the Baron remarked that, as it was his birthday, we should have snap-dragon, and, with his hostess's permission, left the dining-room and prepared it. Presently it appeared in a big antique Worcester bowl, and was placed on the table close to me.

Then the electric light was switched off and the spirit ignited.

Next moment with shouts of laughter, the blue flames shedding a weird light upon our faces, we were pulling the plums out of the fire—a childish amusement.

I had placed one in my mouth, and swallowed it, but as I was taking a second from the blue flames, I suddenly felt a faintness. At first I put it down to the heat of the room, but a moment later I felt a sharp spasm through my heart, and my brain swelled too large for my skull. My jaws were set. I tried to speak, but was unable to articulate a word!

I saw the fun had stopped, and the faces of all were turned upon me anxiously. The Baron had risen, and his dark countenance peered into mine with a fiendish murderous expression.

"I'm ill!" I gasped. "I—I'm sure I'm poisoned!"

The faces of all smiled again, while the Baron uttered some words which I could not understand, and then there was a dead silence, all still watching me intently.

"You fiends!" I cried, with a great effort, as I struggled to rise. "What have I done to you that you should—*poison—me*?"

I know that the Baron grinned in my face, and that I fell forward heavily upon the table, my heart gripped in the spasm of death.

Of what occurred afterwards I have no recollection, for, when I slowly regained knowledge of things around me, I found myself, cramped and cold, lying beneath a bare, leafless hedge in a grass field. I managed to struggle to my feet and discovered myself in a bare, flat, open country. As far as I could judge it was midday.

I got to a gate, skirted a hedge, and gained the main road. With difficulty I walked to the nearest town, a distance of about four miles, without meeting a soul, and to my surprise found myself in Hitchin. The spectacle of a man entering the town in evening dress and hatless in broad daylight was, no doubt, curious, but I was anxious to return to London and give information against those who had, without any apparent motive, laid an ingenious plot to poison me.

At the old Sun Inn, which motorists from London know so well, I learned that the time was eleven in the morning. The only manner in which I could account for my presence in Hitchin was that, believed to be dead by the Baron and his accomplices, I had been conveyed in a motor-car to the spot where I was found.

A few shillings remained in my pocket, and, strangely enough, beside me when I recovered consciousness I had found a small fluted phial marked "Prussic acid—poison." The assassins had attempted to make it apparent that I had committed suicide!

Two hours later, after a rest and a wash, I borrowed an overcoat and golf-cap and took the train to King's Cross.

At Judd Street Police Station I made a statement, and with two plain-clothes officers returned to the house in Burton Crescent, only to find that the fair Julie and her friends had flown.

On forcing the door, we found the dining-table just as it had been left after the poisoned snap-dragon of the previous night. Nothing had been touched. Only Julie, the Baron, the man-servant, and the guests had all gone, and the place was deserted.

The police were utterly puzzled at the entire absence of motive.

On my return to Guilford Street I at once telephoned to Ray, and he was quickly with me, Vera accompanying him.

I related the whole of the circumstances, while my friends sat listening very attentively.

"Well," Ray said at last, "it's a great pity, old chap, you didn't mention this before. The Baron de Moret is no other person than Lucien Carron, one of Hartmann's most trusted agents, while Julie's real name is Erna Hertfeldt, a very clever female spy, who has, of late, been engaged in endeavouring to obtain certain facts regarding the defences of the Humber estuary. She was recalled to Berlin recently to consult Hirsch, chief of the German Intelligence Department. You evidently came across her on her way back, while the old man whom she met at the Gare du Nord was Josef Gleichen, the spy whom I told you was in association with Barker up at Newcastle."

"Ah! I remember," I cried. "I never saw him."

"But he had evidently seen you, and again recognised you," Ray replied. "It seems that he must have followed you to London, where, having told Lucien Carron, or 'the Baron,' of your return, they formed a plot to avenge your action up at Elswick."

"Then I was entrapped by that woman Julie, eh?" I exclaimed, my head still feeling sore and dizzy.

"Without a doubt. The spies have made yet another attempt upon your life, Mr. Jacox," Vera remarked.

"But why did they take me out in a motor-car to Hitchin?"

"To make it appear like a case of suicide," Ray said. "Remember that both of us, old chap, are marked men by Hartmann and his unscrupulous friends. But what does it matter if we have managed to preserve the secret of our new gun? We'll be even with our enemies for this one day ere long, mark me," he laughed, as he lit a fresh cigarette.

CHAPTER X
THE SECRET OF THE CLYDE DEFENCES

A curious episode was that of the plans of the Clyde Defences. It was a February evening. Wet, tired, and hungry, I turned the long grey touring car into the yard of the old "White Hart," at Salisbury, and descended with eager anticipation of a big fire and comfortable dinner.

My mechanic Bennett and I had been on the road since soon after dawn, and we yet had many miles to cover. Two months ago I had mounted the car at the garage in Wardour Street and set out upon a long and weary ten-thousand-mile journey in England, not for pleasure, as you may well imagine—but purely upon business. My business, to be exact, was reconnoitring, from a military stand-point, all the roads and by-roads lying between the Tyne and the Thames as well as certain districts south-west of London, in order to write the book upon similar lines to *The Invasion of 1910*.

For two months we had lived upon the road. Sometimes Ray and Vera had travelled with me. When Bennett and I had started it was late and pleasant autumn. Now it was bleak, black winter, and hardly the kind of weather to travel twelve or fourteen hours daily in an open car. Day after day, week after week, the big "sixty" had roared along, ploughing the mud of those ever-winding roads of England until we had lost all count of the days of the week; my voluminous note-books were gradually being filled with valuable data, and the nerves of both of us were becoming so strained that we were victims of insomnia. Hence at night, when we could not sleep, we travelled.

In a great portfolio in the back of the car I carried the six-inch ordnance map of the whole of the east of England divided into many sections, and upon these I was carefully marking out, as result of my survey, the weak points of our land in case an enemy invaded our shores from the North Sea. All telegraphs, telephones, and cables from London to Germany and Holland I was especially noting, for would not the enemy's emissaries, before they attempted to land, seize all means of communication with the metropolis? Besides this I took note of places where food could be obtained, lists of shops, and collected a quantity of other valuable information.

In this work I had been assisted by half a dozen of the highest officers of the Intelligence Department of the War Office, as well as other well-known experts—careful, methodical work prior to writing my forecast of what must happen to our beloved country in case of invasion. The newspapers had referred to my long journey of inquiry, and often when I arrived in a town, our car, smothered in mud, yet its powerful engines running like a clock, was the object of public curiosity, while Bennett, with true chauffeur-like imperturbability, sat immovable, utterly regardless of the interest we created. He was a gentleman-driver, and the best man at the wheel I ever had.

When we were in a hurry he would travel nearly a mile a minute over an open road, sounding his siren driven off the fly-wheel, and scenting police-traps, with the happy result that we were never held up for exceeding the limit. We used to take it in turns to drive—three hours at a time.

On that particular night, when we entered Salisbury from Wincanton Road, having come up from Exeter, it had been raining unceasingly all day, and we presented a pretty plight in our yellow fishermen's oilskins—which we had bought weeks before in King's Lynn as the only means of keeping dry—dripping wet and smothered to our very eyes in mud.

After a hasty wash I entered the coffee-room, and found that I was the sole diner save a short, funny, little old lady in black bonnet and cape, and a young, rather pretty, well-dressed girl, whom I took to be her daughter, seated at a table a little distance away.

Both glanced at me as they entered, and I saw that ere I was half through my meal their interest in me had suddenly increased. Without doubt, the news of my arrival had gone round the hotel, and the waiter had informed the pair of my identity.

It was then eight o'clock, and I had arranged with Bennett that after a rest, we would push forward at half-past ten by Marlborough, as far as Swindon, on our way to Birmingham.

The waiter had brought me a couple of telegrams from Ray telling me good news of another inquiry he was instituting, and having finished my meal I was seated alone by the smoking-room fire enjoying a cigarette and liqueur. Indeed, I had almost fallen asleep when the waiter returned, saying:

"Excuse me, sir, but there's a lady outside in great distress. She wants to speak to you for a moment, and asks if she may come in." He presented a card, and the name upon it was "Mrs. Henry Bingham."

Rather surprised, I nevertheless consented to see her, and in a few moments the door reopened and the younger of the two ladies I had seen at dinner entered.

She bowed to me as I rose, and then, evidently in a state of great agitation, she said:

"I must apologise for disturbing you, only—only I thought perhaps you would be generous enough, when you have heard of our difficulty, to grant my mother and I a favour."

"If I can be of any assistance to you, I shall be most delighted, I'm sure," I answered, as her big grey eyes met mine.

"Well," she said, looking me straight in the face, "the fact is that our car has broken down—something wrong with the clutch, our man says—and we can't get any further to-night. We are on our way to Swindon—to my husband, who has met with an accident and is in the hospital, but—but, unfortunately, there is no train to-night. Your chauffeur has told our man that you are just leaving for Swindon, and my mother and I have been wondering—well—whether we might encroach upon your good nature and beg seats in your car?"

"You are quite welcome to travel with me, of course," I replied without hesitation. "But I fear that on such a night it will hardly be pleasant to travel in an open car."

"Oh, we don't mind that a bit," she assured me. "We have lots of waterproofs and things. It is really most kind of you. I had a telegram at four o'clock this afternoon that my husband had been taken to the hospital for operation, and naturally I am most anxious to be at his side."

"Naturally," I said. "I regret very much that you should have such cause for distress. Let us start at once. I shall be ready in ten minutes."

While she went back to her mother, I went out into the yard where the head-lights of my big "sixty" were gleaming.

"We shall have two lady passengers to Swindon, Bennett," I said, as my chauffeur threw away his cigarette and approached me. "What kind of car have the ladies?"

"A twenty-four. It's in the garage up yonder. The clutch won't hold, it seems. But their man's a foreigner, and doesn't speak much English. I suppose I'd better pack our luggage tighter, so as to give the ladies room."

"Yes. Do so. And let's get on the road as soon as possible."

"Very well, sir," responded the man as he entered the car and began packing our suit-cases together while almost immediately the two ladies emerged, the elder one, whose voice was harsh and squeaky, and who was, I noticed, very deformed, thanking me profusely.

We stowed them away as comfortably as possible, and just as the cathedral chimes rang out half-past ten, the ladies gave parting injunctions to their chauffeur, and we drew out of the yard.

I apologised for the dampness and discomfort of an open car, and briefly explained my long journey and its object. But both ladies—the name of the queer little old widow I understood to be Sandford—only laughed, and reassured me that they were all right.

That night I drove myself. With the exhaust opened and roaring, and the siren shrieking, we sped along through the dark, rainy night up by old Sarum, through Netheravon, and across Overton Heath into Marlborough without once changing speed or speaking with my passengers. As we came down the hill from Ogbourne, I had to pull up suddenly for a farmer's cart, and turned, asking the pair behind how they were faring.

As I did so I noticed that both of them seemed considerably flurried, but attributed it to the high pace we had been travelling when I had so suddenly pulled up on rounding the bend.

Three-quarters of an hour later I deposited them at their destination, the "Goddard Arms," in Old Swindon, and, descending, received their profuse thanks, the elder lady giving me her card with an address in Earl's Court Road, Kensington, and asking me to call upon her when in London.

It was then half an hour past midnight, but Bennett and I resolved to push forward as far as Oxford, which we did, arriving at the "Mitre" about half-past one, utterly fagged and worn out.

Next day was brighter, and we proceeded north to Birmingham and across once again to the east coast, where the bulk of my work lay.

About a fortnight went by. With the assistance of two well-known staff-officers I had been reconnoitring the country around Beccles, in Suffolk, which we had decided upon as a most important strategical point, and one morning I found myself at that old-fashioned hotel "The Cups," at Colchester, taking a day's rest. The two officers had returned to London, and I was again alone.

Out in the garage I found a rather smart, good-looking man in navy serge chatting with Bennett and admiring my car. My chauffeur, with pardonable pride, had been telling him of our long journey, and as I approached, the stranger informed me of his own enthusiasm as a motorist.

"Curiously enough," he added, "I have been wishing to meet you, in order to thank you for your kindness to my mother and sister the other night at Salisbury. My name is Sandford—Charles Sandford—and if I'm not mistaken we are members of the same club—White's."

"Are we?" I exclaimed. "Then I'm delighted to make your acquaintance."

We lounged together for half an hour, smoking and chatting, until presently he said:

"I live out at Edwardstone, about ten miles from here. Why not come out and dine with me to-night? My place isn't very extensive, but it's cosy enough for a bachelor. I'd feel extremely honoured if you would. I'm all alone. Do come."

Cosmopolitan that I am, yet I am not prone to accept the invitations of strangers. Nevertheless this man was not altogether a stranger, for was he not a member of my own club? Truth to tell, I had become bored by the deadly dullness of country hotels, therefore I was glad enough to accept his proffered hospitality and spend a pleasant evening.

"Very well," he said. "I'll send a wire to my housekeeper, and I'll pilot you in your car to my place this evening. We'll start at seven, and dine at eight—if that will suit you?"

And so it was arranged.

Bennett had the whole of the day to go through the car and do one or two necessary repairs, while Sandford and myself idled about the town. My companion struck me as an exceedingly pleasant fellow, who, having travelled very extensively, now preferred a quiet existence in the country, with a little hunting and a little shooting in due season, to the dinners, theatres, and fevered haste of London life.

The evening proved a very dark one with threatening rain as we turned out of the yard of "The Cups," Sandford and I seated behind. My friend directed Bennett from time to time, and soon we found ourselves out on the Sudbury road. We passed through a little place which I knew to be Heyland, and then turned off to the right, across what seemed to be a wide stretch of bleak, open country.

Over the heath we went, our head-lights glaring far before us, for about two miles when my friend called to Bennett:

"Turn to the left at the cross-roads."

And a few moments later we were travelling rather cautiously up a rough by-road, at the end of which we came to a long, old-fashioned house—a farm-house evidently, transformed into a residence.

The door was opened by a middle-aged, red-faced man-servant, and as I stepped within the small hall hung with foxes' masks, brushes, and other trophies, my friend wished me a hearty welcome to his home.

The dining-room proved to be an old-fashioned apartment panelled from floor to ceiling. The table, set for two, bore a fine old silver candelabra, a quantity of antique plate, and, adorned with flowers, was evidently the table of a man who was comfortably off.

We threw off our heavy coats and made ourselves cosy beside the fire when the servant, whom my host addressed as Henry, brought in the soup. Therefore we went to the table and commenced.

The meal proved a well-cooked and well-chosen one, and I congratulated him upon his cook.

"I'm forty, and for twenty years I was constantly on the move," he remarked, with a laugh. "Nowadays I'm glad to be able to settle down in England."

A moment later I heard the sound of a car leaving the house.

"Is that my car?" I asked, rather surprised.

"Probably your man is taking it round to the back in order to put it under cover. Hark! it has started to rain."

To me, however, the sound, growing fainter, was very much as though Bennett had driven the car away.

The wines which Henry served so quietly and sedately were of the best. But both my host and myself drank little.

Sandford was telling me of the strange romance concerning his sister Ellen and young Bingham—a man who had come into eight thousand a year from his uncle, and only a few days later had met with an accident in Swindon, having been knocked down by a train at a level-crossing.

Presently, after dessert, our conversation ran upon ports and their vintages, when suddenly my host remarked:

"I don't know whether you are a connoisseur of brandies, but I happen to have a couple of rather rare vintages. Let's try them."

I confessed I knew but little about brandies.

"Then I'll teach you how to test them in future," he laughed, adding, "Henry, bring up those three old cognacs, a bottle of ordinary brandy, and some liqueur-glasses."

In a few minutes a dozen little glasses made their appearance on a tray, together with four bottles of brandy, three unlabelled, while the fourth bore the label of a well-known brand.

"It is not generally known, I think, that one cannot test brandy with any degree of accuracy by the palate," he said, removing his cigar.

"I wasn't aware of that," I said.

"Well, I'll show you," he went on, and taking four glasses in a row he poured a little spirit out of each of the bottles into the bottoms of the glasses. This done, he twisted each glass round in order to wet the inside with the spirit, and the surplus he emptied into his finger-bowl. Then, handing me two, he said: "Just hold one in each hand till they're warm. So."

And taking the remaining two he held one in the hollow of each hand.

For a couple or three minutes we held them thus while he chatted about the various vintages. Then we placed them in a row.

"Now," he said, "take up each one separately and smell it."

I did so, and found a most pleasant perfume—each, however, quite separate and distinct, as different as eau-de-Cologne is from lavender water.

"This," he said, after sniffing at one glass, "is 1815—Waterloo year—a magnificent vintage. And this," he went on, handing me the second glass, "is 1829—very excellent, but quite a distinct perfume, you notice. The third is 1864—also good. Of the 1815 I very fortunately have two bottles. Bellamy, in Pall Mall, has three bottles, and there are perhaps four bottles in all Paris. That is all that's left of it. The fourth—smell it—is the ordinary brandy of commerce."

I did so, but the odour was nauseating after the sweet and distinct perfume of the other three.

"Just try the 1815," he urged, carefully pouring out about a third of a glass of the precious pale gold liquid and handing it to me.

I sipped it, finding it exceedingly pleasant to the palate. So old was it that it seemed to have lost all its strength. It was a really delicious liqueur— the liqueur of a gourmet, and assuredly a fitting conclusion to that excellent repast.

"I think I'll have the '64," he said, pouring out a glass and swallowing it with all the gusto of a man whose chief delight was the satisfaction of his stomach.

I took a cigarette from the big silver box he handed me, and I stretched out my hand for the matches.... Beyond that, curiously enough, I recollect nothing else.

But stay! Yes, I do.

I remember seeing, as though rising from out a hazy grey mist, a woman's face—the countenance of a very pretty girl, about eighteen, with big blue wide-open eyes and very fair silky hair—a girl, whose eyes bore in them a hideous look of inexpressible horror.

Next instant the blackness of unconsciousness fell upon me.

When I recovered I was amazed to find myself in bed, with the yellow wintry sunlight streaming into the low, old-fashioned room. For some time—how long I know not—I lay there staring at the diamond-paned window straight before me, vaguely wondering what had occurred.

A sound at last struck the right chord of my memory—the sound of my host's voice exclaiming cheerily:

"How do you feel, old chap? Better, I hope, after your long sleep. Do you know it's nearly two o'clock in the afternoon?"

Two o'clock!

After a struggle I succeeded in sitting up in bed.

"What occurred?" I managed to gasp. "I—I don't exactly remember."

"Why nothing, my dear fellow," declared my friend, laughing. "You were a bit tired last night, that's all. So I thought I wouldn't disturb you."

"Where's Bennett?"

"Downstairs with the car, waiting till you feel quite right again."

I then realised for the first time that I was still dressed. Only my boots and collar and tie had been removed.

Much puzzled, and wondering whether it were actually possible that I had taken too much wine, I rose to my feet and slowly assumed my boots.

Was the man standing before me a friend, or was he an enemy?

I recollected most distinctly sampling the brandy, but beyond that— absolutely nothing.

At my host's orders Henry brought me up a refreshing cup of tea and after a quarter of an hour or so, during which Sandford declared that "such little annoying incidents occur in the life of every man," I descended and found Bennett waiting with the car before the door.

As I grasped my host's hand in farewell he whispered confidentially.

"Let's say nothing about it in future. I'll call and see you in town in a week or two—if I may."

Mechanically I declared that I should be delighted, and mounting into the car we glided down the drive to the road.

My brain was awhirl, and I was in no mood to talk. Therefore I sat with the frosty air blowing upon my fevered brow as we travelled back to Colchester.

"I didn't know you intended staying the night, sir," Bennett ventured to remark just before we entered the town.

"I didn't, Bennett."

"But you sent word to me soon after we arrived, telling me to return at noon to-day. So I went back to 'The Cups,' and spent all this morning on the engines."

"Who gave you that message?" I asked quickly.

"Mr. Sandford's man, Henry."

I sat in silence. What could it mean? What mystery was there?

As an abstemious man I felt quite convinced that I had not taken too much wine. A single liqueur-glass of brandy certainly could never have produced such an effect upon me. And strangely enough that girl's face, so shadowy, so sweet, and yet so distorted by horror, was ever before me.

Three weeks after the curious incident, having concluded my survey, I found myself back in Guilford Street, my journey at last ended. Pleasant, indeed, it was to sit again at one's own fireside after those wet, never-ending muddy roads upon which I had lived for so long, and very soon I settled down to arrange the mass of material I had collected and write my book.

A few days after my return, in order to redeem my promise and to learn more of Charles Sandford, I called at the address of the queer old hump-backed widow in Earl's Court Road.

To my surprise, I found the house in question empty, with every evidence of its having been to let for a year or more. There was no mistake in the number; it was printed upon her card. This discovery caused me increasing wonder.

What did it all mean?

Through many weeks I sat in my rooms in Bloomsbury constantly at work upon my book. The technicalities were many and the difficulties not a few. One of the latter—and perhaps the chief one—was to so disguise the real vulnerable points of our country which I had discovered on my tour with military experts as to mislead the Germans, who might seek to make use of the information I conveyed. The book, to be of value, had, I recognised, to be correct in detail, yet at the same time it must suppress all facts that might be of use to a foreign Power.

The incident near Colchester had nearly passed from my mind, when one night in February, 1909, I chanced to be having supper with Ray Raymond and Vera at the "Carlton," when at the table on the opposite side of the big room sat a smart, dark-haired young man with a pretty girl in turquoise-blue.

As I looked across, our eyes met. In an instant I recollected that I had seen that countenance somewhere before. Yes. It was actually the face of that nightmare of mine after sampling Sandford's old cognac! I sat there staring at her, like a man in a dream. The countenance was the sweetest and most perfect I had ever gazed upon. Yet why had I seen it in my unconsciousness?

I noticed that she started. Then, turning her head, she leaned over and whispered something to her companion. Next moment, pulling her cloak about her shoulders, she rose, and they both left hurriedly.

What could her fear imply? Why was she in such terror of me? That look of horror which I had seen on that memorable night was again there— yet only for one single second.

My impulse was to rise and dash after the pair. Yet, not being acquainted with her, I should only, by so doing, make a fool of myself and also annoy my lady friend.

And so for many days and many weeks the remembrance of that sweet and dainty figure ever haunted me. I took a holiday, spending greater part of the time on a friend's yacht in the Norwegian fjords. Yet I could not get away from that face and the curious mystery attaching to it.

On my return home, I was next day rung up on the telephone by my friend Major Carmichael, of the Intelligence Department of the War Office, who had been one of my assistants in preparing the forthcoming book. At his urgent request I went round to see him in Whitehall, and on being ushered into his office, I was introduced to a tall, dark-bearded man, whose name I understood to be Shayler.

"My dear Jacox," exclaimed the Major, "forgive me for getting you here in order to cross-examine you, but both Shayler and myself are eagerly in search of some information. You recollect those maps of yours, marked with all sorts of confidential memoranda relating to the East Coast—facts that would be of the utmost value to the German War Office—what did you do with them?"

"I deposited them here. I suppose they're still here," was my reply.

"Yes. But you'll recollect my warning long ago, when you were reconnoitring. Did you ever allow them to pass out of your hands?"

"Never. I carried them in my portfolio, the key of which was always on my chain."

"Then what do you think of these?" he asked, walking to a side table where lay a pile of twenty or thirty glass photographic negatives. And taking up one of them, he handed it to me.

It was a photograph of one of my own maps! The plan was the section of country in the vicinity of Glasgow. Upon it I saw notes in my own handwriting, the tracing of the telegraph wires with the communications of each wire, and dozens of other facts of supreme importance to the invader.

"Great heavens!" I gasped. "Where did you get that?"

"Shayler will tell you, my dear fellow!" answered the Major. "It seems that you've been guilty of some sad indiscretion."

"I am attached to the Special Department at New Scotland Yard," explained the dark-bearded man. "Two months ago a member of the secret service in the employ of our Foreign Office made a report from Berlin that a young girl, named Gertie Drew, living in a Bloomsbury boarding-house, had approached the German military attaché offering, for three thousand pounds, to supply him with photographs of a number of confidential plans of our eastern counties and of the Clyde defences. The attaché had reported to the War Office in Berlin, hence the knowledge obtained by the British secret agent. The matter was at once placed in my hands, and since that time I have kept careful observation upon the girl—who has been a photographer's assistant—and those in association with her. The result is that I have fortunately managed to obtain possession of these negatives of your annotated plans."

"But how?" I demanded.

"By making a bold move," was the detective's reply. "The Germans were already bargaining for these negatives when I became convinced that the girl was only the tool of a man who had also been a photographer, and who had led a very adventurous life—an American living away in the country, near Colchester, under the name of Charles Sandford."

"Sandford!" I gasped, staring at him. "What is the girl like?"

"Here is her portrait," was the detective's reply.

Yes! It was the sweet face of my nightmare!

"What have you discovered regarding Sandford?" I asked presently, when I had related to the two men the story of the meeting at Salisbury and also my night's adventure.

"Though born in America and adopting an English name, his father was German, and we strongly suspect him of having, on several occasions, sold information to Germany. Yesterday, feeling quite certain of my ground, I went down into Essex with a search warrant and made an examination of the house. Upstairs I found a very complete photographic plant, and concealed beneath the floor-boards in the dining-room was a box containing these negatives, many of them being of your maps of the Clyde defences, which they were just about to dispose of. The man had got wind that we were keeping observation upon him, and had already fled. The gang consisted of an old hump-backed woman, who posed as his mother, a young woman, who he said was his married sister, but who was really the wife of his man-servant, and the girl Drew, who was his photographic assistant."

"Where's the girl? I suppose you don't intend to arrest her?"

"I think not. If you saw her perhaps you might induce her to tell you the truth. The plot to photograph those plans while you were insensible was certainly a cleverly contrived one, and it's equally certain that the two women you met in Salisbury only travelled with you in order to be convinced that you really carried the precious maps with you."

"Yes," I admitted, utterly amazed. "I was most cleverly trapped, but it is most fortunate that we were forewarned, and that our zealous friends across the water have been prevented from purchasing the detailed exposure of our most vulnerable points."

That afternoon, Gertie Drew, the neat-waisted girl with the fair face, walked timidly into my room, and together we sat for fully an hour, during which time she explained how the man Sandford had abstracted the portfolio from my car and substituted an almost exact replica, prior to sending Bennett back to Colchester, and how at the moment of my unconsciousness—as he was searching me for my key—she had entered the dining-room when I had opened my eyes, and staring at her had accused her of poisoning me. She knew she had been recognised, and that had caused her alarm in the "Carlton."

That Sandford had managed to replace the portfolio in the car and abstract the replica next day was explained, and that he had held the girl completely in his power was equally apparent. Therefore, I have since obtained for her a situation with a well-known firm of photographers in Regent Street, where she still remains. The hump-backed woman and her pseudo-daughter have never been seen since, but only a couple of months ago there was recovered from the Rhine at Coblenz the body of a man whose head was fearfully battered, and whom the police, by his clothes and papers upon him, identified as Charles Sandford, the man with whom I shall ever remember partaking of that peculiarly seductive glass of 1815 cognac.

CHAPTER XI
THE PERIL OF LONDON

Certain information obtained by Ray led us to adopt a novel method of trapping one of the Kaiser's secret agents.

About six months after my curious motoring adventure in Essex I sent to the *Berliner Tageblatt*, in Berlin, an advertisement, offering myself as English valet to any German gentleman coming to England, declaring that I had excellent references, and that I, Henry Dickson, had been in service with several English noblemen.

The replies forwarded to me caused us considerable excitement. Vera was with us at New Stone Buildings when the postman brought the bulky packet, and we at once proceeded to read them one by one.

"Holloa!" she cried, holding up one of the letters. "Here you are, Mr. Jacox! The Baron Heinrich von Ehrenburg has replied!"

Eagerly we read the formal letter from the German aristocrat, dated from the Leipziger Strasse, Berlin, stating that, being about to take up his residence in London, he was in want of a good and reliable English servant. He would be at the Ritz Hotel in four days' time, and he made an appointment for me to call.

"Good!" cried Ray. "You must ask very little wages. Germans are a stingy lot. The Baron has been acting as a secret agent of the Kaiser in Paris, but had to fly on account of the recent Ullmo affair at Toulon. He's a very clever spy—about as clever, indeed, as Hartmann himself. Why he is coming to England is not quite clear. But we must find out."

For the next four days I waited in great anxiety, and when, at the appointed hour, I presented myself at the "Ritz" and was shown into the private salon, the middle-aged, fair-haired, rather elegant man eyed me up and down swiftly as I stood before him with great deference.

I was about to play a dangerous game.

After a number of questions, and an examination of my credentials, all of which, I may as well admit, had been prepared by Ray and Vera, he engaged me, and that same evening I entered upon my duties, greatly to the satisfaction of Vera and her lover.

Fortunately I was not known at the "Ritz," and was therefore able for the first week or so to do my valeting, brushing my master's clothes, polishing his boots, getting out his dress-suit, and other such duties, undisturbed, my eyes, however, always open to get a glimpse of any papers that might be left in the pockets or elsewhere.

Twice he drove to Pont Street and dined with Hartmann. The pair were in frequent consultation, it seemed, for one afternoon the chief of the German spies in England called, and was closeted closely with my master for fully two hours.

I stood outside the door, but unfortunately the doors of the "Ritz" are so constructed that nothing can be heard in the corridors. All I knew was that, on being called in to give a message over the telephone, I saw lying on the table between them several English six-inch ordnance maps.

No master could have been more generous than the Baron. He was tall, rather dandified, and seemed a great favourite with the ladies. Hartmann had introduced him to certain well-known members of the German colony in London, and he passed as the possessor of a big estate near Cochem, on the Moselle. He told me one day while I was brushing his coat that he preferred life in England to Germany. He, however, made no mention of his residence in France and how he had ingeniously induced a French naval officer to become a traitor.

From the "Ritz" we, later on, removed into expensive quarters at "Claridge's," and here my master received frequent visits from a shabby, thin-faced, shrivelled-up old foreigner, whom I took to be a Dutchman, his name being Mr. Van Nierop.

Whenever he called the Baron and he held close consultation, sometimes for hours. We travelled to Eastbourne, Bournemouth, Birmingham, Edinburgh, Glasgow, and other cities, yet ever and anon the shabby old Dutchman seemed to turn up at odd times and places, as though springing from nowhere.

When absent from London, the Baron frequently sent telegraphic messages in cipher to a registered address in London. Were these, I wondered, intended for Hartmann or for the mysterious Van Nierop?

The old fellow seemed to haunt us everywhere, dogging our footsteps continually, and appearing in all sorts of out-of-the-way places with his long, greasy overcoat, shabby hat, and shuffling gait, by which many mistook him for a Hebrew.

And the more closely I watched my aristocratic master, the more convinced I became that Van Nierop and he were acting in collusion. But of what was in progress I could obtain no inkling.

Frequently we moved quickly from one place to another, as though my master feared pursuit, then we went suddenly to Aix, Vichy, and Carlsbad, and remained away for some weeks. Early in the autumn we were back again at a suite of well-furnished chambers in Clarges Street, off Piccadilly.

"I expect, Dickson, that we shall be in London some months," the Baron had said to me on the second morning after we had installed ourselves with our luggage. The place belonged to a wealthy young peer of racing proclivities, and was replete with every comfort. All had been left just as it was, even to an open box of cigars. His lordship had gone on a trip round the world.

On the third day—a very wet and dismal one, I recollect—the old Dutchman arrived. The Baron was out, therefore he waited—waited in patience for six long hours for his return. When my master re-entered, the pair sat together for half an hour. Then suddenly the Baron shouted to me, "Dickson! Pack my suit-case and biggest kit-bag at once. Put in both dress-coat and dinner-jacket. And I shan't want you. You'll stay here and mind the place."

"Yes, sir," I replied, and began briskly to execute his orders.

When the shabby old fellow had gone, the Baron called me into the sitting-room and gave me two cipher telegrams, one written on the yellow form used for foreign messages. The first, which he had numbered "1" in blue pencil, was addressed "Zaza, Berlin," and the second was to "Tejada, Post Office, Manchester."

"These, Dickson, I shall leave with you, for I may want them despatched. Send them the instant you receive word from me. I will tell you which to send. It's half-past eight. I leave Charing Cross at nine, but cannot give you any fixed address. Here's money to get along with. Wait here until my return."

I was sorely disappointed. I knew that he was a spy and was in England for some fixed purpose. But what it was I could not discover.

"And," he added, as though it were an afterthought, "if any one should by chance inquire about Mr. Van Nierop—whether you know him, or if he has been here—remember that you know nothing—nothing. You understand?"

"Very well, sir," was my response.

Five minutes later, refusing to allow me to accompany him to the station, he drove away into Piccadilly with his luggage upon a hansom, and thus was I left alone for an indefinite period.

That evening I went round to Bruton Street, where I saw Ray, and described what had occurred.

He sat staring into the fire in silence for some time.

"Well," he answered at last, "if what I surmise be true, Jack, the Baron ought to be back here in about a week. Continue to keep both eyes and ears open. There's a deep game being played, I am certain. He's with Hartmann very often. Recollect what I told you about the clever manner in which the Baron conducted the affair at Toulon. He would have been entirely successful hadn't a woman given Ullmo away. See me as little as you can. You never know who may be watching you during the Baron's absence."

On the next evening I went out for a stroll towards Piccadilly Circus and accidentally met a man I knew, a German named Karl Stieber, a man of about thirty, who was valet to a young gentleman who lived in the flat beneath us.

Together we descended to that noisy café beneath the Hôtel de l'Europe in Leicester Square, where we met four other friends of Karl's, servants like himself.

As we sat together, he told me that his brother was head-waiter at a little French restaurant in Dean Street, Soho, called "La Belle Niçoise," a place where one could obtain real Provençal dishes. Then, I on my part, told him of my own position and my travels with the Baron.

When we ascended into Leicester Square again we found the pavements congested, for Daly's, the Empire, and the Alhambra had just disgorged their throngs.

As he walked with me he turned, and suddenly asked:

"Since you've been in London has old Van Nierop visited the Baron?"

I started in quick surprise, but in an instant recollected my master's injunctions.

"Van Nierop!" I echoed. "Whom do you mean?"

But he only laughed knowingly, exclaiming:

"All right. You'll deny all knowledge of him, of course. But, my dear Dickson, take the advice of one who knows, and be ever watchful. Take care of your own self. Good night!"

And my friend, who seemed to possess some secret knowledge, vanished in the crowd.

Once or twice he ascended and called upon me, and we sometimes used to spend our evenings together in that illicit little gaming-room behind a shop in Old Compton Street, a place much frequented by foreign servants.

I noticed, however, though he was very inquisitive regarding the Baron and his movements, he would never give me any reason. He sometimes warned me mysteriously that I was in danger. But to me his words appeared absurd.

One evening, in the third week of December, he and I were in the Baron's room chatting, when a ring came at the door, and I found the Baron himself, looking very tired and fagged. He almost staggered into his sitting-room, brushing past Karl on his way. He was dressed in different clothes, and I scarcely recognised him at first.

"Who's that, Dickson?" he demanded sharply. "I thought I told you I forbade visitors here! Send him away. I want to talk to you."

I obeyed, and when he heard the door close the Baron, who I noticed was travel-worn and dirty, with a soiled collar and many days' growth of beard, said:

"Don't have anybody here—not even your best friend, Dickson. You'd admit no stranger here if you knew the truth," he added, with a meaning look. "Fortunately, perhaps you don't."

Then, after he had gulped down the cognac I had brought at his order, he went on:

"Now, listen. In a little more than a week it will be New Year's day. On that day there will arrive for me a card of greeting. You will open all my letters on that morning, and find it. Either it will be perfectly plain and bear the words 'A Happy New Year' in frosted letters, or else it will be a water-colour snow scene—a house, bare trees, moonlight, you know the kind of thing—with the words 'The Compliments of the Season.' Upon either will be written in violet ink, in a woman's hand, the words in English, 'To dear Heinrich.' You understand, eh?"

"Perfectly, sir."

"Good," he said. "Now, I gave you two telegrams before I left. If the card is a plain one, burn it and despatch the first telegram; if coloured, then send the second message. Do you follow?"

I replied in the affirmative, when, to my surprise he rose, and instead of entering his bedroom to wash, he simply swallowed a second glass of brandy, sighed, and departed, saying:

"Remember, you know nothing—nothing whatever. If there should be any inquiries about me, keep your mouth closed."

Twice my friend Stieber called in the days that followed, but I flattered myself that from me he learnt nothing.

On the morning of New Year's day five letters were pushed through the box. Eagerly I tore them open. The last, bearing a Dutch stamp, with the postmark of Utrecht, contained the expected card, with the inscription "To dear Heinrich," a small hand-painted scene upon celluloid, with forget-me-nots woven round the words "With the Compliments of the Season."

Half an hour later, having burned the card according to my instructions, I despatched the mysterious message to Manchester.

That evening, about ten o'clock, Stieber called for me to go for a stroll and drink a New Year health. But as we turned from Clarges Street into Piccadilly I could have sworn that a man we passed in the darkness was old Van Nierop. I made no remark, however, because I did not wish to draw my companion's attention to the shuffling old fellow.

Had the telegram, I wondered, brought him to London?

Ten minutes later, in the Café Monico, my friend Karl lifted his glass to me, saying:

"Well, a Happy New Year, my dear friend. Take my advice, and don't trust your Baron too implicitly."

"What do you mean?" I asked. "You always speak in enigmas!"

But he laughed, and would say no more.

Next day dawned. Grey and muddy, it was rendered more dismal by my loneliness. I idled away the morning, anxious to be travelling again, but at noon there was a caller, a thin, pale-faced girl of fifteen or so, poorly dressed and evidently of the working-class.

When, in response to her question, I had told her my name, she said:

"I've been sent by the Baron to tell you he wishes to see you very particularly to-night at nine o'clock, at this address."

She handed me an envelope with an address upon it, and then went down the stairs.

The address I read was: "4A Bishop's Lane, Chiswick."

The mysterious appointment puzzled me, but after spending a very cheerless day, I hailed a taxi-cab at eight o'clock and set forth for Chiswick, a district to which I had never before been.

At length we found ourselves outside an old-fashioned church, and on inquiry I was told by a boy that Bishop's Lane was at the end of a footpath which led through the churchyard.

I therefore dismissed the taxi, and after some search, at length found No. 4A, an old-fashioned house standing alone in the darkness amid a large garden surrounded by high, bare trees—a house built in the long ago days before Chiswick became a London suburb.

As I walked up the path the door was opened, and I found the old man Van Nierop standing behind it.

Without a word he ushered me into a back room, which, to my surprise, was carpetless and barely furnished. Then he said, in that strange croaking voice of his:

"Your master will be here in about a quarter of an hour. He's delayed. Have a cigarette."

I took one from the packet he offered, and still puzzled, lit it and sat down to await the Baron.

The old man had shuffled out, and I was left alone, when of a sudden a curious drowsiness overcame me. I fancy there must have been a narcotic in the tobacco, for I undoubtedly slept.

When I awoke I found, to my amazement, that I could not use my arms. I was still seated in the wooden arm-chair, but my arms and legs were bound with ropes, while the chair itself had been secured to four iron rings screwed into the floor.

Over my mouth was bound a cloth so that I could not speak.

Before me, his thin face distorted by a hideous, almost demoniacal laugh of triumph, stood old Van Nierop, watching me as I recovered consciousness. At his side, grinning in triumph, was my master, the Baron.

I tried to ask the meaning of it all, but was unable.

"See, see!" cried the old Dutchman, pointing with his bony finger to the dirty table near me, whereon a candle-end was burning straight before my eyes beside a good-sized book—a leather-bound ledger it appeared to be. "Do you know what I intend doing? Well, I'm going to treat you as all English spies should be treated. That candle will burn low in five minutes and sever the string you see which joins the wick. Look what that innocent-looking book contains!" and with a peal of discordant laughter he lifted the cover, showing, to my horror, that it was a box, wherein reposed a small glass tube filled with some yellow liquid, a trigger held back by the string, and some square packets wrapped in oiled paper.

"You see what this is!" he said slowly and distinctly. "The moment the string is burned through, the hammer will fall, and this house will be blown to atoms. That book contains the most powerful explosive known to science."

I could not demand an explanation, for though I struggled, I could not speak.

I watched the old man fingering with fiendish delight the terrible machine he had devised for my destruction.

"You and your friend Raymond thought to trap us!" said the Baron. "But, you see, he who laughs last laughs best. Adieu, and I wish you a pleasant trip, my young friend, into the next world," and both went out, closing the door after them.

All was silence. I sat there helpless, pinioned, staring at the burning candle and awaiting the most awful death that can await a man.

Ah, those moments! How can I ever adequately describe them? Suffice it to say that my hair was dark on that morning, but in those terrible moments of mental agony, of fear and horror, it became streaked with grey.

Lower and still lower burned the flame, steadily, imperceptibly, yet, alas! too sure. Each second brought me nearer the grave.

I was face to face with death.

Frantically and fiercely I fought to wrench myself free—fought until a great exhaustion fell upon me.

Then, as the candle had burned until the flame was actually touching that thin string which held me between life and death, I fainted.

A blinding flash, a terrific explosion that deafened me, and a feeling of sudden numbness.

I found myself lying on the path outside with two men at my side.

One was a dark-bearded, thick-set, but gentlemanly-looking man—the other was Ray Raymond.

Of the house where I had been, scarcely anything remained save its foundations. The big trees in the garden had been shattered and torn down, and every window in the neighbourhood had been blown in, to the intense alarm of hundreds of people who were now rushing along the dark, unfrequented thoroughfare.

"My God!" cried Ray. "What a narrow escape you've had! Why didn't you take my advice? It was fortunate that, suspecting something, we followed you here. This gentleman," he said, introducing his friend, "is Bellamy, of the Special Department at Scotland Yard. We just discovered you in time. Old Van Nierop ran inside again when he met us in the path. He thought he had time to escape through the back, but he hadn't. He's been blown to atoms himself, as well as the Baron, and thus saved us the trouble of extradition."

I was too exhausted and confused to reply. Besides, a huge crowd was already gathering, the fire-brigade had come up, and the police seemed to be examining the débris strewn everywhere.

"You watched the Baron well, but not quite well enough, my dear Jacox," Ray said. "They evidently suspected you of prying into their business, and plotted to put you quietly out of the way. You have evidently somehow betrayed yourself."

"But what was their business?" I asked. "I searched every scrap of paper in the Baron's rooms, but was never able to discover anything."

"Well, the truth is that the reason the Baron came to England was in order to take a house in this secluded spot. Aided by Van Nierop they have established a depôt close by in readiness for the coming of the Kaiser's army. Come with me and let us investigate."

And leading me to a stable at the rear of another house about fifty yards distant, he, aided by Bellamy, broke open the padlocked door.

Within we found great piles of small, strongly bound boxes containing rifle ammunition, together with about sixty cases of old Martini-Henry rifles, weapons still very serviceable at close quarters, a quantity of revolvers, and ten cases of gun-cotton—quite a formidable store of arms and ammunition, similar to that we found in Essex, and intended, no doubt, for the arming of the horde of Germans already in London on the day when the Kaiser gives the signal for the dash upon our shores.

"This is only one of the depôts established in the neighbourhood of the metropolis," Raymond said. "There are others, and we must set to work to discover them. Germany leaves nothing to chance, and there are already in London fifty thousand well-trained men of the Fatherland, most of whom belong to secret clubs, and who will on 'the Day' rise *en masse* at the signal of invasion."

"But the Baron!" I exclaimed, half dazed. "Where is he?"

"They've just recovered portions of him," replied Ray, with a grin.

"But that New Year's card!" I exclaimed, and then amid the excitement proceeded to tell Bellamy and my companion what had happened.

"The message you sent to Manchester was to acquaint Hartmann, who is staying at this moment at the Midland Grand Hotel, with their intended vengeance upon you, my dear old chap. Nierop was a Dutch merchant in the City, and his habit was to import arms and ammunition in small quantities, and distribute them to the different secret depôts, one of which we know is somewhere near the 'Adelaide,' in Chalk Farm Road, another is at a house in Malmesbury Road, Canning Town, a third in Shepperton Street, Hoxton, and a fourth is said to be close by the chapel in Cowley Road, Leytonstone."

"And there are others besides," remarked Bellamy.

"Yes," remarked Raymond, "one is certainly somewhere in Crowland Road, South Tottenham, another near the Gas Works at Hornsey, and others somewhere between Highgate Hill and the New River reservoir. Besides, there are no doubt several in such towns as Ipswich, Chelmsford, Yarmouth, and Norwich."

The police had by this time taken possession of the stable, but no information was given to the public, fearing that a panic might be caused if the truth leaked out.

So the newspapers and the public believed the death of the German and the Dutchman to be due to a gas explosion—at least that was what the police reported at the inquest. Next day the arms and ammunition were quietly removed in closed vans from the house and stable which the spies had rented, and conveyed to safe keeping at Woolwich—where, I believe, they still remain as evidence of the German intentions.

Londoners, indeed, sadly disregard the peril in which they are placed with a hostile force already in their midst—an advance guard of the enemy already on the alert, and but awaiting the landing of their compatriots from the Fatherland.

No sane man can to-day declare that, with our maladministered Navy, the invasion of England is impossible. Invasion is not a "scare." It is a hard fact which must be faced, if we are not to fall beneath the "mailed fist."

The peril is great, and it is increasing daily. The Germans are strenuous in their endeavours to make every preparation for the successful raid upon our shores.

As an instance, in February, 1909, what may well be described as a careful, complete, and systematic photographic survey of the coast between the Tyne and the Tees was conducted, it is stated, by a party of foreigners, three of whom were Germans.

Every indentation of the coast, and especially those in the neighbourhood of the dunes about Heselden and Castle Eden, was faithfully recorded by means of the camera, photographs being taken both at low tide and at high tide at various points.

Considerable attention was given to the entrances to the Tyne, Tees and Wear, and also to the Harbour entrances at Seaham Harbour and Hartlepool; whilst the positions of the various coast batteries and coast-guard stations were also photographed.

Nor did the party, whose operations extended over a period of several weeks, confine their attention solely to the coast line. Railway junctions and bridges near the coast, collieries, and even farm-houses were photographed; in fact, the salient features of the countryside bordering the sea were all included in what was altogether a most exhaustive series of pictures.

A certain number of films were developed from day to day at West Hartlepool, something like two hundred pictures in all being dealt with, but these formed only a tithe of the photographs taken, and the undeveloped films, together with the prints from those that had been developed, were despatched direct to Hamburg and Berlin, while some were sent to the head-quarters of the German espionage in Pont Street, London.

CHAPTER XII
HOW GERMANY FOMENTS STRIFE

Ray Raymond had been engaged watching the house of Hermann Hartmann in Pont Street ever since our discovery of the secret store of arms and ammunition down at Chiswick.

I had been absent at Devonport, keeping observation upon the movements of two Germans who had once or twice paid visits to Hartmann, and who had evidently received his instructions personally. The two men in question were known to us as spies, for with two other compatriots we had found them, only three months before, busily engaged in preparing a plan of the water-mains of East London, in order that, in case of invasion, some of the German colony could destroy the principal mains and thus deprive half the metropolis of drinking-water.

In Leeds they had, we know, mapped out the whole water-supply, as Barker had done at North Shields; and again in Sheffield, the plans of which were in Berlin; but fortunately we had discovered them at work in London, and had been able to prevent them from accomplishing their object. Two of the men had returned to Germany on being detected, and the other two were now at Devonport, where I had been living for a month in irritating inactivity.

One afternoon, on receipt of a telegram from Ray, I immediately returned to London, and as I entered the flat in Bruton Street, my friend said:

"The great *agent provocateur* of the German Government, our friend Hermann Hartmann, has left for Russia, Jack. His employers have sent him there for some special reason. Would it not be wise for you to follow, and ascertain the latest move?"

"If you think so, I'll go," I said readily. "You can take my place down at Devonport. I've been there too long and may be spotted. Where has Hartmann gone?"

"First back to Berlin. He has been ordered to go to Poland on a special mission."

"Then I must pick him up in Berlin," I said.

And thus it was arranged. Next morning I obtained a special *visa* to my passport from the Russian Ambassador, whom I chanced to know personally, and at 2.20 left Charing Cross for Calais, bound for Berlin.

I was puzzled why Hartmann, the most trusted agent of the Kaiser's secret police, should be so suddenly transferred to Russian territory. It was only temporarily, no doubt, but it behoved us to have knowledge of what might be in the wind.

It was winter, and the journey to the German capital was cold and cheerless. Yet I had not been there six hours before I had discovered that Hartmann had left for a place called Ostrog, in Eastern Poland.

Therefore I lost no time in setting forth for that rather obscure place.

Yes, nowadays my life was a strange one, full of romance and constant change, of excitement—and sometimes of insecurity.

For what reason had the great Hartmann been sent so far afield?

On leaving the railway, I travelled for two days in a sleigh over those endless snow-covered roads and dark forests, until my horses, with their jingling bells, pulled up before a small inn on the outskirts of the dismal-looking town of Ostrog. The place, with its roofs covered with freshly-fallen snow, lay upon the slight slope of a low hill, beneath which wound the Wilija Goryn, now frozen so hard that the bridge was hardly ever used. It was January, and that month in Poland is always a cold one.

I had crossed the frontier at the little village of Kolodno, and thence driven along the valleys into Volynien, a long, weary, dispiriting drive, on and on until those bells maddened me by their monotonous rhythm. Cramped and cold I was, notwithstanding the big fur coat I wore, the fur cap with flaps, fur gloves, and fur rug. The country inns in which I had spent the past two nights had been filthy places where the stoves had been surrounded by evil-smelling peasantry, where the food was uneatable and where a wooden bench had served me as a bed.

At each stage where we changed horses the post-house keeper had held up his hands when he knew my destination was Ostrog. "The Red Rooster" was crowing there, they said significantly.

It was true. Russia was under the Terror again, and in no place in the whole empire were the revolutionists so determined as in the town whither I was bound. I saw at once the reason why Hartmann was there—to secretly stir up strife, for it is to the advantage of Germany that Russia should be in a state of unrest. To observe the German methods was certainly interesting.

Ostrog at last! As I stood up and descended unsteadily from my sleigh my eyes fell upon something upon the snow near the door of the inn. There was blood. It told its own tale.

From the white town across the frozen river I heard revolver shots, followed by a loud explosion that shook the whole place and startled the three horses in my sleigh.

Inside the long, low, common room of the inn, with its high brick stove, against which half a dozen frightened-looking men and women were huddled, I asked for the proprietor, whereupon an elderly man, with shaggy hair and beard, came forth, pulling his forelock.

"I want to stay here," I said.

"Yes, your excellency," was the old fellow's reply, in Polish. "Whatever accommodation my poor inn can afford is at your service"—and he at once shouted orders to my driver to bring in my kit, while the women, all of them flat-faced peasants, made room for me at the stove.

From where I stood I could hear the sound of desultory firing across the bridge, and inquired what was in progress.

But there was an ominous silence. They did not reply, for, as I afterwards discovered, they had taken me for a high police official from Petersburg, thus accounting for the innkeeper's courtesy.

"Tell me," I said, addressing the wrinkled-faced old Pole, "what is happening over yonder?"

"The Cossacks," he stammered. "Krasiloff and his Cossacks are upon us. They have just entered the town and are shooting down people everywhere. Hartmann, the great patriot from Germany, has arrived, and the fight for freedom has commenced, excellency. But it is horrible. A poor woman was shot dead before my door half an hour ago, and her body taken away by the soldiers."

Tired as I was, I lost no time. With a glance to see that my own revolver was loaded, I threw aside my overcoat, and, leaving the inn, walked across the bridge into a poor narrow street of wretched-looking houses, many of them built of wood. A man limped slowly past me, wounded in the leg, and leaving blood-spots behind him as he went. An old woman was seated in a doorway, her face buried in her hands, wailing:

"My poor son!—dead!—dead!"

Before me I saw a great barricade composed of trees, household furniture, paving-stones, overturned carts, pieces of barbed wire—in fact, everything and anything the populace could seize upon for the construction of hasty defence. Upon the top, silhouetted against the clear frosty sky, was the scarlet flag of the revolution—the Red Rooster was crowing!

Excited men were there, armed with rifles, shouting and giving orders. Then I saw that a small space had been left open against the wall of a house so that persons might pass and repass.

As I approached a wild-haired man shouted to me and beckoned frantically. I grasped his meaning. He wished me to come within. I ran forward, entered the town proper, and a few moments later the opening was closed by a dozen slabs of stone being heaped up into it by as many willing hands.

Thus I found myself in the very centre of the revolution, behind the barricades, of which there were, it seemed, six or seven. From the rear there was constant firing, and the streets in the vicinity were, I saw to my horror, already filled with dead and wounded. Women were wailing over husbands, lovers, brothers; men over their daughters and wives. Even children of tender age were lying helpless and wounded, some of them shattered and dead.

Ah! that sight was sickening. Never had I seen wholesale butchery such as that in which I was now in the midst. I was looking about to find the German *agent provocateur*, but I failed to find him. Perhaps, having bidden the people to rise, he had himself escaped. Most probably.

Above us bullets whistled as the Cossacks came suddenly round a side street and made a desperate attack upon the barricade I had entered only a few minutes before. A dozen of those fighting for their freedom fell back dead at my feet at the first volley. They had been on top of the barricade, offering a mark to the troops of the Czar. Before us and behind us there was firing, for at the rear of us was another barricade. We were, in fact, between two deadly fires.

Revolver in hand, I stood ready to defend my own life. In those exciting moments I disregarded the danger I ran from being struck in that veritable hail of lead. Men fell wounded all around me, and there was blood everywhere. A thin, dark-headed young fellow under thirty—a Moscow student, I subsequently heard—seemed to be the ringleader, for above the firing could be heard his shouts of encouragement.

"Fight! my comrades!" he cried, standing close to me and waving the red flag he carried—the emblem of the Terror—"Down with the Czar! Kill the vermin he sends to us! Long live Germany! Long live freedom! Kill them!" he shrieked. "They have killed your wives and daughters. Men of Ostrog—remember your duty to-day! Set an example to Russia. Do not let the Moscow fiasco be repeated here. Fight! Fight on as long as you have a drop of life-blood in you, and we shall win, we shall win! Down with the Autocrat! Down with the— —"

His sentence was never finished, for at that instant he reeled backwards with half his face shot away by a Cossack bullet.

The situation was, for me, one of greatest peril. I had had no opportunity of finding the governor of the town to present my credentials, and thus obtain protection. The whole place was in open revolt, and when the troops broke down the defences, as I saw they must do sooner or later, then we should all be caught in a trap, and no quarter would be given.

The massacre would be the same as at Moscow and many other towns in Western Russia, wherein the populace had been shot down indiscriminately, and official telegrams had been sent to Petersburg reporting "order now reigns."

I sought shelter in a doorway, but scarcely had I done so than a bullet embedded itself in the woodwork a few inches from my head. At the barricade the women were helping the men, loading their rifles for them, shouting and encouraging them to fight gallantly for freedom. And suddenly I caught sight of Hartmann's evil face. He was calmly talking to a man who was no doubt also in the German employ. The rising was their work!

A yellow-haired young woman, not more than twenty, emerged from a house close by where I stood and ran past me to the barricade. As she passed I saw that she carried something in her hand. It looked like a small cylinder of metal.

Shouting to a man who was firing through a loophole near the top of the barricade, she handed it up to him. Taking it carefully, he scrambled up higher, waited for a few moments, and then, raising himself, he hurled it far into the air into the midst of an advancing troop of Cossacks.

There was a red flash, a terrific explosion which shook the whole town, wrecking the houses in the immediate vicinity, and blowing to atoms dozens of the Czar's soldiers.

A wild shout of victory went up from the revolutionists when they saw the havoc caused by the awful bomb. The yellow-haired girl returned again and brought another, which, after some ten minutes or so, was similarly hurled against the troops, with equally disastrous effect.

The roadway was strewn with the bodies of those Cossacks which General Kinski, the governor of the town, had telegraphed for, and whom

Krasiloff had ordered to give no quarter to the revolutionists. In Western Russia the name of Krasiloff was synonymous with all that was cruel and brutal. It was he who ordered the flogging of the five young women at Minsk, those poor unfortunate creatures who were knouted by Cossacks who laid their backs bare to the bone. As every one in Russia knows, two of them, both members of good families, died within a few hours, and yet no reprimand did he receive from Petersburg. By the Czar and at the Ministry of the Interior he was known to be a hard man, and for that reason certain towns where the revolutionary spirit was strongest had been given into his hands.

At Kiev he had executed without trial dozens of men and woman arrested for revolutionary acts. A common grave was dug in the prison yard, and the victims, four at a time, were led forward to the edge of the pit and shot, each batch being compelled to witness the execution of the four prisoners preceding them. With a refinement of cruelty that was only equalled by the Inquisition, he had wrung confessions from women, and afterwards had them shot and buried. At Petersburg they knew these things, but he had actually been commended and decorated for his loyalty to the Czar!

And now that he had been hurriedly moved to Ostrog the people knew that his order to the Cossacks was to massacre the people, and more especially the Jewish portion of the population, without mercy.

"Krasiloff is here!" said the man whose face was smeared with blood as he stood by me. "He intends that we shall all die, but we will fight for it. The revolution has only just commenced. Soon the peasants will rise, and we will sweep the country clean of the vermin the Czar has placed upon us. To-day Kinski, the governor, has been fired at twice, but unsuccessfully. He wants a bomb, and he shall have it," he added meaningly. "Olga—the girl yonder with the yellow hair—has one for him!"—and he laughed grimly.

I recognised my own deadly peril. I stood revolver in hand, though I had not fired a shot, for I was no revolutionist. I was only awaiting the inevitable breaking down of the barricade—and the awful catastrophe that must befall the town when those Cossacks, drunk with the lust for blood, swept into the streets.

Around me men and women were shouting themselves hoarse, while the red emblem of Terror still waved lazily from the top of the barricade. The men manning the improvised defence kept up a withering fire upon the troops, who in the open road were afforded no cover. Time after time the place shook as those terrible bombs exploded with awful result, for the yellow-haired girl seemed to keep up a continuous supply of them. They were only seven or eight inches long, but hurled into a company of soldiers their effect was deadly.

For half an hour longer it seemed as though the defence of the town would be effectual, yet, of a sudden, the redoubled shouts of those about me told me the truth.

The Cossacks had been reinforced, and were about to rush the barricade.

I managed to peer forth, and there, surely enough, the whole roadway was filled with soldiers.

Yells, curses, heavy firing, men falling back from the barricade to die around me, and the disappearance of the red flag showed that the Cossacks were at last scaling the great pile of miscellaneous objects that blocked the street. A dozen of the Czar's soldiers appeared silhouetted against the sky as they scrambled across the top of the barricade, but the next second a dozen corpses fell to earth, riddled by the bullets of the men standing below in readiness.

In a moment, however, others appeared in their places, and still more and more. Women threw up their hands in despair and fled for their lives, while men—calmly prepared to die in the cause—shouted again and again, "Down with Krasiloff and the Czar! Long live the revolution! Long live Germany! Give us the Kaiser! Victory for the people's will!"

I stood undecided. I was facing death. Those Cossacks with orders to massacre would give no quarter, and would not discriminate. Krasiloff was waiting for his dastardly order to be carried out. The Czar had given him instructions to crush the revolution by whatever means he thought proper.

Those moments of suspense seemed hours. Suddenly there was another flash, a stunning report, the air was filled with débris, and a great breach opened in the barricade. The Cossacks had used explosives to clear away the obstruction. Next instant they were upon us.

I flew—flew for my life. Whither my legs carried me I know not. Women's despairing shrieks rent the air on every hand. The massacre had commenced. I remember I dashed into a long, narrow street that seemed half deserted, then turned corner after corner, but behind me, ever increasing, rose the cries of the doomed populace. The Cossacks were following the people into their houses and killing men, women, and even children.

Suddenly, as I turned into a side street, I saw that it led into a large open thoroughfare, the main road through the town, I expect. And there, straight before me, I saw that an awful scene was being enacted.

I turned to run back, but at that instant a woman's long, despairing cry reached me, causing me to glance within a doorway, where stood a big, brutal Cossack, who had pursued and captured a pretty, dark-haired, well-dressed girl.

"Save me!" she shrieked as I passed. "Oh, save me, sir!" she gasped, white, terrified, and breathless with struggling. "He will kill me!"

The burly soldier had his bearded face close down to hers, his arms clasped around her, and had evidently forced her from the street into the entry.

For a second I hesitated.

"Oh, sir, save me! Save me, and God will reward you!" she implored, her big, dark eyes turned to mine in final appeal.

The fellow at that moment raised his fist and struck her a brutal blow upon the mouth that caused the blood to flow, saying with a savage growl:

"Be quiet, will you?"

"Let that woman go!" I commanded in the best Russian I could.

In an instant, with a glare in his fiery eyes, for the blood-lust was within him, he turned upon me and sneeringly asked who I was to give him orders, while the poor girl reeled, half stunned by his blow.

"Let her go I say!" I shouted, advancing quickly towards him.

But in a moment he had drawn his big army revolver, and, ere I became aware of his dastardly intention, he raised it to a few inches from her face.

Quick as thought I raised my own weapon, which I had held behind me, and, being accredited a fairly good shot, I fired in an endeavour to save the poor girl.

Fortunately my bullet struck, for he stepped back, his revolver dropped from his fingers upon the stones, and, stumbling forward, he fell dead at her feet without a word. My shot had, I saw, hit him in the temple, and death had probably been instantaneous.

With a cry of joy at her sudden release, the girl rushed across to me, and raising my left hand to her lips, kissed it, at the same time thanking me.

Then, for the first time, I recognised how uncommonly pretty she was. Not more than eighteen, she was slim and petite, with a narrow waist and graceful figure—quite unlike in refinement and in dress the other women I had seen in Ostrog. Her dark hair had come unbound in her desperate struggle with the Cossack and hung about her shoulders, her bodice was torn and revealed a bare white neck, and her chest heaved and fell as in breathless, disjointed sentences she thanked me again and again.

There was not a second to lose, however. She was, I recognised, a Jewess, and Krasiloff's orders were not to spare them.

From the main street beyond rose the shouts and screams, the firing and wild triumphant yells as the terrible massacre progressed.

"Come with me!" she cried breathlessly. "Along here. I know of a place of safety!"

And she led the way, running swiftly for about two hundred yards, and then, turning into a narrow, dirty courtyard, passed through an evil, forbidding-looking house, where all was silent as the grave.

With a key she quickly opened the door of a poor, ill-furnished room, which she closed behind her, but did not lock. Then, opening a door on the opposite side, which had been papered over so as to escape observation, I saw there was a flight of damp stone stairs leading down to a cellar or some subterranean regions beneath the house.

"Down here!" she said, taking a candle, lighting it, and handing it to me. "Go—I will follow."

I descended cautiously into the cold, dank place, discovering it to be a kind of unlighted cellar hewn out of the rock. A table, a chair, a lamp, and some provisions showed that preparation had been made for concealment there, but ere I had entirely explored the place my pretty fellow-fugitive rejoined me.

"This, I hope, is a place of safety," she said. "They will not find us here. This is where Gustave lived before his flight."

"Gustave?" I repeated, looking her straight in the face.

She dropped her eyes and blushed. Her silence told its own tale. The previous occupant of that rock chamber was her lover.

Her name was Luba—Luba Lazareff, she told me. But of herself she would tell me nothing further. Her reticence was curious, yet before long I recognised the reason of her refusal.

In reply to further questions she said: "The Germans are our friends. Two men from Berlin have been in Ostrog nearly a month holding secret meetings and urging us to rise."

"Do you know Hermann Hartmann?" I inquired.

"Ah! yes. He is the great patriot. He arrived here the day before yesterday to address us before the struggle," she replied enthusiastically.

Candle in hand, I was examining the deepest recesses of the dark, cavernous place, while she lit the lamp, when, to my surprise, I discovered at the further end a workman's bench, upon which were various pieces of turned metal, pieces of tube of various sizes, and little phials of glass like those used for the tiny tabloids for subcutaneous injections.

I took one up to examine it, but at that instant she noticed me and screamed in terror.

"Ah, sir! For heaven's sake, put that down—very carefully. Touch nothing there, or we may both be blown to pieces! See!" she added in a low, intense voice of confession, as she, dashed forward, "there are finished bombs there! Gustave could not carry them all away, so he left those with me."

"Then Gustave made these, eh?"

"Yes. And, see, he gave me this"—and she drew from her breast a small, shining cylinder of brass, a beautifully finished little object about four inches long similar to those used at the barricade. "He gave this to me to use—if necessary!" the girl added, a meaning flash in her dark eyes.

For a moment I was silent.

"Then you would have used it upon that Cossack?" I said slowly.

"That was my intention."

"And kill yourself, as well as your assailant?"

"I have promised him," was her simple answer.

"And this Gustave? You love him? Tell me all about him. Remember I am your friend, and will help you if I can."

She hesitated, and I was compelled to urge her again and again ere she would speak.

"Well, he is German—from Berlin," she said at last, as we still stood before the bomb-maker's bench. "He is a chemist, and, being an anarchist, came to us, and joined us in the Revolution. The petards thrown over the barricades to-day were of his make, but he had to fly. He left yesterday."

"For Berlin?"

"Ah! How can I tell? The Cossacks may have caught and killed him. He may be dead," she added hoarsely.

"What direction has he taken?"

"He was compelled to leave hurriedly at midnight. He came, kissed me, and gave me this," she said, still holding the shining little bomb in her small white hand. "He said he intended, if possible, to get over the hills to the frontier at Satanow."

I saw that she was deeply in love with the fugitive, whoever he might be.

Outside the awful massacre was in progress, we knew; but no sound of it reached us down in that rock-hewn tomb.

The yellow candle-light fell upon her sweet dimpled face, but when she turned her splendid eyes to mine I saw that in them was a look of anxiety and terror inexpressible.

I inquired of her father and mother, for she was of a superior class, as I had from the first moment detected. She spoke French extremely well, and we had dropped into that language as being easier for me than Russian.

"What can it matter to you, sir, a stranger?" she sighed.

"But I am interested in you, mademoiselle," I answered. "Had I not been I should not have fired that shot."

"Ah, yes!" she cried quickly. "I am an ingrate! You saved my life,"—and again she seized both my hands and kissed them.

"Hark!" I cried, startled. "What's that?" for I distinctly heard a sound of crackling wood.

The next moment men's gruff voices reached us from above.

"The Cossacks!" she screamed. "They have found us—they have found us!" And the light died out of her beautiful countenance.

In her trembling hand she held the terrible little engine of destruction.

With a quick movement I gripped her wrist, urging her to refrain until all hope was abandoned, and together we stood facing the soldiers as they descended the stairs to where we were. They were, it seems, searching every house.

"Ah!" they cried, "a good hiding-place this! But the wall was hollow, and revealed the door!" and next moment we saw the figures of men.

"Well, my pretty!" exclaimed a big, leering Cossack, chucking the trembling girl beneath the chin.

"Hold!" I commanded the half-dozen men who now stood before us, their swords red with the life-blood of the Revolution. But before I could utter further word the poor girl was wrenched from my grasp, and the Cossack was smothering her face with his hot nauseous kisses.

"Hold, I tell you!" I shouted. "Release her, or it is at your own peril!"

"Hulloa!" they laughed. "Who are you?"—and one of the men raised his sword to strike me, whilst another held him back, exclaiming, "Let us hear what he has to say!"

"Then listen!" I said, drawing from my pocket book a folded paper. "Read this, and look well at the signature. I am a British subject, and this girl is under my protection!"—and I handed to the man who held little Luba in his arms my permit to travel hither and thither in Russia, which the Ambassador in London had signed for me.

The men, astounded at my announcement, read the document beneath the lamp-light and took counsel among themselves.

"And who, pray, is this Jewess?" inquired one.

"My affianced wife," was my quick reply. "And I command you at once to take us under safe conduct to General Krasiloff—quickly, without delay. We took refuge in this place from the Revolution, in which we have taken no part."

I saw, however, with sinking heart, that one of the men was examining the bomb-maker's bench, and had recognised the character of what remained there.

He looked at us, smiled grimly, and whispered something to one of his companions.

Again in an authoritative tone I demanded to be taken to Krasiloff, and presently, after being marched as prisoners across the town, past scenes so horrible that they are still vividly before my eyes, we were taken into the chief police-office, where the hated official, a fat red-faced man in a general's uniform—the man without pity or remorse, the murderer of women and children—was sitting at a table. He greeted me with a grunt.

"General," I said, addressing him, "I have to present to you this order of your Ambassador, and to demand safe conduct. Your soldiers found me and my——"

I hesitated.

"Your pretty Jewess—eh?"—and a smile of sarcasm spread over his fat face. "Well, go on"—and he took the paper I handed him, knitting his brows again as his eyes fell upon the British royal arms and the visa.

"We were found in a cellar where we had hidden from the revolt," I said.

"The place has been used for the manufacture of bombs," declared one of the Cossacks.

The General looked my pretty companion straight in the face.

"What is your name, girl?" he demanded roughly.

"Luba Lazareff."

"Native of where?"

"Of Petersburg."

"What are you doing in Ostrog?"

"She is with me," I interposed. "I demand protection for her."

"I am addressing the prisoner, sir," was his cold remark.

"You refuse to obey the order of the Emperor's representative in London! Good! Then I shall report you to the Minister," I exclaimed, piqued at his insolence.

"Speak, girl!" he roared, his black eyes fixed fiercely upon her. "Why are you in Ostrog? You are no provincial, you know."

"She is my affianced wife," I said, "and in face of my statement and my passport she need make no reply to any of your questions."

A short, stout little man, shabbily dressed, pushed his way forward to the table, saying:

"Luba Lazareff is a well-known revolutionist, your Excellency. The German maker of bombs, Gustave Englebach, is her lover—not this gentleman. Gustave only left Ostrog yesterday."

The speaker was, I afterwards discovered, one of Hartmann's agents.

"And where is Englebach now? I gave orders for his arrest some days ago."

"He was found this morning by the patrol on the road to Schumsk, recognised, and shot, your Excellency."

At this poor little Luba gave vent to a piercing scream and burst into a torrent of bitter tears.

"You fiends!" she cried. "You have shot my Gustave! He is dead—*dead!*"

"There was no doubt, I suppose, as to his identity?" asked the General.

"None, your Excellency. Some papers found upon the body have been forwarded to us with the report."

"Then let the girl be shot also. She aided him in the manufacture of the bombs."

"Shot!" I gasped, utterly staggered. "What do you mean, General? You will shoot a poor defenceless girl, and in face of my demand for her protection. I have promised her marriage," I cried in desperation, "and you condemn her to execution!"

"My Emperor has given me orders to quell the rebellion, and all who make bombs for use against the Government must die. His Majesty gave me orders to execute all such," said the official sternly. "You, sir, will have safe conduct to whatever place you wish to visit. Take the girl away."

"But, General, reflect a moment whether this is not — —"

"I never reflect, sir," he cried angrily, and rising from his chair with outstretched hand, he snapped:

"How much of my time are you going to lose over the wench? Take her away, and let it be done at once."

The poor condemned girl, blanched to the lips and trembling from head to foot, turned quickly to me, and in a few words in French thanked me, and again kissed my hand, with the brief words, "Farewell; you have done your best. God will reward you!"

Then, with one accord, we all turned, and together went mournfully forth into the street.

A lump arose in my throat, for I saw, as the General pointed out, that my passport did not extend beyond my own person. Luba was a Russian subject, and therefore under the Russian martial law.

Of a sudden, however, just as we emerged into the roadway, the unfortunate girl, at whose side I still remained, turned and, raising her tearful face to mine, kissed me.

Then, before any of us were aware of her intention, she again turned, wrenched herself free, and rushed back into the room where the General was still sitting.

The Cossacks dashed after her, but ere they reached the chamber there was a terrific explosion, the air was filled with débris, the back of the building was torn completely out, and when a few minutes later I summoned courage to enter and peep within the wrecked room, I saw a scene that I dare not describe here in cold print.

Suffice it to say that the bodies of Luba and General Stepan Krasiloff were unrecognisable, save for the shreds of clothing that still remained.

Luba had used her bomb in revenge for Gustave's death, and she had freed Russia of the heartless tyrant who had condemned her to die.

But the man Hartmann—the German "patriot," whose underlings had stirred up the revolt—was already on his way back to Berlin.

As in France and Russia, so also in England, German Secret agents are, we have discovered, at work stirring strife in many directions.

One is a dastardly scheme, by which, immediately before a dash is made upon our shores, a great railway strike is to be organised, ostensibly by the socialists, in order to further paralyse our trade and render us in various ways unable to resist the triumphant entry of the foe.

When "the Day" comes, this plot of our friends across the North Sea will assuredly be revealed, just as the truth was revealed to me at Ostrog.

CHAPTER XIII
OUR WIRELESS SECRETS

Something important was being attempted, but what it was neither Ray Raymond nor myself could make out.

We had exerted a good deal of vigilance and kept constant watch upon Hartmann's house in Pont Street since my return from Poland, but all to no purpose.

Vera had been staying in London with her aunt and had greatly assisted us in keeping observation upon two strangers who had arrived in London about a month ago, and who were staying in an obscure hotel near Victoria Station.

Their names were Paul Dubois, a Belgian, and Frederick Gessner, a German. The first-named was, we judged, about forty, stout, flabby-faced, wearing gold pince-nez, while the German was somewhat younger, both quiet, studious-looking men who seemed, however, to be welcomed by many of the prominent members of the German colony in London.

On five separate occasions we had followed the pair to King's Cross Station and watched them take third class tickets to Hull. They would remain there perhaps two or three days, and then return to London.

After a while they had grown tired of their hotel, and had taken a small furnished house at the top of Sydenham Hill, close to the Crystal Palace, a pleasant little place with a small secluded garden in which were several high old elms. They engaged a rather obese old Frenchwoman as housekeeper, and there they led a quiet life, engrossed apparently in literary studies.

I confess that when it came my turn to watch them I became more than ever convinced that Raymond's suspicions were ungrounded. They seldom went out, and when they did, it was either to dine with Hartmann, or to stroll about the suburban roads of Norwood, Sydenham, and Penge.

Late one afternoon, however, while I was down at Sydenham, I saw them emerge from the house, carrying their small suit-cases, and followed them to King's Cross Station, where they took tickets for Hull.

Instantly I rushed to the telephone and informed Ray in Bruton Street of my intention to follow them.

That same night I found myself in the smoke-grimed Station Hotel in Hull, where the two foreigners had also put up.

Next day they called at a solicitor's office at the end of Whitefriargate, and thence, accompanied by a man who was apparently the lawyer's managing clerk, they went in a cab along the Docks, where, at a spot close to the Queen's Dock, they pulled up before an empty factory, a place which was not very large, but which possessed a very high chimney.

The managing clerk entered the premises with a key, and for about half an hour the pair were within, apparently inspecting everything.

I was puzzled. Why they were in treaty to rent a place of this description was an utter enigma.

They returned to the hotel to luncheon, and I watched them engaged in animated discussion afterwards, and I also noticed that they despatched a telegram.

Next day they called upon the solicitor, and by their satisfied manner when they came forth from the office, I guessed that they had become tenants of the place.

In this I was not mistaken, for that same afternoon they went together to the factory and let themselves in with the key, remaining within for over an hour, evidently planning something.

That night I wrote a long report to Raymond, and next morning spoke to him over the telephone.

"Vera wants to know if you want her in Hull. If so, she'll come," my friend said. "I'm just as puzzled as you are. Those two men mean mischief—but in what manner is a mystery."

"If Miss Vallance can come, I'll be only too thankful," I replied. "I fear the men know you, but they don't know her. And she can greatly assist me."

"Very well, Jacox," was his reply. "She'll leave this evening. She'll wire to the hotel. She'd better not be seen with you. So, to the hotel people, you'll be strangers. Meet outside, and arrange matters. 'Phone me when you want me up there."

"Right, old chap," I replied. "I'll ring you up at eleven to-morrow and report. So be in. Good-bye."

And I rang off.

Vera arrived just before eleven that evening. I was in the hall of the hotel when the porter entered, carrying her dressing-case. She passed me and went to the office, but I did not acknowledge her. She wore a neat dark blue travelling gown, well cut by her tailor, and a little toque which suited her face admirably. She possessed perfect taste in dress.

Half an hour later I sent a note up to her room by a waiter, asking her to meet me outside on the railway platform at ten o'clock next morning.

She kept the appointment, and in order to escape observation we entered the refreshment-room.

"The numbers of the rooms occupied by the two men are sixty-eight and seventy-two," I explained. "Perhaps it will be as well if you watch them the whole of to-day. They are at present in the writing-room, so you can at once pick them up."

"Certainly, Mr. Jacox," she said. "Jack is intensely anxious. He's very puzzled as to what they intend doing."

"Yes," I replied, "it's quite a mystery. But we shall discover something ere long, never fear."

Vera laughed as she sipped the glass of milk I had ordered.

Then I briefly explained all that I had discovered, telling her how the two men had evidently taken the factory on a lease, and how they were there every day, apparently making plans for future business.

"But what business do they intend starting?" she asked.

"Ah!" I said; "that's what we have to find out. And we shall do so before very long, if we are careful and vigilant."

"Trust me," she said; "I am entirely at your orders."

"Then I shall wait and hear your report," I said. "When you return to the hotel send a line to my room."

And with that arrangement we parted.

That day I spent idling in the vicinity of the hotel. It was mid-August, and the atmosphere was stifling. That district of Hull is not a very pleasant one, for it is one of mean provincial streets and of the noise of railway lorries rumbling over the granite setts.

The afternoon I spent in playing billiards with the marker, when about six o'clock a page-boy brought me a note from my enthusiastic little friend.

"I shall be in the station refreshment-room at half-past six. Meet me.— Vera."

Those were the words I found within the envelope.

Half an hour later, when I sat at the little marble-topped table with her, she related how she had been following the pair all day.

"They were in the factory from half-past one until four," she said. "They've ordered a builder to put up ladders to examine the chimney. They appear to think it isn't quite safe."

She told me the name of the builder, adding that the contract was to have the ladders in position during the next three days.

"They are leaving for London to-night by the last train," she added. "I heard the Belgian telling the hall-porter as I came out."

"Then we'll wire to Ray to meet them, and keep an eye upon them," I said. "I suppose you will go up to town?"

"I think so. And when they return I will follow them down if Ray deems it best," replied the pretty girl, who was just as enthusiastic in her patriotism as ourselves.

So still mystified I was compelled to remain inactive in Hull, while Vera and the two foreigners whom we suspected of espionage went up to London.

For the next four days I heard nothing until suddenly, at eight o'clock one morning, Ray entered my bedroom before I was up.

"I've found out one thing about those Johnnies!" he exclaimed. "They've been buying, in Clerkenwell, a whole lot of electrical appliances— coils of wire, insulators, and batteries. Some of it has been sent direct to the place they've taken here, and the rest has been sent to their house down in Sydenham."

"What can they want that for?" I queried.

"Don't know, my dear chap. Let's wait and see."

"Perhaps, after all, they are about to set up in business," I said. "Neither of them has struck me as being spies. Save that they've visited Hartmann once or twice, their movements have not been very suspicious. Many foreigners are setting up factories in England, owing to the recent change in our patent laws."

"I know," said my friend. "Yet their confidential negotiations with Hartmann have aroused my suspicions, and I feel confident we shall discover something interesting before long. They came back by the same train as I travelled."

After breakfast, we both strolled round to the factory. The ground it covered was not much, and it was surrounded by a wall about twelve feet high, so that no one could see within the courtyard. It had, at one time, been a lead-mill, but for the past eight years had, we learned, been untenanted.

Even as we loitered near, we saw the builder's men bringing long ladders for the inspection of the chimney.

We watched for a whole week, but as each day passed, I became more confident that we were upon a false scent.

The chimney had been inspected, the ladders taken down again, and once more the German and the Belgian had returned south to that pleasant London suburb.

In order to ascertain what was really in progress I called one morning upon the solicitor in Whitefriargate, on pretext of being a likely tenant of the factory. I was, however, informed by the managing clerk that it was already let to a firm of electrical engineers.

Thus the purchase of electrical appliances was entirely accounted for.

Once again I returned to London. They seemed, by the electrical accessories that had been delivered, to be fitting up a second factory in their house in Sydenham.

That, being a private house, seemed somewhat mysterious.

They had become friendly also with a tall, rather well-dressed Englishman named Fowler, who had the appearance of a superior clerk, and who resided in a rather nice house in Hopton Road, Streatham Hill.

Fowler had become a frequent visitor at their house, while, on several occasions, he dined with Dubois at De Keyser's Hotel, facing Blackfriars Bridge.

In consequence of some conversation I one evening overheard—a conversation in English, which the Belgian spoke fluently—I judged Fowler to be an electrician, and it seemed, later on, very much as though he had been, or was about to be, taken into partnership with them.

As far as we could discover, however, he had been told nothing about the factory in Hull. More than once I suspected that the two foreigners were swindlers, who intended to "do" the Englishman out of his money. This was impressed I upon me the more, because one evening a German woman was introduced to their newly-found friend as Frau Gessner, who had just arrived from Wiesbaden.

Whether she was really Gessner's wife I doubted. It was curious that, on keeping observation that evening, I found that the lady did not reside at Sydenham, but at a small hotel in Bloomsbury, not a stone's-throw from my own rooms.

There was certainly some deep game in progress. What could it be?

Vera had watched Fowler on several occasions, but beyond the fact that he was an electrical engineer, occupying a responsible position with a well-known telegraph construction company, we could discover nothing.

After nearly three weeks in London, Dubois and Gessner returned to Hull, where, while living at the Station Hotel, they spent each day at their "works." They engaged no assistant, and were bent apparently upon doing everything by themselves. They were joined one day by a shrivelled-up old man of rather seedy appearance, and typically German. His name was Busch, and he lived in lodgings out on the Beverley Road. He was taken to the works, and remained there all day.

A quantity of electrical appliances were delivered from London, and Dubois and Gessner received them and unpacked them themselves.

Ray Raymond was down at Sheerness upon another matter—a serious attempt to obtain some confidential naval information—therefore I remained in Hull anxiously watching. Vera had again offered her services, but at that moment she was down at Sheerness with Ray.

Day by day old Busch went regularly to the factory, and by the appearance of the trio when they came forth, it was apparent that they worked very hard. I was intensely inquisitive, and dearly wished to obtain a glance within the place. But that was quite out of the question.

Busch, it seemed, had lived in Hull for a considerable period. Inquiries of his neighbours revealed that he was a well-known figure. He did but little work, preferring to take long walks into the country.

One man told me that he had met him twice away near Spurn Head, at the estuary of the Humber, and on another occasion he had seen him wandering aimlessly along the low-lying coast in the vicinity of Hornsea. In explanation of this, it seemed that he had once lived for a whole summer in Withernsea, not far from Spurn Head, and had grown fond of the neighbourhood. Everybody looked upon him as a harmless old man, a trifle eccentric, and a great walker.

That constant rambling over that low-lying district of Holderness had aroused my suspicions, and I determined to turn my attention to him.

One day the old man did not go to the factory, but instead went forth upon one of his rambles. He took train from Hull to Hornsea, where the railway ends at the sea, and walked along the shore for several miles; indeed until he was three parts of the distance to Bridlington, when he suddenly halted near the little village of Barmston, and producing a neat pocket-camera took a long series of snap-shots of the flat coast, where I saw there were several places which would afford an easy landing for the invader.

The truth was in an instant plain. Old Busch was a "fixed-agent," who was carrying on the same work along the Yorkshire coast as his ingenious compatriots were doing in Norfolk, Suffolk, and Essex. The remainder of that day I kept a sharp eye upon him, and witnessed him making many notes and taking many photographs of the various farms and houses near the sea. He noted the number of haystacks in the farmyards—for his report on fodder stores, no doubt—and made certain notes regarding the houses, of great use, no doubt, when the Germans came to billet their troops.

It was not until nearly midnight that I was back at the hotel in Hull. Then, by judicious inquiry of the hall porter—who had become my particular friend—I ascertained that Gessner had left for London by the last train.

Should I follow, or should I remain in Hull?

I decided upon the latter course, and retired to bed, thoroughly fagged out.

Early next morning I went round to the telephone-exchange, rather than use the instrument in the hotel, and rang up Raymond.

To my delight he answered my call. He was at home.

I gave him a rapid digest of what I had discovered, and told him that the German had returned to Sydenham.

"All right, old chap," came his voice over the wire. "Vera will watch at this end, while you watch yours. If what I guess is right, they're doing something far more serious than surveying that flat coast north of the Humber. Be careful not to betray yourself."

"Trust me for that," I laughed. "Are you going back to Sheerness?"

"Yes. I'll be there all day to-day—and to-morrow I hope to get one of our friends the enemy arrested. That's what I'm trying for. Good-bye—and good luck," and he rang off.

Busch went to the factory where Dubois was already awaiting him. As I stood outside that building of mystery I wondered what devilment was being plotted within. It had not been cleaned or painted, the windows being still thick with soot, and several of them, which had been broken, were boarded up. The place had certainly not been cleaned down for years, and no wonder they had been suspicious of the stability of that chimney which towered so high towards the murky sky.

There was no sign whatever of activity within, or of any business about to be carried on. Thus, day followed day, Busch and Dubois spending most of their time within those high walls which held their secret.

One curious thing was the number of telegrams delivered there. Sometimes they sent and received as many as fourteen or fifteen in a day. How I longed to know with whom they were in such constant communication.

Suddenly, after the third day, the shoal of wires entirely ceased. Busch and Dubois, instead of going to the factory, spent the day in the country, taking train to Patrington and walking through Skeffling went out to Kilnsea, opposite Great Grimsby at the entrance to the Humber.

From the point where I watched I could see that the old man with considerable gesticulation was standing upon the shore facing seaward and explaining something to his companion.

The Belgian apparently put many questions to him, and had become intensely interested. Then presently his companion produced a paper from his pocket—evidently a plan, for he pointed out something upon it.

They both lit their pipes, and sitting down upon a rock discussed something quietly. Apparently Busch was making an elaborate explanation, now and then pointing with his finger seaward.

Where he pointed was the channel through which passed all the shipping into the Humber.

Then, after a time, he rose from where he sat, and seemed to be measuring a distance by taking paces, his companion walking at his side over the level expanse of sand.

Suddenly he halted, pointing to the ground.

Dubois examined the shore at that point with apparent curiosity. With what object I could not imagine.

They remained there for fully an hour, and the sun had already set when they returned to Patrington, and took the train back to Hull.

That old Busch was a spy I had proved long ago, but what part Dubois and Gessner were playing was not yet at all clear.

On the following evening, about ten o'clock, I saw Dubois near the Dock office, and on watching him, followed him to the factory, which he entered with his key. Beyond the gate was the small paved courtyard in which rose the high chimney. Within the factory he lit the gas, for I could see its reflection, though from the street I could not get sight of the lower windows.

The night was bright and moonlit, and as I waited I heard within the grinding of a windlass, and saw to my surprise, a thin light iron rod about six feet long and placed vertically rising slowly up the side of the chimney stack, evidently being drawn up to a pulley at its summit.

Dubois was hoisting it to the top, where at last it remained stationary, its ends just protruding beneath the coping and hardly visible.

Scarcely had this been done when Busch came along, and I had to exercise a quick movement to avoid detection. He was admitted by Dubois, and the door was closed and locked as usual.

I stood beneath the wall, trying to overhear their words. But I could understand nothing.

Suddenly a dull, crackling noise broke the silence of the night, as though the sound was dulled by a padded room.

Again I listened. Then at last the truth dawned upon me.

The spies had put in a secret installation of wireless telegraphy!

Those intermittent sounds were that of the Morse code. They were exchanging signals with some other persons.

Gessner was absent. No doubt the corresponding station was at that house high upon Sydenham Hill to the south of London, two hundred miles distant!

I waited for a quarter of an hour, listening to those secret signals. Then I hurried to the telephone, and fortunately found Raymond at home. I told him what I had discovered, and urged him to take a taxi at once down to Sydenham and ascertain whether they were receiving signals there.

This he promised to do, telling me he would 'phone me the result to the hotel at eight o'clock next morning.

Therefore I returned to the factory, and through the long night-hours listened to their secret experiments.

At eight next morning the telephone rang, and Ray briefly explained that Gessner, who had placed his apparatus upon the high flagstaff in his garden, had been receiving messages all night!

"Have you seen anything of Fowler?"

"No. But Hartmann has spent the night with Gessner, apparently watching his experiments. Couldn't you manage to watch your opportunity and get inside the factory somehow? I'll come north at noon, and we'll see what we can do."

At five o'clock he stepped from the London express, and together we walked down to the Imperial Hotel, to which I had suddenly changed my quarters, feeling that I had been too long in the close vicinity of the spy Dubois.

"It seems that they carry out their experiments at night," I explained. "For in the daytime the wireless apparatus is no longer in position. I see now why they engaged a builder to examine the chimney—in order to place a pulley with a wire rope in position at the top!"

"But Gessner and Dubois are expert electricians, no doubt. Members of the Telegraphen-Abtheilung of the German army, most probably," remarked my friend.

"And who is Fowler?"

"A victim, I should say. He appears to be a most respectable man."

"In any financial difficulty?"

"Not that I can discover."

"But why have they established this secret communication between Hull and London?"

"That's just what we have to discover, my dear fellow," laughed Ray. "But if we are to get a peep inside the place it's evident we can only do so in the daytime. At night they are down there."

"At early morning," I suggested, "after they have left."

"Very well," he said; "we'll watch them to-night, and get in after they leave. I've brought a few necessaries in my bag—the set of housebreaking implements," he added, with a grin.

"Well," I said, "neither of us know much about wireless telegraphy. Couldn't we get hold of an operator from one of the Wilson liners in dock, and take him along with us? A sailor is always an adventurer."

Ray was struck with the idea, and by eight o'clock that evening we had enlisted the services of a smart young fellow, one of the operators in the Wilson American service, to whom, in strictest confidence, we related our suspicions.

That night proved an exciting one. Fortunately for us it was cloudy, with rain, at intervals. Murphy, the wireless operator, listening under the wall declared that we were not mistaken. The men were sending messages in code.

"Most probably," he said, "they have another station across at Borkum, Wilhelmshaven, or somewhere. I wonder what they're at?" he added, much puzzled.

Through those long hours we watched anxiously; but just before the dawn Dubois and Busch lowered their apparatus from the top of the chimney, and a few minutes later emerged, walking together towards the hotel.

As soon as they were out of sight we held a consultation, and it was decided that, while Murphy and I kept watch for the police, Ray should use his jemmy upon the door and break it open. He would admit us and remain himself outside to give us warning.

Those moments were breathless ones.

We parted, the wireless operator walking one way, while I went in the opposite direction. Suddenly we heard the cracking of wood, followed by a low cough.

By that, we knew all was well.

We hurried back, and a few seconds later were in the courtyard of the disused factory. Ray had handed me his jemmy, and with it I broke open the second door of the empty place, flashing a light with the electric torch I carried.

We passed into the small office, but no second glance was needed to show that the place was completely fitted with a wireless installation of the most approved pattern.

"We'll try it," suggested young Murphy, and taking out the apparatus we hauled it up to the top of the chimney. Then re-entering the office, he placed the receiver over his ears, and listened intently, in his hand a pencil he had found ready upon the paper pad.

I stood watching his face. Apparently he heard nothing.

Then he touched the key of the instrument and instantly a great blue spark, causing a crackling noise, flashed across the room.

He was calling.

Suddenly his face brightened, and he was listening. Then he grew greatly puzzled.

Taking the receiver off his head he began to search the table upon which were several books; but at that instant I heard a light footstep behind me, and as I turned I felt a heavy crushing blow upon the top of my skull.

Then the blackness of unconsciousness fell upon me.

I knew no more till, on opening my eyes, I found myself lying in bed with a nurse bending over me.

I gazed around in amazement. There were other beds in the vicinity. I was in a hospital with my head tightly bandaged.

For a whole day and night I lay there, the nurse forbidding me to speak.

Then suddenly there entered Ray, whose arm was in a sling, accompanied by young Murphy.

"The spies came back—unexpectedly, and went for me before I could raise the alarm," Raymond explained. "Dubois hit you over the head with a jemmy, and by Jove! it's a mercy you weren't killed. He's cleared out of the country, however, fearing a charge of attempted murder. I've informed the police, and they are looking for both him and Busch, as well as Gessner, who is missing from Sydenham."

"Yes, but why had they established these two wireless stations?" I asked.

"Yes," replied Murphy, "it's a most ingenious piece of work. By some unknown means both the station here, and at Sydenham, had been tuned with the one which I daresay you've seen stretched across the top of the new Admiralty, in Whitehall, hence they could read all the orders given to the Home and Channel Fleets and the reports received from them, while I have to-day discovered that there is a similar secret station existing somewhere near Borkum also in tune with these, and with our Admiralty. Therefore the Germans are aware of every signal sent to our Fleet! The station at Sydenham was only temporary, but the one here was evidently devised in order that the German admiral in the North Sea, on seizing Hull and establishing a base here, might have constant knowledge of our Admiralty orders and the whereabouts of our ships. When I was listening I was surprised at the code, but the truth was made plain by the discovery of a complete copy of the British naval code lying upon the table. By means of this, the spies could decipher all messages to and from our ships. The Civil Lord of the Admiralty and three officials have arrived in Hull, and I have been with them down at the factory this afternoon. The chief wireless engineer declares that the secret of the exact tuning must have been learnt from somebody in the office of the constructors."

And both Ray and I then remembered the man Fowler, who had, as we afterwards discovered, been on the verge of bankruptcy, and had suddenly gone abroad, a fact which was sufficiently instructive for our purpose.

Next day I was well enough to leave the hospital, and I guided the superintendent of the Hull police and two detectives to Busch's house, where, on searching his room, we discovered a volume of plans and reports of defences of the Humber and its estuary, estimates of food and fodder supplies in the country north of Hull, together with a list of the foreign pilots and their addresses, as well as an annotated chart of the river, showing the position where mines would be sunk at the river's mouth on the alarm of invasion.

But what, perhaps, would have been even more alarming to the general public, had they but known, was the discovery of several great bundles of huge posters ready prepared for posting up on the day of invasion—the Proclamation threatening with death all who dared to oppose the German landing and advance—a copy of which I have given in these pages.

It shows, indeed, what careful preparation our enemies are now making, just as the installation of the secret wireless showed the tactful cunning of the invader.

For our exertions, Raymond, Murphy, and myself received the best thanks of the Lords of the Admiralty, at which, I confess, we were all three much gratified.

CHAPTER XIV
PLAYING A DESPERATE GAME

On the 20th of December, 1908, it rained incessantly in London, and well I recollect it. After lunch I sat in the club-window in St. James's Street, idly watching the drenched passers-by, many of them people who were up from the country to do their Christmas shopping.

The outlook was a gloomy one; particularly so for myself, for I had arranged to spend Christmas with an aunt who had a pretty villa among the olives outside Nice, but that morning I had received a telegram from her saying that she was very unwell and asking me to postpone my visit.

The club was practically deserted save for one or two old cronies. Every one had gone to country houses, Ray was spending Christmas with Vera's father at Portsmouth, and in view of the message I had received I felt dull and alone. It is astonishing how very lonely a man may be at Christmas in our great London, even though at other times he may possess hosts of friends.

I had received fully a dozen invitations to country houses, all of which I had declined, and was now, alas! stranded, without hope of spending "A Merry Christmas," except in the lonely silence of my own bachelor chambers. So I smoked on, looking forth into the darkening gloom.

The waiter switched on the light in the great smoking-room at last, and then drew the heavy curtains at all the long windows, shutting out the dismal scene.

A man I knew, a hard-working member of Parliament, entered, threw himself down wearily and lit a cigar. Then, idler that I was, I began to gossip.

He was going up to Perthshire by the 11.45 from Euston that night, he remarked.

"Where are you spending Christmas?" he asked.

"Don't know," I replied. "Probably at home."

"You seem to have the hump, my dear fellow," he remarked, with a laugh, and then I confided to him the reason.

At last, about six o'clock, I put on my overcoat and left the club. The rain had now stopped, therefore I decided to walk along to my rooms in Guilford Street.

Hardly had I turned the corner into Piccadilly, when I heard a voice at my elbow uttering my name with a foreign accent.

Turning quickly, I saw, to my great surprise, a man named Engler, whom I had known in Bremen. He was a clerk in the Deutsche Bank, opposite the Liebfrauen-Kirche, and popular in a certain circle in that Hanseatic city.

"My dear Meester Jacox!" he exclaimed in broken English in his enthusiastic way. "My dear frendt. Well, well! who would have thought of meeting you. I am so ve-ry glad!" he cried. "I have only been in London since three days."

I shook my friend's hand warmly, for a year ago, when I had spent some time beside the Weser watching two men I had followed from London, we had been extremely friendly.

I told him that I was on my way to my rooms, and invited him in to have a chat.

He gladly accompanied me, and when we were comfortably seated in my cosy sitting-room he began to relate to me all the latest news from Bremen and of several of my friends.

Otto Engler was a well-dressed, rather elegant man of forty, whose fair beard was well trimmed, whose eyes were full of fire, and who rather prided himself upon being something of a lady-killer. He was in London in connection with an important financial scheme in which his brother and a German merchant in London, named Griesbach, were interested. He and his brother Wilhelm were over on a visit to the merchant, who, he told me, had offices in Coleman Street, and who lived in Lonsdale Road, Barnes.

There was a fortune in the business, he declared, which was the discovery of a new alloy, lighter than aluminium, yet with twenty times the rigidity.

That evening we dined together at the "Trocadero," looked in at the Empire, and returned to the club for a smoke.

Indeed, I was delighted to have found an old friend just when I was in deepest despair of the dullness of everything, and of Christmas in particular.

Otto Engler had one failing—his impudent inquisitiveness. After he had left me it occurred to me that all the time we had been together he had been constantly endeavouring to discover my recent movements, where I had visited of late, where I intended spending Christmas, and my subsequent movements.

Why did he desire to know all these particulars? He was a busybody, I knew, and the worst gossip in the whole of that gossip-loving city on the Weser. Therefore I attributed his inquisitiveness to his natural propensity for prying into other people's affairs.

"Ah! my dear friend," he had said as he gripped my hand on leaving me, "they often speak of you in Bremen. How we all wish you were back again with us of an evening at the Wiener Café!"

"I fear I shall never go back," I said briefly. "Business nowadays keeps me in London, as you know."

"I know—I know," he replied. "Remember, you have always had a true friend in Otto Engler—and you always will, I trust."

Then he had entered the taxi which the hall-porter had called for him.

Next afternoon he called upon me at New Stone Buildings, as we had arranged. Ray Raymond was seated with me. I introduced him, and we spent a pleasant hour, chatting and smoking. Ray had also been in Bremen, and the two men had, they found, many mutual friends. Then, when he had left, Ray declared himself charmed by him.

"So different to the usual German," he declared. "There's nothing of the popinjay about him, nothing of the modern military fop of Berlin or Dresden, men who are, in my estimation, the very acme of bad breeding and degenerate idiocy."

"No," I said. "Engler is quite a good fellow. I'm glad he's found me. I expected to be deadly dull this Christmas."

"So do I," replied my friend. "I've got a wire this morning from the Admiral saying he is down with influenza, and the Christmas house-party is postponed. So I shall stay in town."

"In that case we might spend Christmas day together," I suggested.

This was arranged.

My German friend Otto saw me daily. I was introduced to his brother, Wilhelm, a tall, thin, rather narrow-eyed man who, from his atrocious German, I judged was from Dantzig. It was one evening in the Café Royal that I first saw Wilhelm, who was seated playing dominoes with a rather stout, middle-aged man in gold-rimmed spectacles, Heinrich Griesbach.

Both men expressed delight at meeting me, and I invited the trio to my rooms for a smoke and a gossip.

We sat until nearly two o'clock in the morning. Griesbach had been many years in London, and was apparently financing the scheme of the brothers Engler, a scheme which, on the face of it, seemed a very sound undertaking.

All three were thorough-going cosmopolitans, cheery, easy-going men of the world, who told many quaint stories which caused my room to ring with laughter.

Next day was Christmas Eve, and Griesbach suddenly suggested that if I had nothing better to do he would be delighted if I would join their party at dinner on Christmas night at his house over at Barnes.

"I regret very much," I said, "but I've already arranged to dine with my friend Raymond, who shares chambers with me in Lincoln's Inn."

"Oh!" exclaimed Otto Engler, "I'm sure Herr Griesbach would be very pleased if he came also."

"Of course!" cried the German merrily. "The more the merrier. We shall dine at eight, and we'll expect you both. I'll send a note to Mr. Raymond, if you'll give me his address."

I gave it to him, and nothing loath to spend the festival in such jovial company, I accepted.

I entertained a shrewd suspicion that by their hospitality they wished to enlist my aid, because I had one or two friends in the City who might, perhaps, assist them materially in their scheme. And yet, after all, Otto Engler had often been my guest in Bremen.

Next day I heard on the telephone from Ray that he would go down to Barnes with me, and would call for me at six at Guilford Street. Curiously enough, I had become so impressed by the possibilities of the new alloy about to be exploited with British capital, that I had really become anxious to "go in" with them. Ray Raymond, too, was much interested when I showed him the specimen of the new metal which Engler had given me.

"Do you know," said he when he called for me at six o'clock on Christmas evening, "I was about town a lot yesterday and I'm quite certain that I was followed by a foreigner—a rather big man wearing gold spectacles."

"Nonsense!" I laughed. "Why should you be followed by any foreigner?"

"It isn't nonsense, my dear Jacox," he declared. "The fellow kept close observation on me all yesterday afternoon. When I got back to Bruton Street, I looked out half an hour afterwards and there he was, still idling outside."

"Some chap who wants to serve you with a writ, perhaps!" I laughed grimly. "A neglected tailor's bill!"

"No," he said. "He's watching with some evil intent, I'm certain. I expect he's somewhere near, even now," he added.

"Why!" I laughed. "You seem quite nervy over it! Next time you see him, go up to the Johnnie and ask him what the dickens he wants."

Then, half an hour later, I put on my hat and coat, and together we took a taxi past Kensington Church and Olympia, to Hammersmith Bridge, over which we turned off to the right in Castelnau, into a long ill-lit thoroughfare, running parallel with the river. Bare trees lined the road, and each house was a good-sized one, standing in its own grounds.

Before one of these, hidden from the road by a high wall, and standing back a good distance from the road, the cab pulled up, and, alighting, we opened the gate, and passing up a well-kept drive pulled the bell.

Our summons was answered by a thin, rather consumptive-looking German man-servant, who took our coats and ceremoniously ushered us into a big well-furnished drawing-room, where Griesbach and his two friends were already assembled awaiting us. All were smoking cigarettes, which showed that no ladies were to be present.

The instant Ray entered the room I saw that he gave a start, and a few moments later he seized an opportunity to whisper to me that the man who had so persistently followed him on the previous day was none other than our host Griesbach.

"Don't worry over it, my dear old fellow," I urged. "What motive would he have? He didn't even know you!"

And then the gossip became merry in that room so seasonably decorated with holly, while Griesbach assured us of his delight in having us as his guests.

Dinner was served in the adjoining room, and a most excellent and thoroughly English repast it was. Our host had been long enough in England, he told us, to appreciate English fare, hence we had part of a baron of beef with Christmas pudding afterwards, and excellent old port and nuts to follow.

Two young Germans waited at table, and the party was as merry a one as any of us could wish. Only Ray seemed serious and preoccupied. He was suspicious I knew—but of what?

I now openly confess that I pretended a gaiety which I certainly did not feel, for after Raymond had told me that he had recognised Griesbach, a very strange thought had occurred to me. It was this. As we had entered the garden to approach the house, I felt certain that I had caught sight of the figure of a man crouching against one of the bushes in the shadow. At the time I had thought nothing of it, so eager was I to meet my friends. Yet now, in face of Ray's whispered words, I grew very suspicious. Why had that man been lurking there?

When the cloth had been cleared and dessert laid, the elder of the two servants placed upon the table before our host a big box of long crackers covered with dark green gelatine and embellished with gold paper.

"These are German bon-bons," remarked Griesbach, his grey eyes beaming through his spectacles. "I get them each Christmas from my home in Stuttgart."

The conversation had again turned upon the splendid investment about to be offered to the British public, whereupon I half suggested that I was ready to go into the affair myself. Griesbach jumped at the idea, just as I expected, and handed round the box of crackers. Each of us took one, in celebration of Christmas, and on their being pulled we discovered small but really acceptable articles of masculine jewellery within. My "surprise" was a pair of plain gold sleeve-links, worth fully three or four pounds, while Ray, with whom I pulled, received a nice turquoise scarf-pin, an incident which quite reassured him.

Our host refused to take one.

"No," he declared, "they are for you, my dear fellows—all for you."

So again the box was passed round, and four more crackers were taken. That time Ray's bon-bon contained a tiny gold match-box, while within mine I found a small charm in the form of a gold enamelled doll to hang upon one's watch-chain.

As Ray and I pulled my cracker, I had suddenly raised my eyes and caught sight of the expression upon the face of my friend Engler. It struck me as very curious. His sallow cheeks were pale, and his dark eyes seemed starting out of his head with excitement.

"Now, gentlemen," said our genial host, after he had passed the box for the third time, first to his two compatriots, who handed the remaining two bon-bons across the table to us, "you have each a final bon-bon. In one of them there will be found a twenty-mark piece—our German custom. I suggest, in order to mark this festive occasion, that whoever of you four obtains the coin shall receive, free of any obligation, five shares in our new syndicate."

"A most generous proposal!" declared my friend Engler, a sentiment with which we all agreed.

The two Germans pulled their bon-bons, but were unsuccessful. The prize—certainly a prize worth winning—now lay between Ray and myself.

At that instant, however, Griesbach rose from the table suddenly, saying:

"You two gentlemen must settle between yourselves. It lies between you."

And before we were aware of his intention he had passed into the adjoining room, followed by his two friends.

"Well," I laughed to Ray when we were alone, "here goes. Let's decide it!" And we both gripped the long green-and-gold cracker. If the coin were within, then I should receive a very handsome present, worth a little later on, perhaps, several thousand pounds.

At that instant, however, we were both startled by a loud smashing of glass in the next room, curses in German and loud shouts in English, followed by the dull report of a revolver.

We both sprang into the room, and there, to our surprise, found that six men had entered through the broken French window and were struggling fiercely with our host and his friends.

"What in the name of Fate does this mean?" I cried, startled and amazed at that sudden termination to our cosy Christmas dinner.

"All right, Mr. Raymond," answered a big brown-bearded man. "You know me—Pelham of Scotland Yard! Keep an eye on those bon-bons in the next room. Don't touch them at peril of your life!"

"Why?" I asked.

Then, when our host and our two friends had been secured—not, however, before the room had been wrecked in a most desperate struggle—Inspector Pelham came forward to where Ray was standing with me, and said:

"My God, Mr. Raymond! You two have had a very narrow escape, and no mistake! Where are those bon-bons?"

We took him into the dining-room, showed him the remaining two, and told him we had been about to pull them.

"I know. We were watching you through the window. Those men were flying from the house when they ran into our arms!"

"Why?"

"Because they are a dangerous trio whom we want on several charges. In addition, all three, and also the two servants, are ingenious spies in the service of the German General Staff. They've been busy this last two years. They intended to wreak upon both of you a terrible revenge for your recent exposures of the German system of espionage in England and your constant prosecution of their spies."

"Revenge!" I gasped. "What revenge?"

"Well," replied the detective-inspector, "both these bon-bons contain powerful bombs, and had you pulled either of them you'd both have been blown to atoms. That was their dastardly intention. But fortunately we got wind of it, and were in time to watch and prevent it."

"And only just in the nick of time, too!" gasped Ray, pale-faced at thought of our narrow escape. "I somehow felt all along some vague presage that evil was intended."

The three spies were conveyed to Barnes police-station in cabs, and that was the last we ever saw of them. The Government again hushed up the matter in order to avoid international complications, I suppose, but a week later the interesting trio were deported by the police to Hamburg as undesirable aliens.

And to-day, with Ray Raymond, I am wondering what is to be the outcome of all this organised espionage in England.

What will happen? When will Germany strike?

WHO KNOWS?